THE FR

Book 1 in

Christi   ue

Chapter 1

Monday, Week One

At first, Clarke Pettis wondered if the email was a joke, the sort of thing that gets sent around the office on April Fools' Day. But this was November, and joking about terrorism would be in particularly bad taste.

"Tammy, have you seen this?" Clarke propelled her office chair backwards towards her colleague, Tammy Doncaster, and swung round to face her.

"Just reading it now," Tammy said. "Some sort of management game, isn't it?" She brushed her fringe out of her eyes with one hand whilst scrolling down with the other, quickly reading the email until she caught up with Clarke.

Operation Brack Attack

This is a test of corporate resilience. There will be a mock terrorist attack on the company this week to find out how employees react and test whether we would be ready to cope with the real thing if it should ever occur. The "terrorists" will be wearing orange hi-viz clothing. If they tap you on the shoulder, you are out of the game and must proceed immediately to the car park, like for a normal fire drill, and give your name to the organisers.

RUN OR HIDE Please try either to escape the building without the "terrorists" catching you, or find somewhere to hide until the exercise is over. Do not leave your computers unlocked, as that would leave the company wide-open to a cyberattack or information download. Your safety and that of your colleagues is paramount, so helping others will be awarded bonus points.

1

No form of violence towards the officials will be tolerated.
This test will occur sometime this week, without warning.
BE READY

"This might be the most excitement we've had in ages," Clarke said.

"Right," said Tammy, "or it could fizzle out like a damp squib."

"So, do we escape or hide?" Clarke looked down at her long legs, then glanced over at Tammy's voluptuous figure. All the cupboards in this part of the office were about waist height and arranged with shelving, exactly the right size to fit standard A4 ring binder files. They were great for putting stuff on, especially cakes, when anyone in the office had a birthday. Not much use for hiding in. "Neither of us will fit in the cupboards. I guess we'd better escape."

"Third floor," said Tammy. "Only one way out."

"Unless you've got a ladder." Clarke was very much at home going up and down ladders. Before she came to work for Briar Holman, she had been a firefighter. She'd been good at it too, until the accident, until she'd been retired early from the brigade, until she'd been forced to earn a living doing something more sedentary and less exciting.

Clarke looked around the large, open-plan office. Fifty-three people shared the same big space. Finance and human resources to the left, procurement to the right. Nowhere much to hide. They might be able to duck down behind a bank of desks for temporary refuge in the heat of the moment, but they'd be discovered in ten seconds flat. Hopefully, it would make management do something about the space. The room always seemed either too hot or too cold, unless you were the lucky one who got hold of the air conditioning remote control, the one who got to dictate the temperature to all the others. And then, in winter, everyone caught colds and coughs as germs spread around the room, with no partitions to stop their progress. The office echoed too, so the noise levels on a busy day were distracting, and frankly, headache-inducing. All in all, it made for a pretty lousy working environment. Now it seemed the office would also be useless in the event of a terrorist attack.

"So, which day will they do it?" In the brigade, the lads would have run a book on it, bet money on which day the exercise would take place. Clarke wasn't going to suggest that.

"That's easy," Tammy said. "It's bound to be Wednesday."

She sounded so sure. "Do you know something the rest of us don't?" Clarke asked. Tammy was married to Douglas Doncaster, the deputy chief executive. She might actually know something for a fact.

"No way." Tammy leaned back in her chair. "It's obvious, though. They won't do it Friday. Too many people take Fridays off or bunk off early. And you lose the element of surprise by then as there are no more days left in the week. It won't be Monday either. Too soon. Most people won't have even read the email by now. They'll assume the exercise is real and start having heart attacks."

"Real?" Clarke laughed. "Like real terrorists wear orange hi-viz jackets!"

"You ever seen a real terrorist?"

Clarke shrugged. "Ok. So why not Tuesday or Thursday?"

Tammy spun around in her chair, doing a full 360 rotation. "Because the management in this place has no imagination," she said. "They'll go for midweek. Just wait and see."

"Clarke. Tammy." Andrew Hardwicke, the chief accountant, Clarke and Tammy's line manager, called over from his desk in the corner. "Team meeting in ten minutes. Room 3a. Where's Ken?"

Clarke noticed the empty desk on the other side of Tammy.

"He's just walked in the door." Tammy pointed across the room.

Ken Langton ambled towards them. Ten minutes late. Like most other days. He never managed to get up in time to catch the earlier train, didn't appreciate why he should work an extra twenty minutes if he got in early. Unofficially, they were all expected to go above and beyond their contracted hours. Everybody else in the office put in the hours to get the job done and to keep advancing their careers. Ken worked exactly his contracted hours. He didn't see the point of doing more than that. Clarke used to imagine that he led an exciting life out of work, but he never admitted to anything more interesting than watching Netflix boxed sets most evenings and an occasional visit to the local pub.

"Team meeting, Ken," she said. "Ten minutes. You'd better read your emails first." Andrew would want to discuss the mock terrorist attack at the meeting. Better not send Ken in blind.

Clarke spotted Tammy's empty chair and guessed she would have had the same idea as her—a quick visit to the loo before the meeting. She headed for the door.

Tammy was adjusting her hair in front of the bathroom mirror.

"What do you think of this terrorist attack thing?" Clarke said, giving her own hair the once-over and finding it sadly lacking in comparison to Tammy.

"Might be fun." Tammy teased a stray piece of hair back into place. She spent a lot of time perfecting her hair, showing up every day with a different style, a different way of twisting or braiding or curling it. Today, her long black hair was wound into a sleek knot on top of her head. "I'm not sure I'll be able to take it seriously. I mean—people in hi-viz. That's not exactly scary, is it? They might at least give them water pistols." Tammy routed around in her bag until she found a bright red lipstick and touched up her lips. The colour looked stunning against her dark ebony skin.

Clarke laughed. "You can suggest that to Douglas," she said, hoping she wouldn't. Getting sprayed in November in the freezing cold would not be fun. She slipped into a cubicle and closed the door.

From inside, the silence made Clarke wonder if Tammy had left. When she came back out, she was surprised to find Tammy waiting for her.

"There's something I need to tell you." Tammy looked serious.

She spoke quietly, unusual for her. Clarke strained to hear her over the noise of the running tap. She looked up from washing her hands, pausing while Tammy continued.

"You can't tell anyone."

Clarke nodded, worrying now about what the big revelation might be. "Of course not." She wanted to dry her hands but figured the noise of the dryer would drown out Tammy's voice. She dripped a tiny puddle onto the tiled floor as she waited for Tammy to speak.

Tammy turned away. "I've left Doug."

"I'm so sorry." Clarke dropped her wet hands, making a damp patch on each side of her black trousers. That was unexpected. Tammy had never given any indication of a problem with her marriage. Clarke assumed they were sound. "When?"

"August."

Clarke held her breath, stoppering a gasp. Three months ago. Really. "I'm sorry," she repeated, unsure what else to say. She glanced at her watch, trying to do so without Tammy noticing. They were due in the team meeting in less than two minutes, and this conversation needed way longer than that.

"The meeting."

Tammy nodded. "We'd better get back. Andrew hates anyone being late." She moved towards the door, with Clarke tagging along behind her.

The meeting took place in a small room in the middle of the building, with no windows and a row of tables in the centre. Clarke grabbed the chair opposite Andrew.

Tammy seemed to be back to her normal self now, but her news had shocked Clarke. Not so much the fact that Tammy had left her husband. Stuff like that happened, and Tammy undoubtedly had a good reason for leaving. But after three years of working closely together,

Clarke assumed they were friends. It surprised her, shocked her even, that Tammy hadn't told her much sooner. Clarke tried to put that to one side, reminding herself that it wasn't about her, and began to speculate about what had happened with Tammy and Douglas. Whose fault had it been? Where was Tammy living now? Were they heading for divorce or just on a break? She wondered if Tammy would tell her any of this. If she screwed up the courage to ask, when would be the right time?

"A couple of things first." Andrew looked Clarke in the eye.

Clarke shuffled in her chair, uncomfortable under his gaze. Had he realised she hadn't been paying attention?

"Massive congratulations to Clarke," Andrew said.

The heat of Clarke's blushing cheeks burned into her face.

"Clarke passed her exams last month with flying colours and is now a qualified accountant. Well done, Clarke."

"Well done," Ken muttered.

Andrew continued, "And Tammy. Tammy has been promoted into the vacant post of principal accountant and starts her new role today."

"That's brilliant," Clarke said. She noticed Ken glaring at Tammy and wondered if he had applied for the same post. He had certainly worked for the company much longer than Tammy. Knowing Ken, he probably felt entitled. But Tammy had put the work in. She deserved the promotion. Clarke hoped that any resentment from Ken wouldn't put a dampener on Tammy's achievement.

"Yes," said Andrew. "Well done, Tammy."

Tammy gave her widest grin. Perhaps she had seen Ken's evil glare and smiled all the more to annoy him. Clarke was pleased her friend had something to smile about. The last few months must have been tough for her.

Andrew tapped at the computer keyboard in front of him and *Operation Brack Attack* appeared in huge letters on the white wall at the end of the room.

Clarke wondered if she dared apply for Tammy's old post now that it was vacant. She lacked experience, but if she didn't apply, it may be a long time before another opportunity came up.

Andrew cleared his throat and Clarke forced herself to concentrate.

"You've all read the email." Andrew brought up a document on the computer. It projected onto the wall, slightly out of focus.

"What email?" Ken asked.

"If you hadn't got in late, you'd understand exactly what we're talking about." Andrew glared at Ken. "For those of you who can't be bothered." He remained staring at Ken. "Operation Brack Attack is not, as the name might suggest, an attack on Brackford. It's a mock terrorist attack on Briar Holman to test our corporate resilience. What would you do if someone threatened to shoot you, Ken?" Andrew's eyes shot daggers at Ken.

Ken coughed nervously. "I'd run like hell."

"Yes." Andrew's voice boomed in Clarke's ears as he leant towards Ken. "That's exactly the right answer. Corporate policy is RUN or HIDE. Do one or the other, whichever is safest. Unless you want to be cannon fodder." He looked pointedly at Ken again. "And phone for help as soon as you can. Memorise the special phone number on the email. If you can't manage that, carry the number on your person at all times this week. Save it on your phone. That phone number is the company equivalent of 999 for this exercise."

Andrew stood up and paced around the room, then clicked onto the next PowerPoint slide. "Brack Attack is a team competition. Even though we're only a small team, I want to win," he said. "You can win points for not being caught, for escaping the building, for phoning the help number. Points are deducted if you leave your computer screen unlocked or do something really stupid." He turned his attention to Clarke. "Clarke, I'm counting on you to help us out here. Make a plan. Give us some tips. With all your experience, you're our secret weapon."

Clarke grimaced. Just because she was an ex-firefighter, people expected her to be some sort of superhero. Ask her to put out a fire or lead someone out of a burning building and she would know exactly what to do, but terrorist attacks... In any unusual situation, she'd simply followed orders.

"I'm not really trained to handle terrorist attacks."

"Nonsense," said Andrew. "You've had plenty of emergency training. It's all pretty much the same."

It wasn't the same at all. Clarke wanted to protest her lack of qualification for this, but it was futile to go up against Andrew when he got fixated on an idea.

"You've got a cool head on you," Andrew said. "I'm counting on you. Come up with a plan by the end of today."

Clarke nodded. Never one to shirk a challenge, she hoped common sense would be enough to help her produce an acceptable plan. She wanted to impress sufficiently for Andrew to consider her for Tammy's old job.

Ken put his hand up. "When's this attack thing going to happen, Andrew?"

Andrew closed down the computer. "It's going to be a surprise, Ken. Terrorists don't make appointments." He glared at Ken. "My guess is Tuesday, but it might be any day this week."

Clarke looked at Tammy. She smiled. Perhaps she did know something the rest of them didn't, but she couldn't, not if she'd left Douglas.

"Any more questions?" Andrew got up, clearly not wanting to encourage any. "No? Back to work then."

Clarke busied herself with exploring the building. There were five floors and a basement, most of which she'd never visited. She took a notepad with her and started with the fifth floor, making notes on exits and potential hiding places and drawing a plan of each floor. A fire escape on every floor led out to a metal staircase on the outside of the building. She made a note to go outside and check at lunchtime.

When she'd been firefighting, she'd always looked for possible exits, in case the fire got worse or spread in a direction she hadn't anticipated. Locating the best exit was one of the most important things, almost as important as having a Plan B ready. Andrew was right. She did have the training for this—some of it, at least.

Clarke had loved her job. The teamwork, the excitement, the adrenalin rush, and the huge satisfaction when they'd managed to rescue someone or save someone's home and precious possessions from being destroyed. She'd done it for eight years. Then one day she'd slipped climbing down a ladder, losing her footing and falling awkwardly.

Over the course of a year, Clarke had endured three operations to fix her ankle. Huh, Clarke thought, not really a fix, not completely. She still suffered from the pain on lots of days, especially in cold, wet weather, and often still walked with a limp. At least, she would if she allowed herself to. She preferred to grit her teeth and walk through the pain, not allowing the limp to show. Few people even realised she had a problem. If her ankle hurt, she popped a couple of painkillers and got on with it, determined not to let anything hold her back.

She'd sported the exact same attitude when the brigade had assessed her, to test her fitness to return to work. Don't show any signs of pain. Don't show any signs of a limp. But they made her run on a treadmill until she couldn't hide it any longer, until she'd collapsed in agony. Then they'd pensioned her off.

She'd had to take an office job. She had always been good with numbers, so trainee management accountant at Briar Holman had seemed like a good idea. That was three years ago, and now she had qualified as an accountant. Who'd have thought? Certainly not Clarke. Accountancy had never featured in her game plan.

At first, she'd been angry. They'd taken away the job she'd loved. The job had broken her. Chewed her up and spat her out. They'd discarded her like rubbish, albeit with a handsome payout and a pension. Gradually, she began to accept her situation. She saw the sense now in not endangering lives—colleagues and the public—by making them rely on someone whose ankle might give out at any moment. But at the time, the rejection felt raw, and it had pained her to lose what she'd had with the brigade. Eventually, she started to accept her new beginning, set herself new challenges, ones that didn't involve racing into burning buildings. She'd channelled her energy into what she could do instead of grieving for what she couldn't.

Clarke walked down the stairs and made her way towards her desk. She'd been on her feet too long, so her ankle hurt. She would get a coffee and do some of her other work for a bit. No doubt Andrew would still expect her to do all her usual work, as well as working out an escape route for them.

"What's up?" Tammy seemed agitated when Clarke returned to the office.

"Damned computer," Tammy said. "Keeps freezing on me and it's deleted a vital file."

"Have you called IT?" Clarke sat down, relieved to take the weight off her ankle.

"Yes. They said they'd send someone, but he would be at least half an hour."

"I'm sure they'll fix it." Clarke started skimming through her unread emails. Their legal team had sent something late on Friday. They needed her to find a copy of an old invoice urgently. The pain in Clarke's ankle stabbed at her. She'd finish her coffee first. She would be ok by then to take the lift to the basement, where all the old invoices were stored.

The basement archives always smelt dank and dusty. Clarke hated the smell. But she loved the peacefulness. Not many people came down here. Sometimes, when the office became really noisy with fifty-three people all having different conversations and random phones ringing and the buzzing of computers, Clarke would come down here and sit quietly with her eyes closed for ten minutes. There was no time for that today. She needed to find the invoice for legal. Briar Holman was threatening to sue the supplier for supplying substandard electrical components.

Clarke walked up and down the aisles of shelving, looking for the date she needed. She quickly found the relevant file.

Much of the paperwork in this file comprised receipts for expenses. A lot of them related to Douglas Doncaster. Hotel bills, restaurants. She remembered Tammy saying he frequently stayed away on business. Had Douglas been having an affair? Was that why he'd been away so often? Was that why Tammy had left him?

She continued searching through the pile of invoices. A familiar name caught her eye. *Firestop*. She'd worked with them a bit back in her fire brigade days. They made a lot of fire prevention equipment: fire doors, fire escapes, extinguishers, fire blankets. The invoice was for twenty fire doors. Anti-blaze 400 model. Hadn't that model been discontinued while she was still in the brigade because of a flaw in the seals? Clarke had attended a huge fire in a high-rise block of flats. The fire had swept through the block in no time and had taken all night to get under control. Fourteen people dead. This one hadn't been on her patch. Appliances had been drafted in from miles around and she had been one of many firefighters in attendance that night.

Anyway, the fire investigators blamed the faulty fire doors, and they had been discontinued. What was Firestop doing selling faulty fire doors to Briar Holman? Clarke pulled out the invoice and scanned it on the photocopier near the door to the archive room, sending the copy to her email. It wouldn't hurt to double-check. She didn't want anyone else to die because of those doors.

Clarke soon found the invoice she needed for their legal department. She scanned that one as well.

While she was down here, she decided to check out the basement for her Brack Attack plan. A rabbit warren of shelving filled the basement, creating loads of potential hiding places. Clarke found one fire exit door in the far corner. She would check the outside of the building on her way home later to establish where it came out. There must be some stairs back up to ground level outside. She sketched a quick plan of the basement in her notebook. It would make a great place to hide from the attackers. The problem would be getting down here without being seen.

Slowly, Clarke made her way back towards the lift. As she pushed open the final fire door, she wondered if it was one of the defective ones.

Chapter 2

Monday, Week One

When Clarke got back upstairs, Jeffrey Todd from IT had borrowed her chair to sit next to Tammy, leaning in towards her to reach her computer. Tammy shrank away from him uncomfortably.

"I'll log in as the administrator. Then I should be able to get you going," he said, blushing as he briefly locked eyes with Tammy. She shrank back a little more.

Jeffrey turned and noticed Clarke behind him. "Do you need your chair back?"

"No, carry on. I'll get a coffee while you finish." Clarke reached across for her mug.

Jeffrey started typing gobbledygook into the computer. The screen filled with loads more words and numbers as Jeffrey's commands worked their magic.

The kitchen was situated along a corridor and through a fire door. Clarke caught herself looking carefully at the door as she went through. It looked too old to be one of the defective ones on the invoice and she didn't remember any doors on this floor being replaced recently. The huge staff kitchen sometimes doubled up as a spare meeting room, so it contained groups of tables and chairs, as well as a sofa. Clarke headed straight for the sofa, eager to take the weight off her ankle while the kettle boiled. As the room was empty, she swung her bad leg up and rested it on a cushion, hoping no one would come in and see her.

Later, when the office got quieter, she would Google the fire door, check if her memory was correct about the Anti-Blaze 400 model being defective, and confirm that the company had stopped making them. If Firestop was still selling faulty fire doors, she would need to report them. She should also find out which of Briar Holman's buildings had those doors fitted and make sure management replaced them. For a few moments, she closed her eyes and pictured their offices burning down. Would her old crew come out if that happened? Probably not. It would be good to see them, though. She should make the effort to meet up with them one day.

When Clarke got back to her desk, Tammy was in the middle of a total meltdown.

"Don't touch me. Just don't touch me." Tears streamed down Tammy's face as she backed away from Jeffrey.

Jeffrey's face was crimson. "I... I..."

"What did you do?" Clarke put an arm around Tammy to try to comfort and calm her down. Everyone in the office had stopped working to stare. Clarke stared back at some of them and, embarrassed, they turned away quickly, getting back to their work.

"What's going on?" Andrew boomed. "The pair of you, in the corner office now." He pointed towards the far corner of the large office, where one of the few meeting rooms was vacant.

Tammy broke away from Clarke's hold and ran out into the corridor.

"I'm sure there's a simple explanation," Clarke said, trying to calm the situation. With Tammy in such a distraught state, Andrew shutting her in an office with Jeffrey and shouting at the pair of them was really not the sort of sensitive approach she needed. "I should go after her." She didn't wait for a reply. Tammy would probably have bolted to the ladies' loos: the only safe place to escape Andrew. By the time Clarke got to the bottom of this, Andrew would have calmed down and Jeffrey would have gone back downstairs.

Tammy was wiping her eyes in front of the mirror when Clarke caught up with her.

"What happened?"

"He touched me. He's a creep," Tammy said, wiping mascara from her face.

"I'm sorry." Clarke put a hand on Tammy's shoulder. "You don't think it might have been an accident?"

Tammy shook her head. "He pushed his elbow into my breast."

Clarke rubbed Tammy's shoulder sympathetically. Tammy had one of those voluptuous, curvy figures. Not overweight. Well, a little overweight, but attractive. Clarke easily imagined how Jeffrey might have brushed against her by accident. But Tammy never normally got upset like this. She would normally laugh off this kind of thing. So perhaps Jeffrey had done it deliberately.

"Jeffrey's a creep." Tammy made a face.

Clarke was inclined to agree. Jeffrey was a creep. "Yes, he is, but he'll probably lose his job if you make a complaint."

Tammy twisted round to face her. "Whose side are you even on?" she yelled at her. "You don't understand. He's always following me. I saw him near my house last week." Tammy started to cry again.

"That's awful." Clarke tried to calm her down. No way would Tammy be persuaded to walk back into the office now. Not with everyone looking at her. Not with Jeffrey probably still there. "Have you reported it to the police?" she said. "If you're sure. He seems harmless, but you should tell someone." She stopped herself just in time from asking her if she'd told Douglas.

"I'm telling *you*," Tammy said. "He's stalking me. I swear he is."

"Then you should report him." It didn't have to be now, not in the office. Tammy would hate that. "Phone the police when you get home."

Tammy shook her head. "No, I don't want the police."

Clarke looked at her, worried. "But what if things get worse? You need to do something."

"Not the police," Tammy said again. "They'll make me tell them everything. I can't handle that right now. I can't."

Clarke knew the police had specialist officers to deal with victims, people trained to handle things with sensitivity. But she couldn't force Tammy. "Ok," she said. "But you need to keep a diary. Just in case. Write down everything he does. Dates, times, places. Everything. Just in case..." she cut herself off. Just in case one day he goes too far and the police need evidence, she had been about to say. She wouldn't let it go too far. If anything else happened, she would make Tammy call the police. Somehow.

Tammy nodded, wiping her eyes with a tissue. "Yes," she said. "That's the best idea. For now."

Clarke continued to worry about Tammy long after she left work. On Monday evenings, Clarke always went swimming. Before her accident, she used to run fifty miles a week, serious stuff. She'd been pretty good. Not a world-beater, but good enough to run in the county team. 10k cross-country had been her thing, along with a few half marathons. She'd loved that journey from A to B. Track running bored her silly, compared to the enjoyment she got from getting out into the countryside, powering up hills, or splashing through mud and observing the local wildlife at close quarters. Freedom runs, she'd called them. And running had kept her super fit for her job, too. Fit enough to hold her own with the men. Fit enough to save lives.

She hated not being able to run anymore. Even a short distance would make her ankle scream with pain, so now she swam to keep fit.

Swimming bored her. No scenery, no animals, no people, nothing to watch as she swam. Only water. The same blue-bottomed pool, the same up and down, up and down. Stay in your lane. Up and down. Again. And again. And again.

Probably the only thing that swimming had in common with running was its repetitive action. In her running days, Clarke had always used it as thinking time. She would whirl a problem around in her head, going over it dozens of times, looking at every aspect, working through different scenarios, different questions. Then by the end of the run, a solution inevitably came to her. Swimming and running were very similar really, apart from the scenery. She didn't have to concentrate. Nothing to make her switch off. Thinking time.

This evening the problem spinning round in her head concerned Tammy. Why had Tammy got so freaked out about Jeffrey? Could he really be stalking her? He might be the type. A bit geeky, but that on its own didn't make him a stalker. Was he a loner? Probably. She tried to remember her very small number of conversations with him. He wasn't a great talker. She remembered he'd been a bit tongue-tied every time she'd spoken to him, but she'd assumed it was simply shyness. To be honest, he seemed perfectly harmless. But these things often escalated, didn't they?

Luckily the pool wasn't crowded today. Clarke got a lane to herself, so she mulled the problem over while she swam, without having to pay attention to where she was going. She reached the end of the pool and took a breath, diving under the water to turn, pushing herself off the edge of the pool with her good leg.

When did beautiful, bubbly Tammy ever worry about a man fancying her? God knows, she attracted admirers like bees around a particularly sweet honeypot. Crying in the middle of the office seemed way out of character. Maybe Tammy's split with Doug was driving her to depression. Surely things must have deteriorated badly to set her off like that.

Clarke reached the end of the pool again and stopped to take a breather. She'd lost count of the number of lengths she'd swum, as she often did when she let her mind wander. A quick glance up at the big clock on the wall told her she was over halfway through the session. Her ankle felt good, as it always did in the pool. Funny how she could kick her legs as much as she liked when she swam, with no ill effects on her ankle, but weight bearing completely knackered it. Too much standing or walking and she struggled.

She pushed herself off the edge and started another length. Was Jeffrey really developing some sort of obsession with Tammy? Tammy often casually flirted with men. Had she flirted with Jeffrey, not realising that he might take it seriously? That would easily lead him to imagine that Tammy actually liked him. Clarke didn't suppose that a man like Jeffrey got too much attention from women. Would that make him bolder? Probably, but her imagination struggled to picture Jeffrey as a stalker. It must be just a coincidence that Tammy spotted him near her house. It only happened once. Maybe the split from Douglas was responsible for Tammy's heightened sensitivity. Clarke considered Tammy as a friend, not just a colleague, so she found it odd that Tammy had never told her any of this until today. She wondered what else Tammy hadn't told her.

Clarke climbed out of the pool and reached for her towel and flip-flops. This whole situation annoyed her. She liked to find solutions to things. That was what she did—solved problems, found answers. But now she was simply coming up with more and more questions. Questions that still worried her as she walked back to the changing rooms.

"Late tonight?" The lifeguard often stopped to chat with her when things weren't busy, but this evening he remained perched up in his high chair, concentrating on the lanes of swimmers. "Been doing anything exciting?"

"Only work," she said. Clarke didn't like to stop and chat with him when he was on guard duty. What if someone drowned because he didn't spot them? She didn't want that on her conscience.

As Clarke drove home, she realised *she* needed a lifeguard because she was beginning to drown in somebody else's problems.

Chapter 3

Clarke had been right about those fire doors being discontinued. She got into work especially early to investigate the issue before the office filled up. So far, she had discovered that, in the last nineteen months, Briar Holman paid twenty-one Firestop invoices, for a total of around £600k. Clarke printed out the details. She would somehow find time to examine all the others this week, to ensure that all the fire prevention equipment the company bought met safety standards. She couldn't help herself. Once a firefighter, always a firefighter.

Tammy arrived really early, for once.

"Are you ok?" Clarke asked, not sure what to say.

"Of course." Tammy tossed her hair, which today flowed long and loose—the natural look that Clarke knew with Tammy's frizzy afro hair, would have taken an hour with the hair straighteners to achieve.

"It's just, yesterday…"

Tammy cut her off. "Forget yesterday. Just forget everything."

Clarke resisted the urge to question her some more, then Andrew showed up, so she couldn't.

"Operation Brack Attack," he said. "You mark my words. It'll be today." He turned to Clarke. "Do you have a plan yet?"

Clarke squirmed in her chair. She still needed to check out the ground floor and outside of the building, then come up with a few ideas on how to escape, despite having no clue what they would face when the mock attack happened.

"I'm still working on it."

Andrew rapped his phone down on the desk. "Well, hurry up then. We're counting on you. Don't get us 'killed.'" He did the air speech-marks thing with his hands. "Today," he said.

Clarke got up. "I'm on the case," she said, still unsure what the plan was going to be. She had better come up with one soon.

The ground floor housed reception, a big meeting room, and about half of the large IT department. The remaining half of IT sat on the first floor. As well as the normal office computers, Briar Holman's factories ran with a great deal of automation and robotics. They also designed robotics for other companies. Much of the IT department was comprised of specialist robotics experts.

Clarke scouted round the ground floor, counting the external exits. She sketched a plan as she walked around.

"Hi, stranger, what are you doing down here?" The tall redheaded man smiled at her.

Clarke smiled back, trying to remember his name and exactly where she recognised him from.

"Top secret mission," she said, still smiling. "If I tell you, I'll have to kill you."

The redhead laughed. "You're not one of those mock terrorists, are you?" he said. "We're still waiting for that to happen. We're a bit doomed here." He cocked his head and made a face. "They'll probably come in here first as we're right by the front entrance. Sabotage all the computers, bring the company down. That's what I would do if I were a terrorist. Which I'm not," he added quickly.

"Yes, you're probably right," Clarke said. "So how would you escape?" She could use some good ideas. And he'd obviously given the matter more consideration than her.

He pointed across to the far corner of the large room. "See that door?"

Clarke turned. She saw the door, right beside where Jeffrey Todd sat. Jeffrey hadn't noticed her yet, and she wondered if she should make her escape before he saw her. Or perhaps she should go over and talk to him, get his side of the story because, frankly, Tammy's story about yesterday was chockful of holes and none of it made sense. She should ignore Jeffrey and focus on what she came down here for because Andrew expected some amazing stroke of genius from her. She should concentrate on her conversation with the redheaded man and keep her nose out of other people's business.

Redhead finished speaking.

"That's a good idea," Clarke said, realising she had no clue what he'd said.

"Yes, I think so too." He looked pleased with himself.

"Excuse me," Clarke said. "I must just..." She walked towards Jeffrey. She hadn't planned to, but she couldn't stop herself.

Jeffrey saw her coming. "Hi, Clarke." He blushed as he greeted her.

"Got time for a quick coffee?" Discussing the Tammy incident in front of all his colleagues would be a disaster.

Jeffrey nodded and grabbed his half full mug, taking a clean spare mug out of his desk drawer.

The kitchen was empty. Clarke jumped straight in before anyone else came in and before she lost her nerve.

"What happened yesterday, Jeffrey?" she said. "With Tammy."

Jeffrey spooned out the coffee. He was making it much too weak. Clarke needed a decent-sized dose of caffeine to function, especially in the mornings. He stirred the coffee and handed it to her, slopping some over the worktop. Clarke stopped herself from wiping up the wet ring of coffee, trying to pay attention to what Jeffrey said.

"Nothing," he said. "I didn't do anything."

"But Tammy..."

"I was only trying to fix her computer," he interrupted her. "I didn't do anything. Honestly, it was an accident."

Clarke looked at him. The idea of Jeffrey trying to touch up anyone in the middle of a busy office did seem ludicrous. He was far too shy. On the other hand, she'd seen him with Tammy and he definitely had the hots for her.

"Do you know where Tammy lives?" She needed to find out if Tammy's claim about Jeffrey being a stalker held any truth. If it did, she would somehow persuade Tammy to talk to the police.

Jeffrey looked puzzled for a second. "Of course not," he said. "Well, with Douglas Doncaster, I suppose. But I've no idea where that is."

"I should get back." Clarke got up and headed for the kitchen door.

Jeffrey followed her out. "Take the door on the right," he said as she moved towards the left-hand door.

A flight of stairs filled the space beyond the door. Clarke wasn't familiar with this part of the office. "Where do those stairs go?" she asked Jeffrey.

"Fifth floor," he said. "But you can't get through the door at the top without a pass and you're not wearing yours."

Clarke smiled and pulled her company pass out of her pocket. "I'll try it," she said.

The back staircase did indeed go right to the top floor. A fire door provided an exit from the stairwell at ground level, but no access existed on any of the other floors apart from the odd arrangement of the ladies' loos on the fourth floor.

The top floor housed all the senior managers. She passed the biggest office, belonging to the chief executive. Then Douglas Doncaster's office next to it. Douglas's door stood slightly ajar and Clarke fought her impulse to burst in and demand to know what he had done to make Tammy leave him. She forced herself to walk past. After she passed the main staircase and lifts, she headed for the smaller staircase on the other side of the building. It came out in the lobby area that housed the third-floor staff lockers. These internal staircases that went nowhere were weird, Clarke decided. Whoever had designed them should probably be sacked. At least the door to the stairs was close to her team's desks, so it would make a great escape route.

She breathed a sigh of relief to have a proper plan for Brack Attack that would keep Andrew happy. No one would expect them to go up before they went down, and the staircase on the other side of the building wasn't widely known about, being accessible only from the fifth floor. The plan might actually work.

The incident between Tammy and Jeffrey seemed to be unimportant and would hopefully blow over in a couple of days. She wondered why Tammy had made such a big fuss. It really wasn't like her at all.

Andrew had gone to a meeting before Clarke returned to her desk. She decided to go back to the archives in the basement to obtain copies of the other Firestop invoices.

Like before, the basement was deserted, and again, she wondered if the racks of shelving would make a good place to hide for the Brack Attack exercise if they weren't able to leave the building. It might make a good Plan B.

It didn't take too long to find the remaining invoices and scan them. She looked at each of the invoices as she pulled them out, knowing it would be tricky looking at the scans on her computer back in the office. She didn't want Andrew accusing her of neglecting her regular work or probing her about exactly what she was working on now.

The only commonality between the invoices was Bradley Acres' signature on all of them, with a counter-signature from Douglas Doncaster. Clarke found no more of the discontinued fire doors. That first one seemed to be a one-off, but she liked to be thorough. She wondered about emailing Douglas Doncaster a copy. If the company had fitted defective fire doors anywhere, he would be able to find out where and also contact the suppliers to replace them.

But with Douglas's signature authorising the invoice, she didn't want to do that. He was deputy chief executive and rumoured probably to get the CEO job next year when the present CEO retired. It wouldn't exactly help her career to go accusing him of buying lethal fire doors.

She wanted to ask Tammy what she should do. But would that be putting her in an awkward position, with Douglas's signature on the invoice? Tammy hadn't really said how things stood between her and Douglas. From her reaction yesterday, Clarke guessed it wasn't good. Nevertheless, she decided to send Tammy a copy of the invoice for her opinion.

Back at her desk, she typed the email, even though Tammy sat inches away from her. She would send it, then talk to her to explain. She hit the send button.

Next to her, Tammy got up. "I've got a meeting with Brad Acres," she said. "I'll be about an hour."

"Ok." Tammy was working with Brad on some big project and met with him quite a lot. Clarke sighed. The discussion about the dodgy fire doors would wait until Tammy returned.

Tammy wasn't back by lunchtime, so Clarke popped out to get a sandwich. She needed the five-minute walk to the centre of Brackford to get some fresh air. Clarke remembered she needed to buy a present for her brother's birthday on Saturday. She browsed in a couple of shops before settling on some fun cufflinks, with little footballs on them.

When she returned to the office, Tammy was flapping round, trying to find something in her desk drawers. She held up a piece of paper to Clarke. "Where did you get this?"

"What?" Clarke wasn't paying attention, still regretting not getting the cufflinks for her brother gift-wrapped in the shop.

"This." Tammy pointed to her screen, which showed a copy of the Firestop invoice.

"Oh, that." Clarke had momentarily forgotten about the invoice. "I found it by chance," she said. "It's the model of the fire doors. They're wrong."

Tammy got up, locking her computer screen as she did so. She beckoned Clarke to follow her and headed for the corner door and out into the staff locker area.

"That invoice," she said, as soon as the door closed behind them. "I'm going to discuss it with someone later. Can you please forget you've seen it and leave it with me to sort out? Best that you don't interfere in case you jeopardise any court case."

"Court case?" Clarke would be pleased if they pursued Firestop to get the money back, but safety remained her primary concern. "What about—"

Tammy cut her short. "I'm dealing with it."

Clarke shut up. She wouldn't say anything. But she didn't like the way Tammy had spoken to her. Something didn't seem quite right. Clarke wondered if Tammy was trying to protect Douglas for making a stupid mistake. She decided to carry on digging to make absolutely sure nothing odd was going on. And she was curious now. She couldn't leave this alone if she wanted to. But she wouldn't tell Tammy.

Chapter 4

Tuesday, Week One

The afternoon dragged. Clarke tried to concentrate on her work, but the noise in the office made it difficult. Conversation buzzed with one thing only: Operation Brack Attack. When would it take place? What would happen? How would they escape the building? And, of course, it sparked off the usual jokers: Let's put a trampoline outside the window and jump out. How about we borrow Harry Potter's invisibility cloak?

By 4:00 p.m., it became obvious that Brack Attack wouldn't happen today. People with young children started to leave. Others hurried to meetings, as it was the only time of day when one of the ridiculously small numbers of meeting rooms became free. Tammy was probably right. Brack Attack was more likely to happen tomorrow, Wednesday. It wouldn't be too early in the morning. Most people in the office worked semi-flexible hours. Management would allow time for everyone to get in. It wouldn't be too close to lunchtime as many people would have popped out into Brackford town centre. And it wouldn't be too late as people would start to go home. That meant it would start either between ten and eleven in the morning or between two and three in the afternoon. Clarke simply needed to make sure they were all in the right place at those times, not trapped in the kitchen or the toilets.

Andrew came over from his desk in the corner. "I don't think it's going to happen today," he said, forgetting to add how certain he had been that it would. "We should have a rehearsal. Make sure we're all familiar with the escape route, so our team can win."

"Damn. I wanted to go home early," Ken whispered.

Clarke wasn't keen either. She'd been on her feet a lot today already, but now that Andrew had got the idea into his head, resistance was pointless. She would take it easy this evening, phone for a pizza, curl up on the sofa, and watch a film.

"Right, let's all follow Clarke," Andrew said.

Tammy started tidying up her desk and putting things in her drawers.

"Stop that," Andrew said. "You won't get time to do that when we're under attack. They'll take you by surprise and you'll need to get up and go. Instantly. Boom."

Tammy got up. Ken beat her to it and followed Clarke.

"Ken," Andrew shouted in his ear. "Lock your effing computer screen."

Ken fumbled with his keyboard, locking the screen. "So not *instantly*," he murmured to Clarke.

Clarke led them out into the locker area.

"Can I get my bag?" Tammy asked.

Andrew looked like he would explode. "No, absolutely not. You don't seem to appreciate the importance of this exercise. You need to take it seriously."

"But—"

"He's right, Tammy. If we were under attack for real, our lives might depend on it." Clarke was used to stuff like this. Follow the rules. Pay attention. Stick to procedure. Take everything seriously. Otherwise, the fire will win and you'll get burned. Sometimes it truly had been life and death. More times than she wanted to remember.

"Thank you, Clarke," Andrew said. "Glad someone's being professional."

Tammy made a face as Andrew looked away. Clarke struggled to stifle a laugh. "I just don't think Briar Holman is a target for terrorists," Tammy said.

Andrew turned and glared at her. "Briar Holman supplies machinery and components for over sixty percent of the food processing factories in this country," he said in his most pompous voice. "If terrorists disable Briar Holman, the whole of the UK will starve."

Tammy looked as though she might argue with him, then changed her mind. Clarke wouldn't blame her if she wanted to debate the issue. Andrew grossly exaggerated the situation. Actually, if no one could produce cakes and biscuits and ready meals, people would be forced to cook fresh food. They might be a whole lot healthier for doing that. It would take weeks before enough factory machinery started failing to make a difference. Andrew had an extremely inflated opinion of his own importance.

Clarke led the way up the stairs. Two flights. Tammy and Ken started puffing well before they reached the top. Clarke paused under the pretence of explaining the rest of the route. When they both got their breath back, she led them past the senior management offices.

"Blimey," Ken said. "I didn't even realise this existed. Bit plush, isn't it?"

"Don't get used to it, Ken. You're never going to get an office up here," Andrew said.

Clarke suppressed a smile. Andrew was right. Ken had already progressed in the company beyond his abilities. But it still wasn't acceptable for Andrew to demotivate Ken like that.

Tammy speeded up and began to overtake everyone. Clarke observed it happening as they passed Douglas's office and she guessed Tammy didn't want to bump into him. Again, she wondered why Tammy had left him. Was Douglas Doncaster even less charming at home than he appeared to be in the office?

"You must make sure you keep your ID pass on you," Clarke told the others when they reached the door to the stairs. "You can get out by pushing the exit button, but if anything goes wrong, you won't be able to get back in without swiping your pass."

"Ok, everyone wear your pass all the time until this thing happens," Andrew said.

Clarke's pass hung on a lanyard round her neck today, but she noticed none of the others wore theirs, including Andrew.

Andrew looked at his watch. "Six and a half minutes so far," he said. "Can we speed up, please? Let's generate a bit more urgency. We can run down the stairs."

"What, in these heels?" Tammy said. "No chance."

Clarke saw that, as usual, Tammy wore smart stilettoes. She loved Tammy's massive collection of shoes. Today, she wore Clarke's favourites, the zebra print stilettoes. She'd teamed that up with a tight black and white pencil skirt, a wide red belt, and a black jacket. Running was absolutely not an option. That pleased Clarke because her ankle would never cope with running down stairs. Going downhill or down stairs killed her ankle. The extra drop exerted a lot more pressure and negotiating five flights of stairs at speed would be agony. At least now she wouldn't need to make excuses.

Andrew scowled at Tammy. "Tomorrow," he said, "wear flat shoes."

"Flat shoes make me look dumpy," Tammy muttered.

Clarke smiled. She doubted that glamourous Tammy even owned a pair of flats. It didn't matter how much Andrew argued with her to wear flat shoes. It wasn't happening.

Ninety-five steps. Clarke counted them as they descended the five flights of stairs. Could be worse, she figured, and with luck, she'd only need to do it once more tomorrow. She would definitely take the lift for the rest of the week.

She paused by the fire exit. "Tomorrow we'll go out through this exit," she said. "It will set the alarm off if we open it now, but we can go outside and I'll show you where it comes out."

"It may not be tomorrow, Clarke," Andrew reminded her. "Even I don't know when it will be."

Ken, who had been silent until then, laughed. Andrew glared at him.

Clarke led them out through the IT department, relieved not to see Jeffrey while Tammy was with her. Perhaps Tammy did have inside information and Brack Attack would take place tomorrow. But even if she was only guessing, her appraisal of how human nature worked made perfect, logical sense. If they were running a book on it, Clarke would also bet on Wednesday.

A light sprinkling of rain greeted them as they left the building. None of them wore coats, and Clarke regretted her suggestion to come outside. The fire exit they would be using came out on the far side of the large office block.

"The exit is directly opposite us on the other side of the building." Clarke pointed. "Then it's a right turn to get to the car park or left to go into Brackford."

"Should have brought my coat. Could have gone straight home," Ken murmured.

"Well, let's go and check it out." Andrew's enthusiasm wouldn't be dampened.

"It's raining," Tammy pointed out unnecessarily. "We'll get soaked."

"It's just a little shower. We need to get the details right." Andrew's voice sounded more insistent than usual. He would probably enjoy making them all suffer. Bullies always did.

Tammy's prediction proved spot-on. By the time they reached the other side of the building, the rain was chucking down. Clarke shivered, wishing she'd grabbed her coat.

"Should have warned us to bring our coats, Clarke," Andrew said. "And umbrellas."

"And a sodding ark," Ken said.

Stuff them. As soon as they got back upstairs, Clarke intended to get her things and go home. She looked at Tammy for support. Tammy appeared as pissed off with her as the rest of them.

Andrew made a move first. He started running as the rain lashed down. Ken jogged right behind him, puffing loudly.

"Miserable bastards," Tammy yelled at them. Luckily, the noise of the rain drowned out her words.

Clarke was grateful for Tammy's high shoes, which allowed her to keep up easily, without knackering her ankle for the rest of the week.

"Thanks for staying with me," Tammy said. "Female solidarity." Her annoyance at Clarke for causing her to get wet seemed forgotten already.

Clarke tried to wipe the rain out of her eyes, but her hands now felt like soggy blocks of ice. "That's ok," she said. It was her fault they were getting a soaking. Clarke wished again that she hadn't suggested coming outside, but Andrew would have probably insisted on it anyway. At least Tammy had forgiven her.

"My hair's going to be wrecked." Tammy shook her head when they got inside the building, sending droplets of rain flying everywhere, reminding Clarke of her mum's cocker spaniel, shaking off water after a bath.

"Let's go home," Clarke said. "We're both soaked. I need a hot bath and I'm sure you do too." Clarke wondered if she should apologise. What for? For not being a good weather forecaster? For doing her job? For trying to keep their boss happy? They should go home and forget about it. She hoped Operation Brack Attack didn't take too much planning, that the organisers would be able to delay things if it rained. She didn't want to get soaked through two days in a row.

"Good idea," Tammy said. "I'll walk out with you."

They left via the staff locker room. Clarke put her coat on and opened her locker. She always kept her handbag locked away during work hours, so it would be safe, as so many people came in and out of the office during the day. She slung the bag over her shoulder and locked up. Tammy fastened the buttons on her long red coat. Her dark hair looked amazing against the red, even when she was wet and bedraggled.

"I'm looking forward to this mock terrorist thing," Clarke said.

"Really?" Tammy took her bag out of her locker. "It sounds like a real pain to me."

"I miss the brigade sometimes," Clarke said. "I suppose I still crave excitement. Maybe I started my second career too young."

Tammy hit the button to call the lift. "Not as young as me," she said. "I started my second career at the grand old age of twenty-two. One year after Uni."

"I never realised you tried another career." Tammy constantly surprised her. Sometimes she was a total enigma.

"I wanted to be an actress," Tammy said. "Did some amateur stuff at Uni. Thought I could make it."

"What happened?"

"Spent more time waitressing than acting," Tammy said. "That's what happened. I got two small acting jobs in a year. Parents told me to get a proper job or they'd throw me out."

"That's such a shame."

Tammy veered off towards the bus stop at the end of the road, but Clarke kept walking with her, forgetting for a moment that she needed to go to the car park.

"You'd be great on the stage." She would be. Tammy was such a drama queen, and really pretty with it.

"It's tough trying to make it as an actress." Tammy sighed. "Even tougher if you're black. Fewer parts to go for. And, to be honest, I was only ever average. Some things aren't worth the fight to get them."

"That's such a shame," Clarke said again.

"Anyway," Tammy said, "the thing is to make the best of what you've got. I threw myself into becoming an accountant. Sure, accountancy's not the glamourous job I'd dreamed of, but the money's good and I'm very much making the best of it." She smiled.

"Yes," Clarke agreed. "Well done on your promotion."

"So, you must make the best of it too."

"I intend to," said Clarke. They reached the bus stop and Clarke needed to go back to the car park for her car. She wondered if she should ask Tammy. What the hell—she would.

"Tammy," she said, "do you think I should go for your old job when it's advertised? Do you think I stand a chance?" There, she'd asked. Now she wished she hadn't. Tammy would point out her inexperience, would take it as an insult that Clarke thought she deserved to fill her shoes.

Tammy turned to face her. "Someone has to cover that work," she said, "until they can get someone in. Why don't you volunteer to do some of it? If you're doing the job, they'll probably give it to you when you apply."

Clarke wanted to ask her some more about the job, but the bus pulled up and, as the only person waiting, Tammy got straight on. Clarke resolved to quiz her about it some more tomorrow.

Clarke walked slowly back to the car park. She wondered what she would be letting herself in for if she took on some of the extra work. How many more hours would she need to work if she ended up doing nearly two jobs? Would she even be able to do some of it? She'd probably fall flat on her face, then suffer the embarrassment of seeing them give the job to somebody else. The timing was all wrong. Really, she needed another year. But that probably wouldn't stop her from applying. Tammy was right. *This* was her career now, not firefighting. She should grab every opportunity that came her way and make the best of it.

Chapter 5

The sun was trying to shine when Clarke arrived at work on Wednesday morning.

Andrew was already ensconced at his desk, working hard. He gave her a casual wave as she sat down.

"They've emailed some more instructions," he said. "Please, can you read it? Make sure everyone does what it says."

Clarke wondered what he meant by that. She would read the email as soon as she'd made coffee. She didn't function until at least her second cup of coffee of the day.

The Brack Attack exercise now came with all sorts of rules. First, touching was strictly forbidden. Management wanted to avoid any chance of physical violence and the organisers intended to watch on CCTV to make sure nothing escalated.

The CCTV concerned Clarke. She worried that management would probably also use what they saw to assess everyone's performance. If she didn't run at all, would they hold that against her, accuse her of not taking it seriously? She hadn't disclosed any form of disability on her application form when she'd joined the company. In her mind, she was fully able. People should focus on the ability, not the disability, in her opinion. She didn't want anyone feeling sorry for her, making concessions. She coped perfectly well. In fact, she went to great lengths to cope, sometimes hiding her pain, glossing over the extent of her injury, rarely letting herself walk with a limp. She realised that she may need to toughen up and put on a show in front of the CCTV cameras. Just a slow jog. That would be enough to show willing. She rummaged in her desk drawer until she found a packet of paracetamol and swallowed a couple down with a gulp of coffee.

"Ok?" Andrew asked.

"Just a headache," she said. Andrew wouldn't even question that. It was nearly ten o'clock, and with the office now full, the noise levels were dreadful.

Management obviously worried they might spook the residents of Brackford as they now stressed that, once anyone left company premises, they couldn't be 'captured.' Clarke decided the best place to escape to would be the town centre. With luck, she and Tammy could give the boys the slip and go for a coffee.

Clarke tried to get stuck into some work but found it difficult to concentrate. She kept glancing at the main door on the other side of the room. With all the buzz about Brack Attack, she couldn't help herself. The excitement had built since yesterday. Everyone knew Brack Attack would happen soon. Every day that it didn't come made it even more likely that it would occur imminently. Clarke rearranged her coat that hung over the back of her office chair. Her handbag sat under her desk, ready. When the moment came, she would grab both handbag and coat before she left. She didn't plan on getting caught out in the rain with no coat two days in a row.

"Still think it's going to be today?" Clarke asked Tammy.

"Probably."

Tammy seemed distracted. Not just the anticipation of Brack Attack, but something else. Clarke couldn't put her finger on it.

She was still thinking about it when a ruckus in the hallway startled her. A second later, several phones rang simultaneously, including Tammy's.

"They're here," she half shouted, half whispered. "It's started." The whisper raced round the room.

Clarke jumped up. She locked her computer quickly but noticed nobody else did. At the other end of the office, Bradley Acres ushered his team into one of the few small offices. Through the glass panels on the door, Clarke glimpsed them dragging a table across to barricade themselves in, then they switched the lights out.

"Quick," she said to the rest of her team, "the escape route." She grabbed her coat and bag and headed towards the exit at the back of the room, checking to make sure Tammy, Ken, and Andrew followed. The main door to their office needed a pass to unlock it from the outside. The mock terrorists would probably take a pass off of anyone they found in the corridor. They would be inside within seconds.

They made it through the door and started walking up the stairs. A few other people had followed them. Clarke hoped there wouldn't be too many or the 'terrorists' would notice the door and come after them.

Andrew and Ken ran up the stairs two at a time and quickly overtook the girls. "Come on. Run," Andrew urged them. Ken wheezed heavily and Clarke hoped he wouldn't succumb to a heart attack.

"I can't run anywhere in these shoes," Tammy complained.

Andrew kept going, with Ken tagging along behind him and three other people who had followed them out jogging along in their wake. Clarke stayed with Tammy. She didn't want to run unless circumstances forced her, but she wouldn't tell Andrew or Ken that. They should be working as a team, but the two men still charged on ahead, looking after themselves. In the fire brigade, she would have never left any of their team behind like that.

When they reached the top floor, Clarke's common sense told her they should run through to the stairs on the other side. All the important people's offices were on this floor. Any proper terrorist would find that out and head up here first. She urged Tammy on. "Take your shoes off," she said. "You can run on the carpet and put them back on when we get to the stairs again."

For once Tammy obeyed, although Clarke guessed that was probably because she didn't want to risk meeting Douglas.

By the time they reached the stairs to go down on the opposite side of the building, Clarke and Tammy were well and truly straggling behind. The sound of five pairs of running feet echoed down the stairs. She wondered if anyone was stationed at the bottom, waiting for them.

"When we get out," Tammy said, puffing from the unaccustomed exertion, "I need to go. I've got a dentist appointment."

"Ok. We'll see you later," Clarke said, mildly disappointed that her plan to spend the next couple of hours in a coffee shop with Tammy had been scuppered.

"I doubt I'll be back. Can you tell Andrew, please? I forgot to mention it to him."

"Sure."

They descended one floor. The others seemed to be nearly at the bottom of the stairs now. The sound of footsteps echoed up the stairwell, then suddenly the footsteps stopped.

"Brack Attack," someone shouted. Then again, "Brack Attack."

Clarke stopped so abruptly that Tammy nearly ran into the back of her. That was the signal. *Brack Attack.* She tried to remember the email instructions. If someone shouted Brack Attack at you and stuck a sticky label on you, it meant you were 'captured' and henceforth out of the game. Ken, Andrew, and the three others must have been captured. Well, she wouldn't let it happen to her and Tammy.

Clarke's brain flew into overdrive. Plan B. She grabbed Tammy's arm, making a 'shushing' signal to her, and led her off the stairs. Round the corner, just off the fourth floor landing, the ladies' toilets would provide the best place to hide. Clarke worried that the 'terrorists' might come up the stairs any minute now.

Inside the ladies' toilets were four cubicles and a big, walk-in cupboard that contained cleaning stuff. She ushered Tammy into the cupboard and shut the door behind them. The stench of bleach reminded

Clarke of being in hospital. Hopefully, they wouldn't need to stay in here too long. "They won't find us here," she whispered. "The toilets are well hidden on this floor. They'll probably go straight past."

"Quiet," Tammy shushed her as multiple footsteps clattered by outside. The absence of carpet on the stairs sent echoes round the entire stairwell.

It surprised Clarke to notice how fast her heart raced. This was only a training exercise, she reminded herself, but the adrenalin that coursed through her body took her back to the old days. Brack Attack seemed to produce almost the same rush as running through a burning house trying to put out a fire.

After a few minutes, Tammy spoke, "It's quiet out there. Shall we risk it? We could make a run for the bottom and get out of here."

"Might be better if we go slower," Clarke said, surprised that Tammy now seemed keen on running. "We'll make too much noise if we run."

Tammy said, "I'll go out first. If they're still on the stairs, only one of us will get caught."

Clarke nodded. "Thanks."

"I'll come and get you if the coast is clear."

Tammy crept out of the cupboard.

"Good luck." The outer door creaked shut, leaving Clarke alone.

It was deadly silent in the cupboard. With no connecting door to the fourth floor, this area remained pretty well insulated from the rest of the office. It was an odd arrangement, having loos here. The women on the fifth floor had to come down a flight of stairs every time they needed the toilet. Clarke strained to listen for any sound. Nothing. Not even the sound of Tammy coming back. She wondered how long she should wait.

After ten minutes, boredom set in. Tammy must have been captured, or she would have come back to get her. In any case, the stairwell should be clear by now. With luck, Clarke would have a clear run—or *walk*, she hoped—down four more flights of stairs to escape outside. Then she would simply have to get round the building without being seen and head for the nearby shops in Brackford to avoid being caught. For a moment, she wondered if she should stay put. She doubted anyone would find her in here. But the strong smell of bleach made her nauseous, so she really needed some fresh air.

Clarke had been carrying her coat, grabbed in a hurry as she left the office, but now she took the time to put it on before she crept slowly out into the stairwell, being extra careful not to make any noise with her footsteps. She strained to listen, in case anyone might be nearby. Nothing. Suddenly, without warning, the strident ringing of the fire alarm shattered the silence. It must be someone escaping through one of the fire doors. At least, Clarke hoped that explained the alarm going off. She immediately remembered the Internal Audit team barricaded in the small meeting room on the third floor and hoped it wasn't a real fire.

Now that Clarke didn't have to worry about making noise, she soon reached the bottom of the stairs and carefully opened the external fire door, a fraction at first, then seeing no one, she pushed the door wide-open. She walked quickly round the shadow of the building, keeping as close as possible to the wall. A couple of minutes later, freedom successfully achieved, Clarke strolled down the footpath towards Brackford.

Freedom. Clarke finally relaxed and breathed a sigh of relief. She wondered if Tammy had escaped also and felt part pleased for Tammy and part annoyed because she'd forgotten to come back for her. Anyway, at least she had done better than Andrew and Ken.

A chill November wind blustered between the buildings, making Clarke relieved she had taken a second to grab her coat and bag.

In the coffee shop, as Clarke opened her bag to get out her purse, something suddenly stuck her as odd. Tammy hadn't been wearing her coat or carrying a handbag. Clarke knew that for a fact because she'd noticed Tammy this morning with a particularly nice Izzy Miyake handbag. She definitely hadn't brought it out of the office with her. Was that what had happened to Tammy? Had she gone back for it and been captured? If she was going to a dentist appointment, then straight home afterwards, she would need her handbag and coat for sure.

After two long, leisurely coffees, Clarke still didn't know if she should go back to the office. It was well into lunchtime now. She ordered a sandwich, smiling to herself. That was the one big flaw in this mock terrorist attack thing—a bit of a Mock-Up. They'd told everyone to either hide or get out of the office, but they didn't arrange any signal to indicate when it might be safe to go back in. She realised now that she'd switched her mobile off when they were hidden in the cleaning cupboard, in case anyone had come in. Part of her didn't want to switch it back on yet. She didn't often get a chance to switch off totally and relax. Part of her wanted to stay here drinking coffee for another couple of hours and enjoy doing nothing. She pressed the power button and watched her phone fire up.

A minute later, the phone started bleeping with text messages. She flicked through them. One from her brother, Rob, one from her mother, and one from Ken, sent over an hour ago. She opened the last one first.

WHERE THE HELL ARE YOU? the text said. Clarke waited a moment while she read the other texts. Her mum wanted to check Christmas arrangements. That would wait. Rob was inviting her out on Saturday evening to celebrate his birthday. She fired off a quick reply to Rob to say she'd come. Then, reluctantly, she put her coat on and made her way back to the office.

"Clarke, where have you been?" Andrew sounded annoyed. "And where's Tammy?"

It would be great, Clarke reflected, if he'd been just a tiny bit worried about her. But then this was the man, she reminded herself, who had charged off ahead, leaving her and Tammy behind.

"Tammy said she's got a dentist appointment. She's not coming back today." Clarke wondered if Tammy's split with Doug had affected her far more deeply than she'd let on. Tammy would normally have remembered to tell Andrew herself earlier.

"Would have been nice if she'd told me," Andrew said, reiterating Clarke's opinion.

"What happened to you and Ken?" Clarke asked, changing the subject. "Did you escape?" She was certain the answer was *No*.

"We were unlucky." Andrew looked embarrassed. "They ambushed us on the back stairs right before the exit. If you and Tammy hadn't been so slow, we would have got out and missed them."

Or, if you'd waited for us, you may have missed them too, Clarke wanted to say but realised there would be no point. Andrew would spin the truth somehow to make himself look good and they would get into an argument.

Andrew continued, "You're lucky we delayed them so they didn't catch you too."

"Thanks," Clarke said, forcing the word out reluctantly. "We hid in a cleaning cupboard until they'd gone, then we went downstairs and got out. Tammy went to her dentist appointment, and I walked into town and sat in a coffee shop. They said not to hang around the building." Clarke didn't mention that she and Tammy had split up before they left the building. Presumably, Tammy got out. Andrew never listened, anyway.

"Well done, girls," Ken said quietly.

"So what happened to everyone else?" Clarke was interested to find out.

"Internal audit barricaded themselves in the end office," Ken said. "They were still there when we came back in. They wouldn't come out until we'd assured them the game was over. They'd put a kettle and coffee and biscuits in the meeting room on Monday. Sounds like they had a great time. We should have done that, instead of all that running around." Ken looked at Clarke reproachfully.

Clarke ignored him, refusing to comment. She unlocked her computer and checked her emails.

"Douglas Doncaster apparently briefed someone on every floor to phone him as soon as things kicked off," Ken said. "He got out of the building first. But he returned to the office far too early and started working again. The fake terrorists ran straight upstairs when they heard that and zapped him with a sticker. He was livid."

Clarke laughed. "Wish I'd seen that." She opened her latest email, titled *Operation Brack Attack*.

Operation Brack Attack is now over, the email read.

"This is ridiculous," Clarke said. "They've emailed us to tell us Brack Attack is finished and we can all go back into the office."

Ken looked blank. Clarke didn't think he really got the irony of that. He had probably been back in the office already when he'd received the email. Never mind, it would be something for her and Tammy to laugh about tomorrow.

"When will they tell us which team's won?" Clarke didn't suppose it would be their team, since they had split up and half of them got caught.

"Next week probably," Ken said.

The afternoon dragged. After the excitement of Brack Attack, Clarke struggled to settle down to work. She decided to give it up as a bad job and leave on time today. Tomorrow, she would catch up.

At five o'clock, she retrieved her coat from the coat hooks by the staff lockers. As she buttoned it up, she noticed that Tammy's coat still hung in the corner.

She looked more closely. It certainly looked like Tammy's coat, vibrant red, with gold buttons, and really long, reaching halfway down her calves, with Tammy being on the short side. The perfect coat for cold weather, Tammy always said. The coat was particularly distinctive, in true Tammy style. It must be Tammy's. Clarke wondered how she'd managed without it. Tammy had been getting the bus to work lately. Clarke supposed that must be since she left Douglas and moved to Tredington. She'd have frozen waiting at a bus stop without her coat in yesterday's sharp wind.

Clarke remembered that Tammy hadn't taken her handbag with her either. She must have returned inside to get it. But why hadn't she taken her coat at the same time?

Chapter 6

Thursday, Week One

Clarke arrived at the office before eight the next morning. With Brack Attack eating up a large part of yesterday, she'd hardly got any work done. She would need to work flat out today to catch up.

She switched her computer on. It buzzed into life. By the time Andrew and Ken showed up, she was working like a demon, trying to power through the punishing schedule of tasks she'd set herself for the day. Clarke ignored them, also blocking out the general hum of office phones ringing and people talking, and focused on what she needed to do. It was ten o'clock before she realised the desk beside her remained empty.

"Where's Tammy?" she asked.

Ken looked up from his computer. "Dunno. It's a bit late, even for her. She's usually in before me."

Andrew was attending a meeting, so Clarke quickly sent Tammy a text, asking where she was. With a bit of luck, she'd show up before Andrew returned. In the meantime, Clarke desperately needed coffee.

In the kitchen, the conversation was all about Brack Attack. It sounded like a lot of people had been captured. Mostly only those people with a proper plan evaded capture.

"Did you hear about Hugh in marketing?" a tall man with a beard, whose name Clarke forgot, asked her.

Clarke shook her head, not even sure if she knew Hugh in marketing.

"He brought an orange fluorescent jacket into work. Put it on and walked straight out past the fake terrorists," the bearded man said. "They all wore the same jackets. Assumed he was one of them. Genius."

Clarke agreed. It was kind of funny but brilliant.

As soon as she got back to her desk, she checked her phone. No reply from Tammy yet. She texted again. *Are You Ok?*

By 11:30, there was still no reply to Clarke's text message. She grabbed her phone and took it into the corridor. Tammy's number diverted straight to voicemail.

"Tammy, where are you?" she said. "Andrew's going to do his nut. Are you ok?"

It occurred to Clarke that Tammy might already have phoned or emailed Andrew by now. She might be taking the day off sick. Andrew wouldn't be back from his meeting until lunchtime. Tammy was sure to have contacted him by then. Clarke wished Tammy were here now. She was dying to compare notes on Brack Attack, particularly to find out why Tammy hadn't come back for her, but she guessed it would wait until tomorrow.

Clarke went out to the staff locker area. Something was buzzing around her brain. She needed to check if Tammy's coat remained in the same place as yesterday. It might not be Tammy's. If someone else had taken it home, it would probably be hanging on a different peg today, then she could stop worrying about Tammy. Clarke scanned along the row of coats hanging on the wall. The red coat, Tammy's red coat, still hung in exactly the same position as yesterday.

"We should call the police," Clarke said. It was nearly two o'clock now.

"Don't be ridiculous." Andrew sneered at her. "She's probably not well and has gone back to bed and forgotten to phone."

"But she hasn't returned my phone calls or texts." Tammy never let her phone out of her sight. If she wasn't phoning or texting, she was scrolling down Facebook or Instagram or posting stuff on those sites.

"Battery's probably flat," Andrew said. "Anyway, she's a grown woman, and it's only been a few hours. The police will laugh at you. They won't do anything."

"I'm worried," Clarke said, remembering Tammy's coat. "It's not like her."

Andrew snorted. "If anyone should be worried, it's Tammy," he said. "I'm going to give her such a bollocking tomorrow."

As soon as Andrew turned his back, Clarke grabbed her phone and took it to the toilets. She sat down in a cubicle and searched for Tammy's Facebook account. Barely a day passed when Tammy didn't post something on Facebook or Instagram. Clarke used to tease her that she fancied herself as the next big influencer. Was she overreacting over Tammy's failure to show up? Tammy hadn't been her normal self these last few days, which worried Clarke. Looking at Tammy's social media posts might set her mind at rest.

Tammy's last post on Facebook showed photos of her with three of her girlfriends sitting in a restaurant. That was Tuesday evening. She'd written, *Girls' night out. What a fun evening with Keira, Sam, and Josie. Prettiest food in North London. The chef is a star in the making.* She'd tagged in her three friends and the restaurant, Finlays. Clarke scrolled through the photos: a few of her friends, in various combinations, a full-length one of Tammy posing, one of the restaurant's exterior, and one of an exquisite chocolate and raspberry dessert that wouldn't look out of place in an art gallery. Tammy was right. Judging by that dessert, it possibly was the prettiest food in North London.

So far, Tammy had clocked up 167 likes and thirty-two comments. Clarke scrolled down through the comments. All the usual stuff. Tammy had 'liked' the first twenty-one comments and replied to a few. Clarke looked at the timings. They had all been late Tuesday evening and early Wednesday morning. The remaining eleven comments, all posted since mid-morning yesterday, had not yet been liked by Tammy.

Clarke's heart thumped as she stared at her phone. She closed Facebook and opened up Instagram, searching for Tammy's account, *Tammy Loves Trouble*. The same pictures came up. The same wording. She'd almost certainly copied the post between Facebook and Instagram. Ninety-nine likes and sixteen comments. Tammy hadn't replied to any of the comments and it wasn't clear when they had been posted, anyway.

Back at her desk, she replayed everything again and again in her head. Tammy's coat, still hanging in the staff cloakroom, the lack of activity on social media since yesterday morning, failing to answer her phone. It might be unimportant. Tammy may be absolutely fine.

Clarke walked upstairs slowly. Timidly, she knocked at the door of Douglas Doncaster's office.

Douglas sat at his desk, bent over some papers. Clarke noticed a bald patch in the middle of his greying hair before he looked up at her. He seemed especially stern today, as if annoyed by the interruption. Clarke wondered what Tammy had ever seen in him. She struggled to picture lively, fun-loving Tammy with this rather stern man. Hopefully, he transformed his personality and became more fun outside of work. Clarke questioned if she had done the right thing coming to see him, especially as he and Tammy were now estranged.

"Yes," he said, sounding impatient.

Clarke hesitated, unsure what to say. Would he still care about his wife? Or perhaps he would and she should be tactful. "I'm worried about Tammy," she said.

Douglas stopped working. "What's she done now?"

"Nothing." Clarke found Douglas a bit intimidating. She forced herself to get a grip. "She didn't show up for work this morning," Clarke said quickly, eager to spurt everything out before Douglas sent her on her way. "She won't answer her phone and she hasn't posted on social media since yesterday morning."

Douglas laughed. "Well, that is serious, isn't it?"

Clarke nodded.

"NO," he said. "For Christ's sake, can't you recognise a joke when you hear one? Tammy's got a mind of her own. She's probably bunking off having a good time somewhere. Tell me when you find out. I'll make sure we dock her a day's pay if she's skiving." He turned back to the papers on his desk. "Shut the door behind you," he said.

Clarke headed back downstairs. Going to talk to Tammy's husband had been a mistake. She realised she had forgotten to tell him about the coat, but she doubted if that would have made any difference. What a horrid, horrid man. She didn't blame Tammy one bit for leaving him.

If no one would take her seriously, she would be forced to wait until tomorrow. If Tammy didn't show up first thing, she would call the police, regardless. She didn't care what everyone else said. Something wasn't right.

Chapter 7

Detective Constable Paul Waterford drove slowly into the Briar Holman car park, as if delaying the issue would make it go away. He wished his sergeant had allocated this misper case to someone else, but the rest of CID was busy on a drugs raid and Paul had just finished tying up some loose ends on a burglary case, so he was free. He'd expected to be assigned to help out with the raid, but then this had come up and there was no one else.

"You all right, mate?" DC Kevin Farrier asked.

"Just looking for a parking space." Kevin—Kev to his friends, of which Paul really didn't want to be one—was new to CID. His likeness to a yapping puppy, keen and excitable and needing to be kept on a very short leash, annoyed Paul. Not only did Paul dread this particular meeting, but he was lumbered with babysitting the newbie as well.

Paul was about to ask for her in reception when she appeared. They both spoke at once.

"Clarke."

"Paul."

He noticed for an instant that aura of vulnerability, of uncertainty, of shock. That same appearance she'd had four years ago when he'd dumped her.

"You're here about Tammy?" Clarke said.

Paul nodded. She had recovered herself quickly. This might not be as bad as he'd feared. He hoped she'd moved on, put their relationship behind her. For the first time, he appreciated the presence of *Kev The Puppy*. Anything would be better than being left alone with Clarke.

"Is there an office where we can talk?" he asked.

Clarke led them to the lift and took them to a small room on the third floor.

Paul sat opposite Clarke. Kevin plonked himself down next to him, like a shadow that was glued to his side.

"You always wanted to be in CID, didn't you?" Clarke said.

Paul ignored her. "Tell me about Tammy, from the start. What happened?" He would keep it professional. They were here to do a job, and he didn't want to take a trip down Memory Lane with DC Bloody Farrier listening in. It was none of his business.

"She's been missing for two days," Clarke said. "I'm really worried about her."

"Since Wednesday then." Paul noticed how upset Clarke seemed. The last time he had seen her like that... He forced himself to concentrate, so he could leave as soon as possible. "What's her full name?" he asked. "Address, age, family?" He would need all the details to file in his report.

"Tammy Doncaster. Her husband is the deputy chief executive here, Douglas Doncaster," Clarke said. "He can give you the rest."

"Why hasn't he reported her missing then?" Kevin asked.

Paul glared at him. He had been about to ask that. Now he looked like an idiot.

Clarke addressed Kevin. "She's left him," she said. "Tammy's living in Tredington, in her parents' old house."

Paul shifted in his seat, trying to get comfortable in a chair that felt like sitting on a board. "Can you tell me what happened on Wednesday, the last time you saw her?"

"We had a terrorist attack," Clarke said.

Paul looked up from his notes. Kevin Farrier looked like he was about to explode out of his chair with excitement.

"Not a real one," Clarke added quickly. "A mock one, as a training exercise, to test our resilience."

Paul smiled as he watched Kevin deflate like a saggy balloon. "Go on," he said.

"It happened on Wednesday morning. I'd come up with a plan to escape down the back stairs. Andrew and Ken, the other members of our team, went on ahead and it sounded like they'd been caught, so Tammy and I turned around and hid in a cleaning cupboard for a while." Clarke paused. "Tammy said she'd go out first and come and get me if the coast was clear."

"And she never came back?" Paul asked.

"No." Clarke shook her head. "I waited for ages. It seemed like ages. Probably ten or fifteen minutes."

"Did you see her afterwards?"

"No," Clarke said, "but I wasn't expecting to. Tammy was going straight to a dentist appointment, so she wouldn't come back." Clarke paused. "The thing is, she hadn't mentioned it until just before she left me."

"When you got out of the building, did you see her anywhere?" Paul asked.

Clarke considered for a moment. "No," she said, "but to be honest, I didn't really look. I just wanted to get away, so I headed towards the shops in Brackford. Tammy would have gone the other way, to the bus stop near the car park entrance."

"And you weren't expecting her back," Paul said. "So when did you realise she was missing?" He accidentally caught Clarke's eye but looked away quickly.

"Yesterday," Clarke said. "She didn't show up for work. We waited, in case her bus was stuck in traffic. I phoned her a couple of times, but the phone went straight to voicemail."

"Her husband didn't report her missing."

"I told you, she left him. Three months ago."

"Is there any reason she would want to disappear?" Paul asked.

Clarke shook her head. "I don't know," she said. "What sort of reason?"

"Did Tammy have any problems? Money worries? Any signs of depression? Had she upset anyone?"

"No. Everybody liked Tammy," Clarke said, "and she was usually really happy. She got upset when she told me she'd left her husband, but nothing like actual depression."

"Was she seeing anyone?" Paul asked.

"I don't think so."

Paul wondered how close Clarke really was to Tammy. She seemed very concerned about her, but she didn't seem aware of anything about her life outside of work. He stood up, cringing as Kevin got up almost in sync with him. "We'll need to talk to her colleagues," he said. "Perhaps we can start with the husband." With a bit of luck, Tammy's husband would give him something more useful and he'd wrap up this case before lunchtime.

"Her colleagues are over there." Clarke pointed to a bank of desks nearby. "You need to talk to Andrew and Ken, but they probably won't know any more than me. Her husband is on the fifth floor."

"DC Farrier, stay here and make a list of anyone on this floor who spoke to her on Wednesday." He turned to Clarke. "Can you take me upstairs to the husband, please?" he said, regretting his decision as soon as the words left his mouth. He should take Farrier with him.

Clarke led him out towards the stairs. "She left her coat," she said. "It was freezing outside, and she left her coat."

"Is it still here?" Paul would take the coat with him. It might be important.

Clarke turned and pointed back in the direction they had come. "I'll show you."

"Thanks."

"I wondered," she said, "if her handbag might still be in her locker. I don't remember her having it with her when we left the office."

"Are you sure?" Paul decided it wouldn't hurt to check. Disappearing without her coat and handbag suggested either she wouldn't have left of her own accord, or alternatively, she might be suffering from extreme depression. There may be more to this than he had first assumed.

"I'll get the key. The office manager keeps them. Tammy's coat is the red one on the end." Clarke pointed towards a rack of coats before going in search of Tammy's locker key.

Paul picked out Tammy's coat easily, there being only one red one. He put some gloves on to remove it from the peg. The coat looked designer. Expensive. He wondered how much she earned. Her husband would certainly be on a massive salary, so no doubt he could afford Tammy's designer tastes. Perhaps he had done her in to avoid an expensive divorce settlement.

He checked the coat pockets. Empty.

Clarke came back with the key to open Tammy's locker.

"Who has access to Tammy's key?" he asked.

"No one," Clarke said. "Tammy has one and the office manager has one, but she keeps that locked away. She only gave me the key because you're police."

Paul pulled at the locker door. It opened reluctantly, its hinges squeaking in protest.

"That's it," Clarke said. "That's the handbag she brought in on Wednesday morning. It's Izzy Miyake. I noticed it because it's my favourite one of hers."

Paul took the handbag out. Another expensive designer item. How the other half lived. He opened it up. Purse, credit cards, iPhone, house keys, a pair of gloves, and a pen.

Clarke seemed distressed. "She can't have gone anywhere without money," she said. "And Tammy would rather have her hand chopped off than be parted from her phone. Please find her, Paul. Something's happened to her."

Paul nodded. "Try not to worry. There's probably some very simple explanation." It was starting to look bad for Tammy, but he didn't want to panic Clarke. He surmised that, without her coat and handbag, Tammy may have been abducted, but why? "Can you take me to meet her husband now, please?" The sooner he spoke to Douglas Doncaster, the better.

Paul followed Clarke up the stairs. He was pleased to see she didn't walk with a limp. He remembered the doctors had believed that she would. At one stage, they thought she might not walk at all. Their footsteps clattered on the uncarpeted stairs. "I'm sorry," he said, pausing halfway up the staircase. It needed saying. He should have said it before.

Ahead of him, Clarke stopped dead, turning to face him. She stood several steps above him and the extra height gave her the upper hand. Paul wouldn't blame her if she pushed him. He deserved it. For a moment, he imagined himself falling backwards onto the hard stairs, rolling down, landing at the bottom in a twisted heap. Yes, he deserved it.

"I was in hospital, Paul. I didn't know if I'd be able to walk properly again, didn't know if I'd lose my job, my career. I was in terrible pain and about to have surgery."

She looked at him blackly. She didn't need to, Paul thought. He already felt guilty as hell.

"I was about to undergo major surgery. You must have realised how terrified I would be, and you dumped me."

Paul had never seen her so angry. His sweet, lovely Clarke. Feisty yes, determined and stubborn, definitely, but not angry. Never angry. He didn't blame her.

"I'm sorry," he said again. He wasn't sure what else to say. "I was young. I couldn't handle it." He'd been terrified that she might lose her leg. It wasn't what he'd signed up for. He'd regretted his stupidity for a long time. At least he should have waited, not ditched her when she needed him the most.

Clarke turned and carried on walking up the stairs. "Just find her, Paul. Find Tammy."

"I'll try," he said. "If you remember anything else, anything at all..." Paul noticed Clarke's hesitation. "There is something, isn't there?"

"No."

Her answer was too quick. "I can't find Tammy if you don't tell me everything," Paul said.

Clarke stopped and turned around.

Paul noticed she was gripping the banister. "Clarke?"

For the first time, she looked at Paul properly. "You're right. I don't want to tell you this," Clarke said, "but only because I think she's wrong."

"Who's wrong?" Paul asked. "You need to tell me everything. It might help. Anything might help."

Clarke resumed walking. They were almost at the top of the stairs now. "Tammy believed one of the guys in IT was stalking her." They reached the top. Clarke paused, her fingers resting on the door handle into the offices.

Paul caught up with her. "Did she say who?"

Clarke nodded. "I'm just not sure I should say."

"Did he ever do anything? Did he threaten her?"

"No. I don't think he's a threat at all. "

"So, who?" Paul put a hand on her arm. "It might help."

She shook his hand off. "It was Jeffrey. Jeffrey Todd. He works on the ground floor. But I really don't think he'd do anything. In fact, I'm sure he wouldn't."

Paul could tell Clarke already regretted telling him this, like she no doubt regretted a lot of things concerning him. He reminded himself he was here to do a job, and that meant checking out Jeffrey Todd, regardless of Clarke's opinion of the man. The nicest people sometimes turned out to be psychopathic murderers. You could never tell. He hoped he wasn't searching for a killer.

Clarke led him down a corridor and knocked on one of the doors. She opened it without waiting for a reply.

"Mr Doncaster," she said. "This is Detective Constable Waterford. He needs to talk to you about Tammy."

Paul entered the office as Clarke retreated, shutting the door behind her.

"Tammy?" Doncaster said. "Where is she?"

Douglas Doncaster's office was spacious enough for several extra chairs. Paul pulled one out and sat down opposite Doncaster without waiting to be asked. Several photos hung on the walls, mostly of Doncaster himself, plus some framed certificates. Otherwise, the room looked pretty bare. There were no photos of Tammy displayed, Paul noted. Had he taken them away after she'd left him? Or had there never been any?

"Your wife seems to have gone missing," Paul said. Although no one had actually checked her house yet. He needed to get the address. She might be bunking off work, making idiots of them all. He glanced down at the coat and handbag scrunched up in the evidence bag on his lap and knew that happy scenario was wishful thinking.

Doncaster hesitated. Was that a hint of concern on his face? It appeared only for a split second, then any trace of caring vanished.

"You're aware we've split up?" Doncaster sat back in his chair and folded his arms.

"Yes," Paul said. Clarke had told him Tammy had left. "Was it amicable?"

Doncaster sneered. "Hardly. She's seeing another man," he said. "I threw her out. You should ask her boyfriend where she is."

"I will," Paul said. That didn't tie up with Clarke's version. He wondered which version was true. "What's his name?" Hopefully, Tammy was bunking off with the boyfriend for a few days and this could all be resolved within hours.

Doncaster unfolded his arms and thumped his hands on the table. "No idea, and I don't bloody care." He composed himself rapidly. "I'd rather be blissfully ignorant as far as that's concerned."

"You must have some inkling. Do you know anything about him?"

"No."

"Then how can you be sure he even exists?" Paul said.

"I suspected something. She didn't deny it."

Paul changed tack. "Tell me about Brack Attack. That's when Tammy went missing, during Brack Attack. Tell me about the reason behind it. It might be significant."

Doncaster looked embarrassed. "It was just a game," he said, "just a game. Management wanted to find out how our employees would react in that sort of situation. It's useful information. Who's calm in an emergency, who might be future higher management material."

"I see." Paul still wondered if it could be of any significance.

Doncaster continued. "Mostly, it was intended to raise awareness of security issues. We've had problems recently with some employees letting strangers tailgate them into the building through the security door. And nearly everyone in the building walks away from their desk to go to lunch or meetings and they don't bother to lock their computer screen. Cyber-crime's a big thing now."

Paul nodded, pretending he understood Douglas Doncaster's worries. It struck him as odd that Doncaster showed somewhat less concern for his wife's whereabouts and well-being than he did about a potential bit of computer hacking. Presumably, the split was even less amicable than Doncaster had admitted. He made a mental note to add Doncaster to his list of suspects. As he was the husband, he would go to the top of the list.

Doncaster coughed, clearing his throat. "I suppose I should tell you. Tammy received some death threats."

Paul jerked his head up, his attention fully focused again. "What death threats? When?" What was it with the people in this company? First Clarke, then Doncaster, thinking they should hold back crucial information.

"Tammy came to me a couple of weeks ago and told me she'd been getting death threats," Doncaster said. "Just a couple of letters. They'd been posted to the office. I tried to make her go to the police, but she wouldn't even consider it."

"So where are the letters now?"

Doncaster shook his head. Paul attempted to catch his eye directly to try to detect if he was lying, but Doncaster carefully avoided any eye contact.

"No idea," Doncaster said. "She took the letters back after she showed them to me. They used those scary-looking newspaper print cut-outs. It really rattled her."

"What did the letters say?" Paul wondered what Tammy had done with them. If they could find them, they might give some clue to her current whereabouts.

"Just the usual stuff. I can't remember," he said. "Anyway, Tammy was scared. She said she didn't feel safe at work. That's why I brought Operation Brack Attack forward. I was planning the exercise for the spring, when the weather's better, but I hoped it might make her feel safer if she saw we were doing something."

Paul wondered if he still cared about Tammy, or if he was simply covering his corporate ass if anyone tried to kill her.

"I ordered an extra security lock on one of the access doors too," he said, "so it can only be opened with an employee pass. It's being fitted next week. Then it will be impossible for anyone to access the building without a pass."

"But you can now?" Paul asked. Had someone got into the building in the middle of all the confusion of Brack Attack and abducted Tammy?

"Yes, I guess I was too late."

Paul detected a glimmer of a smile, but it disappeared almost instantly. He resolved once again to investigate Douglas Doncaster thoroughly.

"Do you think you'll find Tammy?"

"I hope so," Paul said. It had been a couple of days now. He didn't like to say that it was becoming more likely with every minute that, if they did find Tammy Doncaster, she might not still be alive.

"What's Tammy's current address?" he asked. He really needed to check that out before he did anything else. And, if she wasn't home, at least it might give him some clues to her whereabouts.

"I don't know."

Paul wondered how Doncaster could care so little for his wife that he hadn't even bothered to find out where she now lived, especially when they still both worked for the same company. Surely, they must run into each other, working in the same building.

"Someone suggested Tammy may be living in Tredington," Paul said. "Does that area mean anything to her? Does she have any friends living there?"

Doncaster looked at his watch like he had to be somewhere soon. "Her parents used to live in Tredington. But they're both dead. Her mother died back in March this year."

"What's the address?" Paul said. She might live there if she'd inherited the house. It would be the most obvious place.

"She won't be there," Doncaster said. "Her parents lived in a council flat. Never bought it. They could have got it at a huge discount. I offered to help them pay for it, but they didn't want the responsibility. The council took the flat back to re-let it a couple of days after my mother-in-law died." He picked up the phone and dialled. "Wendy, come through, please," he said, hanging up quickly. He turned back to Paul. "Try human resources. I'm sure they'll give you Tammy's address."

A petite blond woman came into the office.

"Wendy, can you take this gentleman down to HR, please?" He turned back to Paul. "I'm sorry. I have an important meeting." Doncaster got up.

Paul was a bit put out at being dismissed so easily. Doncaster really didn't seem at all concerned about his wife, but he may be still pissed with her for cheating on him. That didn't mean he'd done her in. On the other hand, cheating on him provided the perfect motive. Interesting that Tammy came from a council estate background. Doncaster's whole persona screamed public school through and through. Chalk and Cheese?

He remembered DC Farrier and asked Wendy to make a detour to collect him. Best not leave him too long on his own, in case he did something stupid.

Wherever Tammy was living now, she hadn't bothered to inform HR. Paul had asked for Doncaster's address too, in case he needed it later. The two addresses were the same. He decided to talk to Clarke again.

"No, I've never been there," Clarke said when Paul asked her about Tammy's house in Tredington. "But she showed me photos. It used to be her parents' house. She renovated it after they died. She's been showing me pictures all summer. I assume that's where she's moved to."

Paul wasn't sure what to think. That was the second lie Tammy had told Clarke, assuming he believed Douglas Doncaster.

Clarke continued. "It looked pretty big," she said. "Four bedrooms. And a beautiful garden, with a pink rose bush near the gate and clematis growing up the wall by the door."

Paul sighed. That would be easier to find in the summer, not in November, if he knew what a clematis even looked like. He would send Farrier to check the electoral register. Or she may be paying council tax wherever she lived now, probably with the boyfriend. It should be easy

enough to trace her. She might even show up at work tomorrow. Then
he remembered today was Friday.

"Were you aware that Tammy received some death threats?"

"What? No. When? Why didn't she tell me that?"

"Recently," Paul said. "She told her husband. That's why he set up
the security exercise you did."

"Brack Attack."

"Yes. He reckoned it might make her feel more secure if he did
something positive. He thought it might make people more vigilant
too. But it seems like it just created chaos and made it easier for someone to get to Tammy. Douglas says there's a way in without needing an
employee pass."

Clarke nodded. "Yes. It's round the back of the stairs. We all use it
when we've forgotten our pass." She paused for a moment, then said,
"Why would anyone want to kill Tammy?" A tear dripped down her
cheek. "Do you think she's dead?"

"We can't rule that out."

Clarke appeared to be pretty shocked, so Paul tried to tread carefully, but it seemed to be the most likely scenario. It had been two days
with no sign of Tammy Doncaster. He wished she'd reported the death
threats to the police. Then she might still be here now.

"I'm really worried about her, Paul."

"We'll find her." Paul immediately regretted making a promise to
Clarke that he wouldn't be able to keep. Tammy might not even be alive
by now, and there were no guarantees that they would find her, dead or
alive. But Clarke seemed to need reassuring, and he didn't want to let
her down this time. He may not even be allowed to do much. He'd get
into trouble if he spent money on this case unnecessarily. It wasn't certain it was a missing person investigation yet. It might just be a grown
woman, with a new boyfriend, gone AWOL for a few days. He can-
celled that thought from his head. The death threats made it serious.
They would have to pull out all the stops to find her. The IT guy con-

cerned him too. He would check him out first. If this Jeffrey was really stalking Tammy, he might even be able to tell Paul where she lived.

Chapter 8

On Saturday evening, Clarke's younger brother, Rob, celebrated his birthday with some friends in Brackford. There were twelve of them, in Tricolore, his favourite pizza restaurant. Rob and a few of the party had already been on the beers before Clarke arrived, so it promised to be a rowdy night.

"Hi, Sis." Rob got up and hugged her. "This is my beautiful big sister," he announced to his friends.

"Happy Birthday." Clarke kissed Rob on the cheek and sat down at the empty place next to him. She recognised a couple of his friends, but most of them were unfamiliar. She hoped he wouldn't try to set her up with any of them. It wouldn't be the first time.

The party had a big table by the window and, through the one-way glass, Clarke got a great view of the street outside. The restaurant was in Brackford's historic marketplace. In the summer evenings, people often sat outside at the front to eat—all the advantages of a pavement café but with no traffic.

When the conversation turned to football, Clarke watched the people walking past the window, making up stories in her head about where they might be going.

"Nice restaurant, isn't it?" one of Rob's friends said.

"Yes, I come here a lot." Clarke nibbled at an olive. "I work a few minutes round the corner."

Clarke ordered the same pizza she always did, Fiorentina. Spinach, black olives, and a whole egg on top. She loved it, especially when she improved it by adding an extra topping of sun-dried tomatoes.

The waiter put the pizza down in front of her. Tricolore made the most enormous pizzas in Brackford. She'd forgotten how big they were. Clarke waited for the waiters to bring everyone else's food before she started eating. Outside, a large group of people walked past the window. Four couples, all hand in hand and laughing. They disappeared out of sight and a woman opposite the restaurant caught Clarke's attention. The woman wore a dark coat and a blue woolly hat. Clarke instantly recognised the hat, with its distinctive pattern. She stood up to get a better view. The woman looked very much like Tammy. Clarke stared at her for a few seconds longer. It was Tammy for certain. Even in the dark at that distance. Her height, her weight, the way she carried herself when she walked. That woman was Tammy. It must be.

Clarke jumped up and dashed for the door, nearly colliding with a waitress. Rob called her name, but she ignored him. She needed to get outside before Tammy disappeared.

"Tammy." She scanned the marketplace. The woman had moved farther away now. "Tammy," she called again. The woman in the distance didn't react. She mustn't have heard her. Clarke shouted again, louder this time. There was a man walking right behind Tammy. Clarke hadn't noticed him before. Were they together? It seemed odd not to be walking side by side. They both turned into an alleyway. Had Tammy even noticed the man behind her? Clarke began to run.

By the time she reached the alleyway, it was empty.

It must be Tammy. Clarke was so sure. Seeing her alive and well was a massive relief. But why didn't she stop when Clarke called her? Had that man been following her or threatening her even? Clarke should phone Paul, in case Tammy was in danger. He could check the CCTV in the area and prove it really was Tammy. Maybe. As Clarke walked back to the restaurant, she already doubted herself. It was dark outside. The woman had been some distance away. Suddenly, Clarke wasn't so sure.

She took a deep breath and composed herself before she went back into the restaurant, to make sure Rob didn't notice how much her ankle hurt her now. He would start getting protective and Clarke wanted him to enjoy himself tonight, not waste the evening worrying about her.

Rob came to meet her as soon as she got through the door. "What's got into you, Sis?" He put his arm around her. "You're freezing."

"I'm sorry. I thought I saw someone I recognised." Clarke hadn't told Rob yet about Tammy's disappearance. Tonight was the first time she'd seen him since and she didn't want to discuss anything so serious on his birthday and ruin the atmosphere.

"Really, Sis. You don't get up in the middle of dinner and rush out in the freezing cold without a coat and without saying a word to anyone just to say hi to a friend," Rob said. "What's going on?"

"It's ok," Clarke said. "I had a bit of a moment, that's all. My imagination ran wild." She flashed him a big smile to show she was all right. "Come on. It's your birthday. Let's enjoy the evening."

They sat down. Clarke shivered, still reacting to the cold outside. Her ankle ached like crazy now from the running and she needed some painkillers. If only she hadn't drunk that glass of wine.

"Your food's cold," Rob said. He waved at a waitress. "Please, could you warm this up?" he asked, giving the waitress his most charming smile.

Clarke realised Rob hadn't let this go and she would need to give him a full explanation at some point. She was thankful for now that he didn't make a fuss in front of everybody.

Chapter 9

Sunday, Week One

Clarke got up late on Sunday. It had been a good night on the whole, but she had definitely drunk too much. Thankfully, Rob had insisted she take a taxi to and from the restaurant. She was trying to decide what to cook for lunch when the doorbell rang.

Rob looked like he'd just tumbled out of bed with his tousled hair and sleepy appearance. "Hi, Sis," he said. "Can I come in?"

Clarke decided against proper cooking and opened a couple of tins of soup for lunch, putting the contents into a saucepan to heat.

"How's work?" Clarke asked. Rob invented computer games.

"Great," he said. "My latest is all about trying to break into MI5. It's getting rave reviews."

Clarke laughed. As a teenager, Rob had tried to hack into the MI5 computer system using one of the school computers. Of course he'd failed, but Clarke always believed that was because of the lack of power of the school's computer rather than any lack of ability on Rob's part. He'd successfully hacked into his head teacher's emails and got them both into all kinds of trouble over it. Luckily, his teachers had managed to steer his skills towards something more productive. After a couple of years of working for one of the top games manufacturers, he'd set up his own company. Clarke's delight with Rob's success was only surpassed by her relief that he'd avoided getting into trouble.

They sat down to eat the soup. "What was last night all about?" Rob asked. "The running off thing in the middle of dinner?"

Clarke tensed. She'd been expecting that question, but she still wasn't sure what to tell him.

"Do you remember Tammy, from work?"

"Of course I do. How could I forget gorgeous Tammy?"

Clarke blew on her soup while she considered how much to tell Rob. "She's gone missing."

"What? When?" Rob appeared genuinely worried.
"She left work on Wednesday in the middle of a terrorist attack..."
"Terrorist attack?"

Clarke explained quickly about Brack Attack. "But she never got her coat and bag from the office."
"Did she keep spares in the car?"
"She took the bus. It was freezing out. She wouldn't have lasted long without her coat. And she literally never even moved without her phone and that was still in her bag." Clarke took the empty soup bowls and put them in the sink, ready to wash up.
"Four days," Rob said. "There must be a reasonable explanation. Could she have forgotten to tell anyone she'd booked a holiday?"
Clarke shook her head. "Tammy was always so on the ball. She'd never have forgotten anything like that." She realised she was talking about Tammy in the past tense and stopped herself.
"Perhaps she took a sickie but forgot to phone in? That's what I'd do."
"Rob! Most people don't do that. Tammy's a responsible adult." Was she? Clarke wondered. "Tammy wouldn't do that." Or would she? She didn't know anymore. She didn't have a clue what Tammy would or wouldn't do.
"So, last night, you thought..."
"I thought I saw Tammy walking across the marketplace," Clarke said. "I was so sure. She even wore clothes I'd seen her wear before." Rob would think she'd gone mad, imagining things that weren't real. "Then she disappeared down an alleyway and I lost her."

"Did you tell the police?" Rob said. "About Tammy's disappearance, I mean?"

"Yes, of course, but not until Friday. Nobody else worried about her when she didn't show up on Thursday. They said I was overreacting."

"That's bad," Rob said, taking a gulp of his water. "Got any beer?"

Clarke took some cans out of the fridge. "The police came on Friday." She hesitated. "They sent Paul."

Rob looked at her. "I hope you kicked the bastard in the balls."

Clarke smiled. "Bit uncivilised," she said. She'd intended to phone Paul last night to tell him about seeing Tammy. Now she wasn't even sure if it had been Tammy.

"I found some fraudulent invoices," Clarke said, eager to change the subject away from her ex. "Someone's been embezzling money from the company."

"Wow." Rob popped the ring pull on his beer and took a gulp out of the can.

"The thing is," she said, "I showed one of them to Tammy. She said she intended to discuss it with someone."

"So?"

"So, I show her the invoice, she tells someone, and then she disappears," Clarke said. "Don't you think that's suspicious?"

Rob took another gulp of his beer. "What do the police say?"

Clarke passed him a table mat to put his beer can on. "I haven't told them yet. Not about the fraud. I'm looking for more invoices. I'm sure there are others."

"Clarke." Rob sounded worried. "You must tell them. If Tammy disappeared because she knew something about a fraud, she may actually be in danger. So might you."

"I'm ok," Clarke said. She needed to find more invoices first. Enough so the police believed her and would investigate properly. "Anyway, apparently Tammy got some death threats recently, so that's probably what happened to her."

"You think she's dead?" Rob's face paled noticeably.

"I hope not, but it seems likely." Clarke tried not to cry. It didn't seem real, not yet.

Rob came over and hugged her, which did make Clarke cry. "Hey, Sis, it'll be ok. Tammy will probably walk into the office on Monday and tell you what a great holiday she's had."

Clarke doubted that very much, but she appreciated Rob's efforts to comfort her.

"Where's your laptop?" Rob asked. "I have an idea."

Clarke got her laptop from the bedroom.

Rob opened up the laptop. "Can you log into the Briar Holman network on this?"

"Yes. I do it when I need to work from home." Clarke tapped in her username and password.

Rob pulled the laptop back towards him. He started typing.

"What are you going to do?" Clarke almost didn't dare ask.

"I'm going to try accessing Tammy's emails," he said. "That may give us some idea of who she told about the invoice."

"Hacking, you mean?" It worried Clarke that Rob might be doing something illegal.

"*Accessing's* a much nicer word." Rob continued to tap at the keyboard. "Pretty good security system," he said after a few minutes.

Clarke walked round to his side of the table. "Does that mean you can't get in?"

Rob looked up at her and grinned. "Really?" he said. "You think that?"

Clarke looked at the screen. Tammy's email account. She'd never really doubted Rob. Well, perhaps a little, but she wouldn't tell him that.

"You search through them. I'll watch the football," he said, picking up the remote control.

Tammy's emails numbered in the hundreds, if not thousands. Clarke pictured her own inbox. She always methodically read everything and dealt with it, then archived it or deleted it. Tammy clearly took the more chaotic approach. It would be impossible to read through everything. Clarke concentrated on the last month. Mindful that this was illegal, she wasn't at all comfortable about searching through Tammy's emails. Rob seemed to have no worries at all, which concerned Clarke. She remembered his past exploits and wondered if he was still hacking. One day soon, she must discuss that with him properly to make sure he wasn't doing anything stupid. Anyway, she skimmed through Tammy's emails as fast as possible. The sooner she logged out, the less likely that anyone would catch her at it. Even rushing flat out, it took Clarke over an hour to check a month's worth of emails.

She searched for any reference to Firestop or to that particular invoice. Then she also looked at any personal emails to check if Tammy had been arranging to meet someone.

She found a couple of emails from one of the friends that Tammy had met up with on Tuesday evening. Clarke made a note of the email address, in case she wanted to contact her. But nothing she found pointed to any problems, and she didn't come across anything about Firestop.

Rob poked his head round the door. "Find anything?" he said.

"Not a thing." It had been a complete waste of time. She hated that she had allowed Rob to break the law, encouraged him even, and all for nothing.

"Sorry, Sis. Did she delete it? Have you tried the trash folder?"

"That gets automatically emptied when we log out," Clarke said.

Rob nodded. "Perhaps," he said, "you should search for what's *not* there."

Clarke jumped up and hugged him. "You're a genius." She should have noticed it earlier. She hadn't found a single email from Bradley Acres. Tammy had been working with him quite a bit and having lots of meetings with him, but there weren't any emails between them. None.

She let go of Rob and returned to her laptop to double-check. She checked Tammy's sent emails as well. Not one email to Bradley or from him. How likely was that? It waved a red flag a mile high. Something must have been going on. Had Tammy been investigating Bradley? He had signed off all the invoices. Perhaps Tammy knew much more than she had let on to Clarke. After all, Clarke had found those invoices. Perhaps Tammy had too.

Chapter 10

"Arrested?" Shock ricocheted through Clarke as she tried to take in the news.

"Yes, who'd have thought. Jeffrey Todd." Ken seemed to find the news amusing. "But then he did have that incident with touching Tammy last week."

"That was all a stupid misunderstanding." Clarke regretted now ever mentioning it to Paul. She'd wished she'd kept quiet as soon as the words had left her mouth. Jeffrey was just a geek with a crush on Tammy. He didn't deserve to get arrested.

Ken didn't care one iota about Jeffrey, but he seemed to relish being the bearer of bad tidings. "Police must think he's done her in," he said.

Clarke shuddered. "Ken, don't say that, please. We can't be certain Tammy's dead. She can't be dead." Today was Monday. Tammy had been missing for nearly five days. *Please, God, don't let her be dead.* Clarke wondered if she'd been wrong about Jeffrey. The police wouldn't have arrested him for no good reason.

Clarke sneezed. The basement archives seemed to be getting dustier. Searching through the huge racks of old invoices was becoming a never-ending job at the moment. She wasn't even sure what she was searching for.

She had looked up Firestop on the Companies House website. That's when she started to get really suspicious about the invoices. On all the invoices, it said Firestop Ltd. But the Firestop she had known was Firestop (UK) Ltd. They were two completely different companies.

Firestop Ltd was registered in the Cayman Islands and owned by a shell company. Something was very wrong about the whole thing. Clarke was in no doubt now that these invoices were fraudulent. And the person behind them almost certainly worked for the Briar Holman.

Clarke spent all day yesterday worrying about it. She felt responsible for sending Tammy a copy of that first invoice. What if Tammy had shared it with the wrong person? What if they had harmed her? Was it the man who had been following her the other night? She really should have told Paul about that, but, after a while, she'd been so unsure of the woman's identity. It would have wasted Paul's time, when he should be using it to follow up more likely leads. If she discovered anything more, then she promised herself she would tell Paul. There was no point in putting the culprit on their guard if they didn't have enough evidence to stop him.

She shuffled through a bunch of papers. Clarke had decided to check an entire month's worth of invoices. Most of Briar Holman's invoices were paid through an online system now. Each supplier logged in through a portal, the relevant Briar Holman manager authorised their invoice online, and the system paid it automatically. A much smaller number of invoices were paid manually. Clarke was pretty sure that it would be easier for someone to get fraudulent invoices through the manual system. She was only checking the manual invoices. At least they numbered hundreds instead of thousands, which made it a manageable task, but still onerous, and she could only spare an hour while Andrew attended a meeting. If she disappeared at any other time, he would interrogate her about where she'd been. She would prefer to avoid questions like that.

The invoices for Firestop averaged about one per month. If there were others, for other companies, they would probably be similar. Clarke pulled out all the high value invoices, over twenty thousand pounds, and scanned them as quickly as possible.

She was only halfway through checking the month when the alarm on her phone sounded, reminding her to go back to her office if she didn't want to risk Andrew asking awkward questions.

As Clarke entered the office, Ken came over to meet her. She noted with relief that Andrew's desk was empty.

"Where have you been?" Ken said. "The police were here looking for you." He thrust a business card at her. "He says to phone him."

Clarke took it. Paul. "Did he say what he wanted?"

Ken shook his head. "Could be he's going to arrest you."

Clarke faked a laugh. "Thanks, Ken." After Jeffrey's experience, that really wasn't funny. If she waited until lunchtime, she could sit in her car to get some privacy to phone Paul. She considered whether to tell him about the fraudulent invoices. Not yet, she decided. If she stayed late this evening, she could go back to the basement to continue her search.

Paul answered on the first ring. He didn't sound pleased to hear from her, even though he had asked her to phone. "Why did you arrest Jeffrey?" Clarke asked.

Paul didn't reply. Clarke pictured him staring at the floor, like he always used to do during difficult decisions.

"I can't tell you that," he said.

"Paul. You owe me that at least."

Another pause. "Clarke, that wasn't why I wanted to talk to you."

"Stop changing the subject. Why did you arrest Jeffrey Todd? Did you find any evidence?"

"Clarke."

"You did, didn't you?" She could tell from his voice that Paul was holding something back. He really hadn't changed in the last four years. He was still her Paul.

Clarke pulled herself together. He would never be hers again and she wouldn't want him anyway, not after the way he'd treated her. "Please, Paul. What have you got on Jeffrey?"

Paul sighed. "I shouldn't be telling you this," he said. "I might lose my job if I do."

Clarke waited. If she waited long enough, he wouldn't be able to resist filling the silence.

"We found a hair scrunchie in his desk," he said. "We think it's Tammy's."

Clarke didn't know what to say. The scrunchie might belong to anyone. Jeffrey might have picked it up anywhere. Paul interrupted her thoughts.

"Clarke, you need to tell me again about where Tammy's living now," he said. "We can't find her address."

Clarke checked the rearview mirror as she heard a car pull into the parking slot behind her.

"I told you," she said. "She lives in Tredington. That's all I know." Surely the police would be able to track her down. There must be records.

"Think," Paul insisted. "Any little detail may help."

Clarke repeated all the same things she had already told him. As she spoke, a picture formed in her head of the front of the house. Then another picture of Tammy showing her the photos and telling her about the renovations. She'd seen photos of the kitchen and bathroom too. Clarke had assumed Tammy was doing the house up to sell it. It didn't occur to her then that Tammy might be living there.

"I don't know any more," Clarke said.

"If you think of anything..."

"I'll call you." She hung up. Why couldn't the police find Tammy's house? Maybe she should visit Tredington this evening. She could probably find the house herself if she walked around the area for a while. There couldn't be too many that looked like that. But what hope would she stand of finding it in the dark? Better if she headed over there now and searched in daylight. If it helped to find Tammy, she'd risk being late back from lunch. It may not be much use. Tammy wouldn't be there. But Paul could get access and hopefully find some clue as to where she'd gone and why.

Tredington was several miles down the A10 towards central London. Clarke assumed parking would be a nightmare, so she took a bus. That had been a mistake. Eight miles was a long enough drive in a car in London traffic, but on a bus: the bus rolled along at its own pace like a great lumbering beast and took forever. When she got closer, she got a great view of the houses. Except that the bus stayed on the main roads in the area and she doubted that Tammy's house, with clematis growing over the door, would be on a main road. Now she realised with dismay exactly how much walking she would need to do.

She found her phone and dialled Ken's number.

"Where are you?" he said.

Clarke put her hand over the phone, hoping to block out the noise of the traffic. "I'm on my way home," she said. No way would she make it back to the office before lunch ended. "I've got a dreadful migraine. Can you tell Andrew, please?" She hated lying. "I'm sure I'll be fine if I can lie down for a few hours."

"Sure," Ken said. "I'll tell him. Wish you better."

Clarke hung up. Ken needed to work on his sincerity.

She got off the bus in the middle of Tredington. She wished now she'd made up a better excuse. What if someone saw her and reported her to Andrew? What if...? Then she remembered she'd left her car in the office car park.

Clarke stood at the bus stop. This plan kept getting worse. Why didn't she think things through first? This business of Tammy going missing was making Clarke do all sorts of things she would never normally do. Normally, she'd take her time and plan everything properly. But nothing seemed to be normal anymore. If anyone commented on her car, she would say she'd been too ill to drive. Anyway, she was here now, so she may as well make the best of it.

Tredington was a smart area of north London, nearly as trendy as neighbouring Islington. Every other building in the High Street seemed to be a coffee shop or a restaurant. Clarke needed to explore the residential parts of the area.

Logically, she should probably start with the area near the park. Would that be a more likely location for houses with flowers in the front garden? She needed to start searching. It would be dark in about three hours.

One hour later, only seven roads searched and Clarke's ankle ached like crazy. She found a nice coffee shop and sat at a table on her own. She rummaged around in her handbag until she found a paracetamol and swallowed one with a big gulp of coffee.

"Do you mind if I sit here?" A youngish man in a suit put his coffee and briefcase on the table and, without waiting for an answer, pulled out the chair opposite her.

Clarke looked up. The place was filling up fast, so it would be rude to say no. "Please do," she said.

"Do you work near here?" the man asked.

Clarke shook her head. "I'm searching for my friend," she said. "But I can't remember her address, only what her house looks like. It's impossible. I need a helicopter." She laughed. "It's the only way I'm going to find the house before dark. I'm knackered already."

"I can tell," the man said. "You look like you've been walking for hours."

Clarke flinched. She hoped she didn't look that bad.

The man looked her up and down. "What you need," he said, "is Google Earth."

Clarke smiled. Of course. She should have thought of Google Earth. "That's brilliant," she said. She could search the whole neighbourhood from the comfort of the coffee shop well before dark. "Thank you so much."

With a little help from Google Earth, Clarke explored the whole area. The most likely looking houses were situated in Queen Elizabeth Avenue, near the smaller park, not the one she'd circumnavigated earlier. She gulped down her remaining coffee, which was now barely tepid. At least it would keep her going a bit longer.

She reached Queen Elizabeth Avenue in minutes and, halfway along the road, she hit the jackpot.

This must be the right house, Tammy's house. The same royal blue front door, the same leaded windows, and despite it being November, they were definitely roses in the small front garden, and that looked like a clematis climbing up over the door. Clarke paused for a minute. The flicker of a light coming from the front room suggested someone watching TV. Clarke breathed a sigh of relief, imagining that Tammy might actually be at home. But then why hadn't she phoned the office? Had she perhaps been so ill that she couldn't? Clarke marched up to the front door and rang the doorbell.

An elderly lady with silver grey hair answered the door.

Clarke smiled at her. "Is Tammy here?" she said.

"Sorry, who?" The old lady looked confused.

"Tammy," Clarke said, wondering if the woman had been listening. "Tammy Doncaster."

"I'm sorry, there's no one of that name here." The woman started to close the door.

Clarke acted quickly, putting one foot in the doorway. Perhaps Tammy had sold the house since she'd shown Clarke the photos. "Do you have a forwarding address for her?" she said. "Please. I need to find her."

The old lady looked puzzled. "I'm sorry, but you've got the wrong address. I've lived here for nearly forty years and there's no one called Tammy here."

Reluctantly, Clarke stepped back to allow the old lady to close the door. She had been so sure about this house. Could there possibly be another house like it, or had she hit a dead end? If Tammy didn't live here, where was she?

Chapter 11

Clarke got into work extra early on Tuesday. After yesterday's wild goose chase and afternoon off, she needed to catch up on her work. She also wanted to spend some more time looking up invoices before Andrew got in. She was increasingly convinced that the fraudulent invoices must be in some way connected with Tammy's disappearance. Tammy had vanished the day after Clarke had sent her a copy of the first invoice and Tammy intended to show it to someone. If only she'd said who. Clarke wondered if that someone could have been Bradley Acres. As head of internal audit, he was the most logical person to approach about a fraud. Bradley's signature authorised all the fake invoices. Could he be the person behind the fraud? What would he have done to Tammy if she'd confronted him? Clarke was getting more and more frustrated. All these questions and no answers.

The office was deserted at this time of day. Even the couple of people in HR who always arrived first were probably still in bed this early in the morning. Clarke printed out her lists of invoice numbers. She had found three more companies with similar names to well-known companies, but which were registered in the Cayman Islands. That made forty-one invoices to find. It would take ages.

The basement archives seemed spookier today, probably because the office hadn't woken up yet. The only other people in the building were cleaners, who came in at 5:00 a.m. every morning so they didn't disturb anyone working. Clarke put her list and pen on an empty shelf and pulled out a file. As she flicked through the pile of invoices, she wondered about Jeffrey. Perhaps he really had been stalking Tammy. He undoubtedly had a secret crush on her. But his extreme shyness surely prevented him from ever doing anything about it, and Clarke struggled to imagine him murdering Tammy. Could he have finally plucked up the courage to accost her and it got out of hand? Could he have killed her by accident?

Clarke shuddered. For the first time, she allowed herself to believe that might be true. Tammy may be dead. But she couldn't accept the premise for more than a fleeting moment. Clarke hoped Tammy had been kidnapped, then the police would find her. Or, better still, she might simply be at home, wherever that may be. Or possibly she'd been in an accident and was in hospital. There were so many possibilities. Tammy might be anywhere, but not dead. Please, not dead. It had been six days now. Clarke was painfully aware of the implications of that. Rob had told her, since Paul was afraid to upset her.

Clarke examined the latest invoices as she scanned them. Every one of them was authorised by Bradley Acres and Douglas Doncaster. The invoices were getting more frequent and larger as time passed, a sure sign that the fraudster was getting bolder. They were still all under £50,000. Anything over that amount would more likely be scrutinised by the external auditors during the annual audit. But the average amount was growing.

She reached for her pen to tick off the invoices she had found so far and clumsily knocked the pen off the shelf. It jangled on the concrete floor, echoing around the basement room. With a deep breath to calm herself, Clarke picked up the pen and carried on. Another couple of minutes and she ticked off two more invoices. All too soon, 7:45 a.m. arrived. Time to stop. She resolved to finish later, after Andrew went home.

Clarke wondered how much longer she could put off telling Paul about these fraudulent invoices. She wanted to be absolutely certain before she involved the police. The last thing she needed was to look like an idiot in front of Paul if she turned out to be wrong. She was mulling over the decision when a loud thud on the other side of the room made her jump. It sounded like something falling off a shelf. Her heart started to beat rapidly, and she wondered if she should go straight back to the office. No, she chided herself. So what if someone else was down here? It was probably just someone else like her, come down to retrieve some old paperwork.

"Is anyone there?" she called out.

The room was silent. Clarke couldn't see anyone as the shelves were jam-packed full of files, and not even a crack of light pierced the non-existent gaps. She crept round the end of the shelving, trying not to make any noise and wishing now that she'd kept quiet. Suddenly, the silence was shattered by the sound of the door slamming shut. She ran around the shelves towards it, fumbling with the handle, eager to get out as quickly as possible.

The corridor was empty, so Clarke proceeded towards the stairwell. Heavy footsteps clattered up the stairs above her, but she was too far behind to see who it was. Who had been so keen to get away? Was she being paranoid? Other people did use the archives. It must be a coincidence, nothing to worry about at all. Clarke made her way up the stairs slowly, not wanting to set off her ankle pain. At least she had scanned nearly all the invoices she needed, so she resolved to hand everything over to Paul tonight. It was stupid spooking herself like this. Let the police investigate the matter properly.

As Clarke got back up to the ground floor, she decided to take a detour out to the car park. There were only four cars parked so far. Hers. A silver Audi that she assumed belonged to Douglas Doncaster as it took up his reserved space. Andrew's white BMW. And a dark blue Ford Focus.

Clarke shivered, uncertain whether it was from the cold or something else entirely.

Andrew was taking his coat off when Clarke got back upstairs.

"Sorry about yesterday," Clarke said.

Andrew nodded. "Hope you're ok now. I need you to help with some of Tammy's work."

"Of course." It would be a good opportunity for her if she wanted to apply for Tammy's old job. It seemed disloyal, planning her career when Tammy might be dead. She wondered if Andrew had been given any information. "Have the police found Tammy yet?" she asked.

"I don't think so." Andrew shuffled uncomfortably at his desk. "Bad business," he said. "Bad business."

Clarke agreed. "I'm really worried about her." She grabbed her mug, desperate for coffee.

"We all are," Andrew said.

There was no emotion in his voice. Clarke wondered how much concern he really felt. A sudden horrible notion overcame her. What if Andrew was responsible for Tammy's disappearance? Andrew could have been watching her in the basement this morning too. What if he was the person behind the fraudulent invoices and Tammy had shown that first invoice to him? Clarke wished she had never involved Tammy. Was this all her fault? She hoped and prayed that, wherever Tammy was, she would come home safely.

Clarke logged in to her computer. The first email that caught her eye in her inbox detailed the results of the Brack Attack exercise. Clarke read it quickly. Even the mention of Brack Attack gave her the creeps now. Had the chaos of Brack Attack made it easier for someone, in all probability the same someone who sent the death threats, to snatch Tammy? It couldn't be a coincidence that she had disappeared in the middle of Brack Attack. But Clarke still couldn't figure out why. Why would anyone want to kill Tammy? Did she know more about the fraudulent invoices than she'd let on to Clarke? Or did someone want to get at Douglas, someone who didn't realise they'd split up?

RUN, HIDE, TELL. Clarke looked at the words in big bold capitals at the top of the email. The instructions they'd all been given to help them survive Brack Attack. Had Tammy run? Was she hiding? Or had someone found her before she'd got the chance?

The email said that 72 percent of Briar Holman employees had been *captured* during the exercise. Clearly, management were disappointed with that number as they planned to repeat the exercise in a few months. They stated that they took the security of their employees very seriously and would be taking steps to protect them further. They didn't say what steps. They didn't mention Tammy. They hadn't managed to protect her.

Clarke really missed Tammy. There seemed to be a lot less laughter and chatting in the team without her. Tammy's bubbly personality brought the office to life, especially when she would suddenly break off from her work and tell Clarke about some hilarious recent exploit. Clarke tried to remember some of Tammy's latest funny stories in case one of them might give a clue to where she may be, but her mind had gone blank.

At lunchtime, she tried to phone Paul from the car park but got his voicemail. It started to rain as she walked back to the office. The sound of footsteps running up behind her made Clarke swing round in a panic to check who it was. She was definitely getting noticeably jumpy. "Hi, Jeffrey," she said, smiling at him.

"You told them, didn't you?" he shouted. "You told them I upset Tammy."

Clarke took a step back, unused to seeing Jeffrey angry. She glanced around the car park, looking for support, but they were alone. "I'm sorry." Immediately she regretted admitting to it. He must only be guessing it was her. She should have denied it.

He stepped closer, blocking any escape as her back was against the wall. "They kept me in a cell overnight. Do you have any idea how horrible that is?" Jeffrey's face grew redder, and he seemed close to losing control.

Clarke reached in her coat pocket for her phone but wasn't sure how she would have time to use it. She wished she owned a rape alarm or a mace spray.

"I would never hurt her," Jeffrey said, shaking his fists at Clarke. "I would never hurt Tammy."

Clarke shivered. The rain pelted down like baby bullets hitting her face. Hopefully, the weather would drive Jeffrey back inside. "Please, Jeffrey, I know you wouldn't hurt Tammy." Clarke hoped he wouldn't hurt her either. "The detectives made me answer their questions. All I want, all we both want, is to find Tammy," she said. *Stay calm*, she told herself. If it was a fire, she'd be calm. All her training would kick in and she'd do her job. She tried to ignore the fear by pretending to be in the middle of a fire.

"But how could they think that I...?"

Jeffrey started wringing his hands together and Clarke couldn't help imagining that he would have liked them to be around her neck. Was that how it had happened? Had he got over emotional and put his hands around Tammy's neck when she rejected him? She started to worry that the police were wrong to let him go. He certainly wasn't doing himself any favours acting like this. Suddenly, Clarke caught sight of someone running across the car park. She took a deep breath of relief, keeping one eye on the moving figure. Should she shout out to him?

A clap of thunder drowned out Jeffrey's next words. Clarke continued to watch the running man. He would come right past them. The man changed the position of his umbrella and Clarke recognised Douglas Doncaster. She made a move towards him, ready to scream if Jeffrey tried to stop her.

They all three reached the door of the building together.

"Mr Doncaster," Clarke said, "have they found Tammy yet? Is there any news?" If anyone had been told anything, it would be him, Tammy's husband.

Douglas Doncaster turned towards her. She noticed Jeffrey lag back, which was a huge relief, although her stress levels remained sky-high.

"The police haven't said anything," he said. "I'm sorry. I can't help you." He shook out his dripping umbrella. "Damned rain."

Clarke jogged to keep up with his long stride. She wanted to get into the lift with him, in case Jeffrey tried to follow her upstairs.

Doncaster said nothing in the lift, too busy brushing rainwater off his suit. Clarke didn't know what else to say to him. She tried to work out if he was worried about Tammy or whether getting a soaking concerned him more. Tammy and he were separated after all. Was Clarke really expecting him to be upset? If Tammy was never found, it would save him from a very expensive divorce, which provided a pretty good motive. The husband always did it, didn't he? Or was that only on TV? She seemed to suspect everyone these last few days. Douglas didn't acknowledge her when she got out of the lift at the third floor.

"Clarke, you look like a drowned rat," Andrew said as she sat at her desk.

"Thanks." She took off her jacket and hung it over the radiator. Then she put her coat on, which she had stupidly left hanging over the back of her chair while she had been outside getting a soaking. Her thick coat might help warm her up, then perhaps her body temperature would dry out her blouse

The incident with Jeffrey had scared her. Clarke wanted to grab her phone and go somewhere quiet to call Paul. But Andrew was watching her like a hawk after her unscheduled afternoon off yesterday. Otherwise, she would have sneaked out. She looked through her emails, hoping that Andrew would have a meeting to attend soon.

"Here, you look like you need this." Ken hardly ever made her a drink, but amazingly he held out a steaming hot mug of coffee.

"Thanks, Ken, that's exactly what I need." After the last few minutes, a glass of vodka would be welcome, but coffee was the next best thing. Clarke smiled at Ken, wondering if he had an ulterior motive or if she looked even wetter than she felt.

She sipped her coffee gratefully as she worked through one of Tammy's extremely complicated spreadsheets. Andrew wanted her to update the figures, but she wasn't even sure what half of these figures meant. She wasn't just out of her depth, she was drowning. No doubt she was being over ambitious even considering applying for Tammy's old job. She steeled herself to ask Andrew for help with the spreadsheet later. The hot drink slipped down her throat, warming her up. She held the cup tightly, letting the warmth permeate her hands. Even the aroma of the coffee was driving out the cold. Sod Jeffrey, making her get so wet and scaring her half to death. Clarke was glad now that Jeffrey had got arrested. He deserved it.

By four o'clock, Clarke was longing to go home. Tired from her early start and still not fully dried out, there was no question of her working late tonight. She didn't want to risk being alone in the car park with Jeffrey again, so she waited for someone else to leave the office, so she could follow them out.

Ten minutes later, two of the women across the office in procurement started putting their coats on. Quickly, Clarke shut down her computer and left with them. As she walked down the stairs, Clark's phone rang. Paul.

Clarke shivered as soon as she stepped outside. The residual dampness of her clothes made the wind unbearably cold, and she just wanted to get in the car, lock the doors, and turn the heater up to full blast, followed by a long soak in the bath the minute she arrived home. She clutched the phone to her ear.

"Have you found Tammy?" She guessed the answer before Paul replied. Why didn't they try harder? Nobody vanished into thin air, did they?

"Clarke, we should talk," Paul said. "I don't want to leave things like this."

His voice sounded shaky, betraying his fear of anything remotely touchy-feely. Clarke guessed he would have struggled to get those words out, unless he'd changed drastically in the last four years. Well, he could struggle a bit more. Why should she make it easy for him?

"We're talking now. What do you want to say?" she said. He would need to do more than grovel and apologise if he wanted to earn her forgiveness.

"Not now." Paul hesitated. "How about this evening? Can we meet for a drink? Talk properly."

"I can't," Clarke said. "I'm busy." She didn't want to spend an evening with him. It would be awkward. Uncomfortable. And, most of all, she worried that she might succumb too easily and fall in love with him all over again. She really should tell him about the fraud, but not while she was on some personal agenda of his. She didn't need that after the day she'd had.

Clarke reached her car and juggled her phone, handbag, and car keys, trying to unlock the door, whilst still scanning the car park for any signs of Jeffrey. Dusk threw shadows everywhere, making her see demons in every corner. Once she got into the car and locked the doors, her over-worked imagination would calm down.

Paul refused to give up. "Clarke, please. If you won't come out tonight for me, come for Tammy. We can talk about her. Any little detail you might remember could be crucial. It might help us find her."

Clarke tossed her handbag onto the passenger seat, pulling the door shut and quickly clicking the central locking button. She felt safe now. The encounter with Jeffrey earlier had shaken her up more than she'd realised.

"Ok," she said, giving in far more easily than she'd intended. "Ok." At least it would give her the chance to tell Paul about the fraudulent invoices. She would finish checking them before she left to meet him and present Paul with something complete, something she was certain about.

She hung up. Turning the heating up as high as it would go, she reversed out of her parking space. A dark-coloured car stopped to allow her out. Clarke put her hand up to thank them, even though there was no light for them to see her. Never mind, it was the thought that counted. Now to get home.

The journey normally took half an hour. Two junctions on the M25, followed by a short drive northward. As soon as she got onto the motorway, the traffic report on the radio said something about an accident up ahead.

"Damn." Clarke rapped the steering wheel with her hand. With luck, the accident would be minor. A bad accident would cause a massive hold-up, especially at this time of day. Worst-case scenario would be closing the motorway. If that happened, she'd be lucky to get home inside of five hours.

Her fears were quickly realised as the overhead signs changed to forty miles per hour. In less than a minute, the traffic ground to a halt. "Damn. Damn. Damn." Clarke turned the volume up on the radio, hoping for another traffic report soon, something to tell her how long she might be stuck here. The traffic didn't move. She pulled her handbrake on and knocked the car out of gear. She really didn't need this.

After a while, the cars ahead of her started to creep forward. Quickly, Clarke put the car in gear and edged forward, searching for a gap to pull over to the inside lane, in case she wanted to exit the motorway at the next junction.

A familiar looking car ducked in behind her. It was the same colour and shape as the one that let her out of the car park. Was it the same one? Had it been behind her all the time? Clarke looked in her wing mirror, wondering if she would recognise the driver, but there were no overhead lights on this section of the motorway so, despite the plethora of headlight beams, she only made out a vague outline. This was ridiculous, she told herself, thinking she might have been followed, and anyway, it could be some friendly colleague who happened to be going the same way. Instantly, her mind flicked back to her earlier encounter with Jeffrey. If it turned out to be him, she would report him straight to the police.

A burst of horn tooting behind her made her realise there was now a large gap ahead of her. It would be better to get off the motorway. Clarke pulled forward and began indicating, waiting for someone in the inside lane to let her in. She had nearly closed up the gap with the car in front when a space opened up beside her and a flash of headlights invited her to move into it. Clarke flicked her hazards on to thank the driver and glanced over to try to get a clearer view of the person in the car behind her. The dark saloon car had vanished and been replaced by a white Mini Cooper.

Clarke spent the next couple of minutes scolding herself for imagining anyone would follow her. But it still unnerved her, losing track of the dark saloon. Suddenly, she looked forward to meeting Paul later tonight instead of tomorrow. But she would still need to go home to her empty flat first. Again, she told herself to stop being ridiculous and overreacting just because Jeffrey had shouted at her. She needed to take back control. If she stayed in the inside lane, and if the dark car really intended to follow her, the driver might pull off the motorway at the next junction if he thought that was Clarke's plan too. Then she could continue on the motorway at the last minute and wait out the delay. Nothing would happen to her here, surrounded by people. She felt safe.

By the time Clarke arrived home and spoiled herself with a long soak in the bath, it was nearly 6:00 p.m. She put some pasta on to boil and started chopping up vegetables. Onions, tomatoes, yellow peppers. She found a small piece of fresh tuna in the fridge—she hated the tinned stuff. Some chilli and a few straggly basil leaves that grew in a pot on the windowsill, despite the lateness of the season, and she made a delicious meal in less than fifteen minutes.

She couldn't get her mind off Tammy so, after dinner, she switched on her computer. Earlier she'd emailed the scanned invoices to her personal email address. Briar Holman's rules forbade them to do that. The company considered it to be a security risk. Clarke had deleted the sent email from her work account, so hopefully no one would ever realise she'd sent it. She didn't want to get sacked. But she always liked to plan for every possibility, so she wanted more than one copy of the evidence. Planning was Clarke's forte. As a firefighter, she'd planned everything. Some people rushed headlong into danger. Clarke took a couple of minutes to assess the situation and work out how best to tackle things. She'd still ended up injured, so a fat lot of good that approach did her.

With time to spare before she met Paul, she decided to put all the invoice information on a spreadsheet to check if that threw up any similarities. *Get you, girl.* She even thought like an accountant now. She was determined now to make a success of this new career that had been forced upon her. Perhaps tomorrow she would ask Andrew about Tammy's old post. Clarke shuddered. It still seemed wrong, asking about Tammy's former job, with her missing, even if it wasn't actually Tammy's current job. She should be patient, see how things turned out. How could she be planning how to advance her career when her friend was missing? She should wait. And if Tammy turned out to be dead, Clarke might not even want to stay at Briar Holman.

Clarke listed all the invoice details. They were all between twenty and fifty thousand pounds. There was only one thing in common, exactly as she'd already noticed. Every single invoice was signed off by Bradley Acres, the head of internal audit and counter-signed by Douglas Doncaster, Tammy's husband.

Clarke sat staring at the screen for several minutes. Was Bradley Acres behind this? His professional expertise would certainly help him to avoid being caught. Clarke recalled the first invoice. She had spotted it by chance. The wrong model of fire door. How many other people would be aware of that discontinued line? No one probably. It was pure luck that she had been the one to find it. And most of the other invoices consisted of lists of parts, identified only by serial numbers. Were those numbers real or fake? It probably didn't matter. No one would ever check.

Her thoughts turned to Douglas Doncaster. Were they in this together, he and Bradley? Tammy always admired Douglas's ambition, even when he cared about his career more than he did about her. So why would he jeopardise that career? Clarke got up and started pacing back and forth across her small living room. Douglas had been deputy CEO when Clarke joined the company three years ago and some time before that as well. Was he disillusioned not to get the CEO's job yet? Surely, he would simply go to another company. None of this quite added up. She hoped Paul would make sense of things when she showed him what she'd found.

Chapter 12

Tuesday, Week Two

Clarke finished her drink, which she had been nursing for ages, trying to make it last. She checked the time. Paul should have got here half an hour ago. From where she sat in the corner of the pub, she constantly watched the door, hope turning to disappointment with every new arrival. So it seemed much longer than half an hour. She debated with herself whether to order another drink, give Paul some extra time in case something urgent had held him up at work, perhaps a vital new clue in the search for Tammy. It would be annoying if Paul didn't show, when she was dying to ask him about the case, about Tammy.

The bright pink memory stick burned a hole in her pocket. She'd be relieved to hand that over to Paul, with all the scanned copies of the invoices saved on it, but she needed to explain everything when she gave it to him, to make sure he understood. He surely must show up soon.

She looked at her watch for the millionth time. She'd finally concluded that Paul wasn't coming. As she got up, her phone vibrated, and she fumbled in her handbag to find it.

"Clarke?"

"Paul, where are you?" She tried to hide some of her annoyance at being kept waiting for so long.

"I'm really sorry, Clarke." Paul sounded flustered, although she struggled to make out his words over the general chatter around her. "I'm still tied up at work. I'm afraid I'll need to cancel. Sorry."

"Is it a breakthrough in Tammy's case? Have you found her?" Clarke asked quickly.

"No."

Clarke always knew when Paul tried to lie to her. The way his voice faltered slightly gave him away every time. And the way he always paused before he told a white lie, as if considering whether he should, whereas with an accomplished liar, the lies tripped off the tongue with no guilt attached.

"I can't tell you," he said.

Clarke began to protest but realised there would be no point. If Paul was at the police station, the prospect of being overheard would make him clam up.

"Let's meet up tomorrow." He rang off without even waiting for her answer.

Clarke snapped the phone shut, tempted to be busy tomorrow night, even if only with washing her hair. She fingered the memory stick in her pocket and realised she would have to show up.

With time to spare, Clarke didn't really want to go home and spend the evening on her own. Thoughts of Tammy buzzed constantly inside her head. If the police couldn't find her, perhaps *she* could try. She turned around before she reached her car and walked in the opposite direction. Five minutes later, Clarke boarded a bus bound for Tredington. It made perfect sense, she convinced herself. She was part of the way there already.

As a sociable, fun-loving woman, if Tammy lived in the area, she would definitely go out some evenings. Clarke made a plan to visit as many bars and pubs as she could. She found pictures of Tammy on her phone from someone's leaving do a few weeks ago. It would be easy to show them around and ask if anyone recognised Tammy. At least she'd be doing something.

She got out her phone and Googled bars and pubs, finding sixteen of them in the area. She'd never visit that many in a couple of hours, so she narrowed it down to the venues that seemed more upmarket or lively. Those would be the most likely places for Tammy to frequent. It left her with a reasonable number to get through.

An Irish band belted out a popular folk tune at the first pub she found. Tammy would probably hate that type of music, but the pub was certainly lively, so worth a try. She showed Tammy's photo to several people, but no one admitted to seeing her before.

Next, she visited a wine bar. She showed the photos to the bar staff, hoping they would be more likely to recognise Tammy if she was a regular customer.

"A small glass of Sauvignon Blanc, please?" Clarke realised she shouldn't, not if she intended to drive again later, but one small glass might give her the courage to approach a bunch of strangers to ask if they recognised Tammy, and the alcohol would have worn off by the time she got back to her car. She leaned over the bar while the bartender poured her wine. "I'm looking for my friend," she said, pushing her phone, showing the photo of Tammy, in front of him. "Have you ever seen her in here?"

He shook his head. "That'll be four pounds please," he said. "Beautiful lady. If I'd seen her, I'd remember for sure." He grinned at the photo.

Clarke took a gulp of her wine. This would be much quicker, showing Tammy's photo at the bar in each place. Although, at these prices, if she ordered a drink in each place, it would be an expensive evening.

The next pub looked more hopeful. Clarke showed Tammy's photo to a group of young black guys. "Foxy lady," one of them said, licking his lips.

His girlfriend grabbed the phone from Clarke. "I've seen her," she said.

"Where? When?" Clarke tried not to sound too frantic.

"Not here," the girl said. "She goes to the same hairdresser as me. She's always in there." The girl picked up a beer mat and wrote a name on it. "Hairdresser's on the High Street," she said, "near the station."

"That's great. Thank you." Clarke put the beer mat in her handbag. "Can you remember when you last saw this woman?"

"She's not in any trouble, is she? Are you police?"

"No. No, of course not." Clarke smiled. "I'm worried about her. I need to find her." That much was true. Clarke's anxiety about Tammy grew by the second. The longer Tammy stayed missing, the more worried Clarke became. It terrified her that she might never see her friend again.

The hairdresser might have Tammy's address if she was a regular. What a pity it would be closed now. She would pass on the information to Paul to check out.

Clarke visited a few more pubs, but no one else remembered ever seeing Tammy. It was getting late, so she caught the bus back to where she'd parked her car. The walk across the deserted car park where she'd left it felt all too spooky in the dark. Clarke kept looking round to check for anyone following her. This whole situation had made her really jumpy. As soon as she reached the safety of her car, she got inside quickly and locked the doors.

There were no vacant parking spaces remaining near Clarke's flat when she arrived home, so she parked in the neighbouring street and walked round the corner. As soon as she'd left the car, Clarke sensed someone lurking. When she almost reached her front door, a sound behind her made her jump. Quickly, she spun round but couldn't see anyone. Twice, three times, she checked behind her. Nothing. This was ridiculous. She speeded up her walk, nearly running the last few steps.

Fumbling with the door key seemed to take forever, but as soon as the door opened, Clarke launched herself inside, slamming the door shut and double locking it behind her, relishing the safety of her flat.

After so much walking this evening and eating early, Clarke was starving. She searched the fridge and found some chicken liver pate and a bag of rocket leaves. Half a loaf of bread sat on the kitchen worktop. Quickly, she fixed herself a sandwich. That would do nicely.

Clarke poured herself a glass of water, grabbed the plate with her sandwich, and took both into her living room, flicking the light switch on with her little finger. Suddenly, a loud crash and the sound of breaking glass made her scream and drop both plate and glass. An icy blast swept across the room and Clarke noticed with horror that her window was broken. She shrank back into the doorway. The light was still on, and the curtains not yet drawn shut. Anyone outside would be able to see her clearly. Quickly, she turned the light out, but not before she saw the brick lying on the floor below the window. Clarke shuddered. Why? Why would anyone do that to her? Had there been somebody waiting outside when she'd walked back from the car? Had they done this? The culprit might still be in the street, and it would be much easier for them to get in, with the window broken. She reached for her phone and dialled 999.

"Police, please." As she gave them her details, she wondered if she should have called Paul directly. But he may be too busy to answer, and she needed help now. Anticipating the worst, Clarke scanned the room for something to use as a weapon. A baseball bat or a poker would be great. She found nothing that useful. The voice on the other end of the phone carried on talking, but Clarke hadn't heard a word he'd said since she'd given her address. She forced herself to concentrate.

"Someone will be with you shortly. Please stay on the line," the voice said. Clarke hung up and raced to the kitchen. She kept a big wooden rolling pin in one of the drawers. That would do nicely.

Clarke stayed away from the windows and left the lights off. Gradually, her eyes became accustomed to the dark. Luckily, she kept the flat tidy. If she needed to move in the dark, at least she knew her way around and there was nothing to trip over. Except she was frozen to the spot now, petrified with fear, unable to move at all. She listened for any noises that might signal someone trying to get in, but the only sound was her heart pounding, thud, thud, thud, at a million miles an hour. How long would it take for the police to arrive? Quicker if they weren't coming from the station. There might be a patrol car in the area. She hoped so. Now she wished she hadn't hung up the phone. Then she would still have some moral support. She stayed rooted to the spot, willing the police to hurry, both her hands firmly gripped round the rolling pin.

Breathe, she reminded herself. No one was trying to get in. She would hear them if they did. Probably some drunken teenagers broke the window for a dare, and she was their unlucky random victim. It was stupid to be so afraid. Then Clarke remembered all the times in the last few days when she imagined she was being followed. Had she dug up something when she'd been searching for Tammy this evening? Perhaps someone followed her home from one of the pubs she visited.

She put the rolling pin down and dialled Paul's number.

Chapter 13

Tuesday, Week Two

Paul arrived two minutes after the uniformed police. He took charge and sent one of them to the kitchen to make Clarke a coffee and the other to chase up someone to board up the broken window and make the flat secure.

"What happened?" he said.

Clarke sat down. She started to pour out all the things that had been happening. The trip to find Tammy's house. Jeffrey scaring her. Tonight's outing to search for Tammy. Her sensation of being followed home.

"I thought I saw her," she said.

"Tammy?"

"Yes. Saturday evening in Brackford. I was convinced I saw her. I left the restaurant to run after her."

"And...?"

"I lost her. Now I'm starting to wonder if I imagined it."

"The mind can play tricks when you're worried," Paul said. "We're doing everything we can. Leave everything to us. Don't put yourself at risk."

Clarke had stopped listening when Paul had indirectly suggested she might be crazy. "Where is she, Paul?"

Paul sat down beside her. "We can't find any trace," he said. "It's like Tammy doesn't exist. The only address we've found connected to her is her husband's address, and he says he threw her out over three months ago."

"He threw her out? No, that's wrong," Clarke said. "Tammy left him."

"He threw her out when he found out about her affair. That's what Douglas Doncaster said and I believe him."

"What about her parents' house?"

"Council owned it," Paul said. "They took it back when Tammy's parents died and moved in a new tenant, so she couldn't have been living there."

"I found it," Clarke said. "The house in the photos she showed me. Queen Elizabeth Avenue, next to the park. But the old lady who answered the door said she'd lived there forty years and had never heard of Tammy."

"No," Paul said, "that's not right. Her parents lived on the other side of Tredington, practically in Hackney, in a flat, not a house. It looks like she's lied to you about everything."

"But why? Why would she?"

"I don't know," Paul said. "She's your friend. You tell me. Why would she lie?"

Clarke pondered the question. "She is extremely proud," she said. "Tammy wouldn't want to admit to anyone at work that her parents lived in a council flat. If that's where she came from, it's a world apart from her life with Douglas."

"That makes sense."

Clarke finished her coffee. She'd needed that. "I don't suppose Tammy would want the whole office talking about her splitting up with Douglas either. She never talked about him much. It made things tricky, them both working at Briar Holman. She didn't want people to think she'd only got the job because of her husband. She was always trying to prove herself."

Paul nodded.

"I've got the address of her hairdresser. She might know where Tammy lives." Clarke pulled the beer mat with the address scrawled across it from her handbag and handed it to Paul.

With Paul here, staying calm proved much easier. "Could Tammy have gone to live with her new man? Perhaps she didn't want Douglas to find out the boyfriend's address. It might have been the boyfriend following her on Saturday night?"

Paul looked doubtful. "But why would she disappear, if she was shacked up with this other man?"

Paul was right. It didn't make much sense.

"You think he's hurt her, don't you?" Clarke said.

He remained silent, never a good sign with Paul. "The thing is," he said at last, "Tammy hasn't used her bank card or credit cards since she disappeared. She couldn't, since they were still in her handbag, but we checked anyway, in case she'd got replacements."

Clarke shuddered. "You think she's dead, don't you?"

"We ought to start looking at that possibility," he said.

Even though that scenario had occurred to her many times in the last few days, Paul speaking it aloud made it far too real.

"We're questioning Douglas Doncaster again," Paul said.

Clarke put her hand in her pocket and touched the memory stick that had been there all evening. In the drama of the evening's events, she'd forgotten about it. "You need to see this," she said, pulling it out of her pocket and holding it out towards him.

Paul took it. "What's on it?"

Clarke got up and switched on her laptop, waiting for the machine to boot up. Paul came across the room and plugged in the memory stick.

Clarke opened the first file. "They're fraudulent invoices," she said. "I showed Tammy the first one I found the day before she disappeared. She planned to show it to someone. I think she may have shown it to Bradley Acres, our head of internal audit."

"Makes sense," Paul said.

Clarke started to explain to Paul how the company names seemed very similar to legitimate companies, but with a small difference, and the companies were all registered in the Cayman Islands.

"So far, I've found over one and a half million worth," Clarke said.

Paul whistled. He stared at the screen. "These signatures," he said. "They're authorising payment."

"Bradley Acres and Douglas Doncaster."

"They're all the same," Clarke told him.

"All of them? Are you sure?"

"See for yourself."

Paul pulled out his phone. "Sarge, is Doncaster still at the station?"

Paul stood up and pulled the memory stick from Clarke's computer. The screen went blank. "Damn," he said to Detective Sergeant Prosser on the phone, "never mind."

He turned to Clarke. "I need to go."

"No." She didn't want to stay here on her own. The uniformed officers had already left.

"I'll chase up the contractor who's coming to board up your window." Paul pulled out his phone again and dialled a number.

"He'll be here in a couple of minutes," he said. "I can stay until he gets here."

Clarke worried if she would be ok when Paul left her on her own. She'd hoped he would stay a lot longer. Only because she didn't want to be by herself. But of course that wouldn't happen. She needed to stop being pathetic. She'd be absolutely fine on her own. She would have to be.

Half an hour later, when the broken window was boarded up, Clarke's confidence returned. She convinced herself that the broken window was down to some rowdy teenagers larking about. They probably scarpered as soon as the police car showed up. She certainly didn't need to worry about them. They wouldn't be back. She turned on the TV and flicked the channel to MTV. She ought to go to bed, but she was too wound up. The strong coffee hadn't helped. Some music would make the house safe and welcoming.

Paul had been very excited about the fraudulent invoices. She suspected he might focus on that now and forget about finding Tammy.

Tammy disappeared nearly a week ago. Was she dead? Clarke didn't want to believe that she would never see her friend again, never hear her bubbly laughter that brightened up the dullest days in the office. Was her disappearance connected to the fraud? Who had Tammy told about that first invoice? Bradley Acres? As head of internal audit, he was the obvious person to tell. Except that all the invoices were authorised by Bradley, which certainly incriminated him. Tammy didn't realise that, of course. But she did know that he had signed that first one, didn't she? Perhaps she hadn't spotted it. Had Bradley tried to kill her? Had he succeeded?

Clarke shivered. Tammy was feisty. She would have fought back.

The Brack Attack exercise had been when it all started. Clarke remembered the couple of days prior. They'd been sent so many emails with advice. The same advice every time. RUN, HIDE, TELL. Those words were imprinted on Clarke's brain after so many repetitive emails. Hopefully, the advice had got into Tammy's head too. Had she run? Had she hidden? Could she still be alive?

The TV blasted out a video of some new boy band's first hit. They'd obviously done the video on the cheap, just the band running around chaotically. Clarke imagined herself exactly like that right now, running around in circles, trying to make some sense of everything, get some order. But everything still looked a jumbled-up mess.

Douglas Doncaster convinced Paul that Tammy was having an affair. Clarke wondered why Tammy hadn't confessed it to her, not while she was still living with Douglas, but after they split up. Then she remembered Tammy hadn't even told her they'd split until three months after and she'd lied about where she lived. So many secrets. The police seemed to assume that Tammy was lying, but perhaps it was Douglas not telling the truth. The police only had his word for it about the affair. They hadn't found the mystery man.

In the kitchen, Clarke poured herself a glass of vodka and orange, hoping it might help her to relax and take her mind off things.

It didn't. The only thing on her mind now was Tammy and what might have happened to her.

Clarke looked up at the TV screen, where two people were kissing while a well-known male crooner sang something about love. Suddenly, it reminded her of something. Tammy and Bradley in the office, coming out of a meeting together. There'd been something about them. Was Bradley the mystery man? Clarke tried to remember exactly how he and Tammy had looked together. Tammy smiled a lot, certainly, but that was Tammy, bubbly and happy. And, in the right mood, she could flirt with a piece of furniture, let alone a good-looking man. Clarke longed to see the two of them together again now, to search for signs of anything going on between them. Had Tammy been flirting? Had it been sexual tension? Or was it simply Tammy being Tammy?

Chapter 14

Wednesday, Week Two

Clarke didn't sleep well. So many things tossed and turned in her head that her brain seemed to be permanently wired. Was Tammy having an affair with Bradley Acres? Was Bradley Acres involved with the fraud? Was Tammy still alive? When Clarke did eventually doze off, she dreamed of Tammy, Bradley, and Douglas Doncaster all lying together in a big pool of blood.

She woke up with a start. For a moment, she forgot where she was until she saw the familiar green curtains of her bedroom in the faint glow of the streetlamp outside. She took some deep breaths to calm herself down.

The alarm clock glowed 4:45 a.m. Her mind began to buzz again. There was no point in trying to go back to sleep. She rolled out of bed and grabbed her dressing gown.

The heating hadn't come on yet, so Clarke wrapped herself up in her fluffy dressing gown while she washed in lukewarm water. She needed to do something other than sit around worrying, so she decided to go to work early. She might find something more if she poked around the office before anyone else arrived.

Less than an hour later, she drove into the office car park. Clarke made a plan on the journey. She couldn't access Bradley's locker, and the police would probably have searched it already. But she wanted to check his desk and the storage cupboards that he used. There was file storage all around the office. It was meant to be a paperless office, but some paperwork always needed to be kept and some people still need-ed to buy fully into the corporate line on office storage. Searching the

106

cupboards might prove futile, but it would be better than doing nothing.

The silence in the office gave Clarke the creeps. She'd never been here this early before and she wasn't sure exactly what time people would start to arrive, so she headed straight for the cupboards behind Bradley's desk. Locked.

The cupboards throughout the office were identical and there were only four different keys for them. These four keys, between them, opened every single cupboard. Clarke hurried back to her end of the office and found the keys to her team's two cupboards in their hiding place under Andrew's desk. She returned to Bradley's cupboard.

Damn. Neither of the keys fit. She searched round the other cupboards. Some people left keys in the cupboard doors. Even after the Brack Attack exercise, some people were still remarkably lax about locking their cupboards at the end of the day. She found three more keys. She took them one at a time so she would remember to return them to the right place.

The second key she tried opened Bradley's cupboard. It was nearly empty. Maybe he had adopted the paperless ethos. A lone lever arch file lay on its side next to some personal stuff, tea bags, mugs, and an umbrella. Clarke pulled out the file. It only contained two pieces of paper. The first was a print from their accounting system. It showed a budget report of the cost centre that had been used to pay the fake invoices, dated two days after Tammy's disappearance. On it was handwritten in big scrawly writing, *need to find out who the cost centre manager is for this code—no one allocated.*

The other piece of paper listed all the company's departments, with managers' names against most of them.

Clarke took out both pieces of paper and scanned them. The photocopier-scanner seemed to take forever to warm up and Clarke regretted not turning it on sooner. She kept looking behind her at the door, in case someone came in, every time telling herself not to be so stupid, that no one would show up this early. Her blood-drenched dream flashed into her head. It might be just the cold making her shiver. Too early for the heating to come on here.

At last, the scanner burst into life and Clarke returned the file to Bradley's cupboard. She was about to lock the door when she sensed someone come up behind her.

"What are you looking for?"

"Bradley. Hi." What on earth was he doing in the office this early? Clarke thought quickly. "I'm desperate for a stapler. I can't find the key to our cupboard and this cupboard had the key in the door. Sorry."

"It's ok." Bradley smiled at her. "You're looking in the wrong cupboard anyway." He pulled a bunch of keys out of his pocket, jiggled it around, then picked out a small silver key. "I got keys cut for the team," he said, unlocking the adjacent cupboard. He pulled out a stapler and held it out for her.

"Thanks. I'll bring it back as soon as I'm done." Clarke turned to walk back to her desk, wondering if he really believed her story.

"Have the police found Tammy yet?"

Clarke swivelled round to face Bradley. "No. Not that I'm aware."

"I'm worried about her," he said.

Bradley seemed genuinely concerned. Deep worry lines etched across his face, and Clarke tried to remember if they had existed before last week. Perhaps something *had* been going on between him and Tammy.

"Me too," Clarke said. "I hope they find her soon."

They both stood for a moment, awkwardness filling the atmosphere. Did he want to discuss Tammy more and what she should say if he did? Quickly, she returned to her desk and stapled a few random pieces of paper together.

When Clarke took the stapler back, Bradley was sat at his desk. "I wondered," she said, "what you were working on with Tammy. I'm covering some of her work. Perhaps it's something I can help with."

"It's not important. It will wait."

Clarke returned to her own end of the office, trying to remember which cupboard she'd borrowed the key from to unlock Bradley's cupboard. Hopefully, no one would miss it and kick up a fuss. In any case, it was too late to rectify it now. If she was lucky, it would be ages before Bradley's team noticed that they now had an extra key for the cupboard. And, if necessary, she would swear that the key was already in the door when she found it.

It was 7:00 a.m. already. Clarke switched on her computer. She wished now that she had turned it on as soon as she got in. What if someone checked the big difference between the time her pass opened the car park barrier and the time she logged in to her computer? Did they ever do that? Probably not, unless some automatic programme highlighted discrepancies in things like that. Too late to change things now. At least CCTV didn't cover anywhere *inside* the office.

When Andrew arrived twenty minutes later, Clarke was busy working and sipping a very strong cup of coffee.

"Early start?" he said, taking his coat off and switching on his computer.

"Not sleeping well at the moment," Clarke said. "Figured I may as well come in." She swivelled her chair round to face him. "I'm so worried about Tammy," she said. She watched Andrew's face carefully to check his reaction.

"Bad business," he said, shaking his head.

"What do you think's happened to her?"

Andrew paused, as if he'd hardly given the matter any consideration until now. He typed his password into his computer and it sprang to life. He spoke slowly, "I don't know." He paused again.

Clarke waited for him to fill the silence.

"It's usually the husband, isn't it?" he said.

Clarke opened her mouth to speak but remembered just in time that Andrew knew nothing about the fraudulent invoices. She wondered whether to tell him but decided against it. What if he was involved? Her thoughts turned to Paul. How was he progressing with investigating the fraud? She should have told him sooner. If she'd told him about the fraud last week, Tammy might be home by now.

"What was Tammy working on with Bradley Acres?" Clarke asked. "They've met loads of times to discuss it. Do I need to pick up the work?"

"Just some new procedures. Tammy's been working on it for a while. She wanted Bradley's input."

So Tammy had instigated the meetings. She normally knew exactly what she was doing. Not a great one to ask for help, she preferred to work stuff out on her own or research independently on Google. Had she been having an affair with Bradley? Was it just an excuse for them to spend some time together?

Andrew got up and headed towards the kitchen. Clarke didn't suppose she'd get anything more useful of out him that morning.

The clock on the wall ticked over to 7:45 a.m. It promised to be a very long wait until lunchtime.

Clarke needed to do two things at lunchtime. First, she must phone Paul. And secondly, she needed to talk to Jeffrey Todd. She was certain, assuming Tammy was still alive, she would be in Tredington. Tammy swore she had seen Jeffrey near her house—she'd actually said that Jeffrey had been stalking her, but Clarke no longer believed that. So Jeffrey might be able to tell her which part of Tredington he'd been in. If he really was stalking her, he'd know where she lived. Not that she would be there. If you were hiding from something, the first place people would look would be your home. But the police hadn't found her address. Maybe no one else had either.

She would get Jeffrey away from the office by asking him out to the pub at lunchtime. A beer might relax him, make him talk more. She would go downstairs later this morning and suggest it. Her mind flashed back to Jeffrey pinning her against the wall in the car park a few days ago. Was she more afraid of being alone with Jeffrey or Jeffrey turning her down and refusing to talk to her? A vision of Tammy, her bubbly laughter and fabulous hair, popped up in her head, making her smile. She would give it her best shot, for Tammy.

Chapter 15

DC Paul Waterford drove into work carefully. He needed time to decide how to play this. At the moment, neither Acres nor Doncaster were aware that he knew anything about the fraud. He'd looked at the stuff on Clarke's memory stick last night. Their signatures approved every payment. Was one or both of them involved? Clarke had provided some amazing stuff, but Paul realised he needed more evidence before he could charge anyone.

He stopped at a red light. His sergeant would probably hand the fraud case over to the experts to investigate. That would be disappointing, but it needed to be done as soon as Paul got to the station, before Acres or Doncaster could destroy further evidence.

Paul went straight to talk to DS Prosser in his office. Let him pass the evidence to the fraud squad if he must. Paul needed to concentrate on finding Tammy Doncaster.

DS Prosser flicked through the scanned images on his computer screen and tapped his fingers on the desk. "You say there might be more?"

Paul nodded. "Yep, Clarke did well to find this many, but we need to get the whole lot looked at." Paul felt a surprising glow of pride in Clarke, that she had uncovered a big fraud and got some evidence. "There's a roomful of invoices in the basement." Clarke had explained the significance of the paper invoices and the £50,000 limit, although he wasn't sure he'd really understood it himself. Let Prosser figure it out.

"The fraud squad will want to lead on this," he said. "They'll get someone over to the office, box up everything, and move it somewhere they can examine it properly. Let's keep quiet about this until those invoices are secured."

"Yes, sir."

"Has the girl told anyone?"

"Clarke," he said. "Clarke Pettis." He repeated her name to emphasise the fact that she wasn't just *the girl*. Paul's protective instincts had kicked in, big time. "Clarke says she only told Tammy. God knows who Tammy told. Whoever it was probably killed her."

DS Prosser turned off his computer. "We can't be sure that Tammy Doncaster is dead," he said. "Our priority is still to find her. She may have vital information, and she may be in danger if she does."

Paul drove into the Briar Holman car park with two more unmarked cars behind him, thanks to Prosser's decision to delay calling in the fraud squad. He wanted the credit for this one himself. Paul smiled. Prosser shouldn't be taking any credit. Clarke had done all the hard work and handed it to them on a plate.

"What's that grin for?" Prosser asked as Paul pulled into a parking space.

"Nothing, sir."

They intended to get the invoices secured and take Doncaster and Acres in for questioning at the same time. That way, neither of them could start removing evidence nor warn each other.

The posse of police officers barged straight past reception, flashing passes on the way. Paul and Prosser took the stairs to the fifth floor to find Doncaster. DC Farrier showed a couple of other DCs the way to the third floor to bring Bradley Acres in. The remaining pair in the team headed straight to the basement archive.

Paul reached the top floor first. Prosser puffed loudly as he ran up the stairs. Paul ran on ahead and threw open the door to Doncaster's office.

"What the blazes...!" Doncaster got up, then recognised Paul and regained his composure. "What do you want?" he said.

DS Prosser entered the room, still breathing a little too heavily. "We'd like you to come down to the station, please, sir, to answer a few questions." He moved towards Doncaster.

"Is this about Tammy? I've already told you everything I can."

"There's another matter we need to discuss," Prosser said.

"I'm busy." Doncaster reached for the phone on his desk. Paul cut him off before he dialled.

"Best if you cooperate, sir," Paul said. At this rate, he'd be forced to arrest him, which he really didn't want to do due to the lack of evidence so far. He was relying on calling Doncaster's bluff.

Doncaster gave an impatient sigh. "Let's get on with it then," he said.

"Thank you, sir," Paul said. Was Doncaster guilty or did he simply want to avoid the indignity of being arrested and led out of the building in handcuffs? Either way, Paul intended to stick to Doncaster like a limpet until he got him safely in the car.

Kevin Farrier was waiting in reception when they got downstairs. "Bradley Acres isn't in the office," he said. "He's gone out to a meeting. Nobody seems sure where."

Paul watched Doncaster to see if he reacted to hearing that they were looking for Acres. He couldn't be sure if Doncaster's expression displayed surprise or worry. Either way, it was a fleeting moment, then his face became blank again.

Prosser's expression proved much easier to read. "Find him," he yelled at Kevin.

Kevin ran towards the stairs. Hopefully, he would discover someone upstairs who knew of Acres' whereabouts. They didn't want two missing people on their hands. Paul hoped Kevin wouldn't ask Clarke for help. She'd done enough already. He didn't want her involved in this anymore. Somehow, he needed to keep her safe.

An hour later, Paul came out of the interview room feeling despondent. Doncaster had been unhelpful. Even though he wasn't actually under arrest yet, he'd insisted on waiting for his solicitor, which delayed things to no end. Then he couldn't—or wouldn't, Paul thought—provide answers to any of their questions.

He didn't seem too concerned about his wife, so perhaps their split had been more acrimonious than he'd let on. The fraud charges wouldn't stick either. They needed more evidence of his involvement, more than just his signature. Paul would bet that Doncaster probably signed whatever his PA put in front of him, although maybe that ought to be a crime. Acres was still AWOL. He'd allegedly left his meeting at another office and should be on his way back. Paul wondered how to detain Doncaster for longer when they couldn't arrest him. They didn't want to risk him phoning Acres to warn him. They'd been idiots. Someone should have double-checked that both men were in the office before they'd ploughed in.

Chapter 16

It took a great deal of cajoling on Clarke's part to overcome Jeffrey's resistance to come to the pub. He finally agreed and now they were walking together through the subway to the nearest pub, in the marketplace.

At noon, the subway was deserted, still waiting for the lunch rush from the Briar Holman office to start. Clarke shuddered as her mind flashed back to Jeffrey losing his temper with her in the car park. She should have arranged to meet him in the pub.

"I really appreciate this, Jeffrey," she said. She kept walking, making her steps purposeful as she tried to maintain the conversation and keep everything calm. It would only be for a minute. Once they reached the marketplace, it would be busy.

"I'm only doing it for Tammy," Jeffrey said, "but I don't see how I can help."

The Red Lion pub faced them as they exited the subway. Clarke stopped holding her breath. Her phone rang. Paul. She rejected the call. Hopefully, she would have more to tell him later.

The Red Lion could never be accused of being trendy. Its minimal décor, with lots of dark wood furniture, made the whole place seem dingy and old-fashioned. It didn't even have a decent wine list. She bought Jeffrey a beer and herself a sparkling water, then found a table at the back of the pub.

"I'm trying to find Tammy," Clarke said, unsure how to broach the subject of Tammy's sighting of Jeffrey in Tredington, without accusing him of being a stalker. She decided to start at the beginning and hoped, by the time she got to that bit, she'd be struck by inspiration.

"Police think she's dead," Jeffrey said bluntly. He took a big gulp of his beer, slopping it onto the beer mat as he put the glass down clumsily.

Clarke took a sip of her water, regretting her decision to stay alcohol-free today. "What if she's not?"

Jeffrey shrugged. Clarke wondered how to interpret his gesture. She carried on.

"What if she's not dead? I think she's been living in Tredington," Clarke said. "But the police can't find her address."

"If the police can't find her, I'm sure you won't."

"Jeffrey." Clarke looked at him, trying to decide if he actually gave a damn. "Do you ever go to Tredington?" Clarke realised she was holding her breath again, frightened of how he might react, wondering if he would even tell the truth.

"My auntie lives there."

She hadn't expected it to be so easy, but at least Jeffrey had a reason for being somewhere near Tammy's house. At least it gave Clarke hope that he wasn't stalking Tammy. She took another sip of her drink. Her brain kept flashing back to the incident with Jeffrey in the car park. How she needed something alcoholic to calm her nerves. For a moment, she pretended that the mineral water was neat vodka.

"Tammy said she saw you in Tredington a while ago." She waited for a reaction. None came. She wondered if Jeffrey had heard her. "Did you ever see Tammy there?"

Jeffrey took another gulp of his beer, nearly draining the glass. "No," he said. "No."

"Which road does your aunt live on?" Clarke got the impression he was lying about seeing Tammy.

"It's Higham Street," Jeffrey said, "but I didn't see Tammy there."

Clarke realised she was wasting her time. She would find Higham Street on the map later, but she would still be looking for a needle in a haystack. Half a needle. Half a very small needle.

Jeffrey downed the rest of his beer in one and got up to go. "I did see Tammy once," he said, "but not near my auntie's house. She was in Park Road."

Clarke started to ask him how long ago and which direction she had been going in, plus a whole load of other questions, but she ended up talking to an empty space. Jeffrey was already on his way out of the pub. She wondered why he'd changed his story. He'd been adamant at first that he'd never seen Tammy in Tredington. Could she trust anything he said? She began to wonder if perhaps he really had hurt Tammy.

Chapter 17

Clarke left work on the dot of five, reminding herself that she had worked over eleven hours already that day with hardly any sleep last night. She intended to spend the evening looking at maps on the internet to work out where to search for Tammy. Seeing Jeffrey at lunchtime hadn't been a complete waste of time. As she walked out to her car, she tried phoning Paul again, but her frozen hands kept hitting the wrong icons on her phone.

She unlocked the car and pulled the door open, throwing her handbag onto the passenger seat. Why did November have to be so dark and cold and horrible? As soon as the engine warmed up, she would turn the heating on full blast. She might actually stop shivering by the time she arrived home. This morning she'd parked the car against the hedge at the back of the car park. Now she wished she'd taken a minute to reverse into the space. The cars on either side of her were much too close, so it would be tight reversing out and turning.

Clarke reached for her seat belt and had just clicked it shut when she spotted the piece of paper under her windscreen wiper. Cursing, she undid her seat belt and got out of the car to remove the paper. People were cheeky sometimes, and they sneaked into the company car park to put flyers on the car windscreens. They were trespassing, but they didn't seem to care.

This one was wrapped in a plastic bag. Unusual for a flyer, but it rained pretty much constantly at the moment, so she guessed they'd waterproofed everything to stop them from disintegrating. Clarke tossed it into the passenger footwell. It would be the usual rubbish. Did anyone ever actually buy stuff from windscreen flyers? She wondered why they bothered. As soon as she got home, she would bin it.

By the time Clarke shuffled the car out of its tight spot, the heating started to work. She turned it up, blasting hot air as she pulled out of the car park.

Clarke nearly fell asleep a couple of times on the journey home, despite the early hour. She supposed she shouldn't be surprised, when she'd got up at stupid o'clock. A quick nap on the sofa would sort her out, except the icy cold temperature of her living room made that impossible. The boarded-up window seemed secure enough, but an arctic draught flicked through the small gaps round the edges. After twenty minutes of Googling on her phone and calling glaziers and begging them, she managed to arrange someone to come out that evening and replace the glass.

She found some prawns in the fridge that needed using up. Clarke cooked them quickly with some pasta and a tomato sauce. She had just dished it up when the glazier arrived.

"What happened here?" the glazier asked when he saw the window.

Clarke shrugged. "Just one of those things," she said. She didn't want to tell a stranger about the brick being thrown through her window. That would make her feel vulnerable. Better to pretend she was absolutely fine. Anyway, it was none of his business.

The prawn pasta was already semi-cold. If she warmed it up in the microwave, the prawns would taste like rubber, so she opened a bottle of prosecco and poured a glass. Prosecco would help it taste better, even if it didn't make up for the tepid temperature.

A frozen blast engulfed the living room as the glazier took the boarding off the window and removed the remaining glass. Clarke ate quickly, then busied herself with cleaning the kitchen.

The glazier finished sooner than expected. He hoovered up the mess before leaving, but Clarke got her vacuum cleaner out and did the job again to be certain that no broken glass clung to the carpet. Her plans this evening were all going wrong. She started to pour herself another glass of prosecco, then remembered she needed to look at a map of Tredington. Clarke put the bottle back in the fridge and pulled out her laptop.

She decided to try Google Earth again to get a better idea of the area. Clarke's growing expertise on Google Earth meant she found the street she wanted in record time. Park Road contained a long row of houses, with a block of flats at the end. The flats looked to be six storeys high and Clarke wondered how many flats were in the block. Add that to the number of houses and it presented plenty of possibilities. Of course, Tammy may simply have been walking through on her way to somewhere else. Park Road would be a long shot, but it was the only shot she had. She would go at the weekend and knock on every single door if necessary until she found someone who recognised Tammy.

As soon as Clarke got into bed, she remembered the windscreen flyer she'd left in her car. She'd intended to take it out and throw it in the dustbin. She laughed. With everything going on in her life, it should have been the last thing to worry her. But her OCD was kicking in. Even the idea of it littering up her nice tidy car upset her. And it was wet. The carpet would be dirty now. Arrrhhhh.

She pulled the green patterned duvet up under her chin and tried to forget about the flyer. It would be perfectly ok to remove it in the morning.

Her thoughts turned back to Tammy. Should she tell Paul about Jeffrey seeing Tammy in Tredington? She doubted if Jeffrey would have already volunteered the information, not after his arrest. That decided things for Clarke. She had already caused poor Jeffrey enough grief. Better for her to go at the weekend and check it out for herself. It would no doubt be a complete waste of time, another wild goose chase. But if she discovered anything definite, she would tell Paul then.

Chapter 18

Thursday, Week Two

Clarke overslept. She would be late for work. Too many early mornings, she told herself. She decided to skip breakfast and get a coffee in the office. If she really got a move on, she would be out the door in ten minutes.

A light frost shrouded her windscreen. Clarke cursed as she scraped it off. Now she was even later and colder. She got into the car, shutting out the chill November wind, and leaned over to put her ice scraper in the passenger door where she kept it in winter.

That annoying windscreen flyer still lay on the floor in front of the passenger seat. She picked it up. If she put the flyer on the seat, she wouldn't forget to bin it.

The paper flicked over as she tossed it onto the seat. Now that she saw it in daylight, it looked more like a note than a flyer. That explained the plastic bag. Quickly, she took it out of the bag, gasping as she unfolded the piece of paper.

It wasn't a note. Not exactly. Four words stared at her from the piece of paper. Instead of being handwritten, they were carefully cut out of newspaper print. Some of the letters were individually cut out. Others were whole words. Clarke stared at it for a minute, trying to take it in, then she realised she was shaking. She read the words again and again. *MIND YOUR OWN BUSINESS.*

She rummaged in her handbag for her phone and dialled Paul. He would know what to do.

Paul didn't answer. Clarke decided on a short detour to call into the police station on her way to work. Paul might be there and, if not, she would show the note to someone else working on the case. It must be connected to the fraudulent invoices or her search for Tammy. This whole damn mess was connected, for certain. The police would need to fingerprint the note. It occurred to her that her fingerprints would be all over it now. Still, they may find something.

Clarke pulled herself together and started to drive. However much she tried to focus on the route, her thoughts kept drifting back to the note. She wondered why someone would send that note to her. A horrible thought hit her. Could it be the same person who had sent death threats to Tammy? Whoever was responsible, they clearly recognised her car. Had they been watching her? Or was it someone she knew?

Because of the later time, the traffic was worse than normal. Clarke debated whether she should go straight to work and phone Paul from there. She glanced over at the note and decided to go directly to the police station. What did the note even mean? Mind your own business. Mind your own business, or what? What would happen if she didn't mind her own business?

A lorry hooted at her and she realised she'd run a red light. It snapped her out of her daze and she turned left up the road to the police station. She managed to find a parking space and walked back the hundred metres to the station entrance. This better not take too long or she really would be late for work. Her hand gripped the note in its plastic bag. Work was the least of her worries right now.

DS Prosser came out to the front desk to meet Clarke. Paul had gone out, but DS Prosser assured her of his expertise on the case. He looked at the note and immediately ushered her into a small interview room.

"When did you find it?" His big bushy eyebrows moved up and down expressively as he spoke.

Clarke considered for a moment. "I left work at five," she said. "And I definitely didn't see it at lunchtime. So that narrows it down to between one and five p.m."

Prosser nodded, making his eyebrows dance like hairy caterpillars. "And the message," he said. "What do you think it means?"

Clarke wondered how much he knew of her involvement and whether she should tell him about her efforts to find Tammy. She hadn't even told Paul everything yet.

"You're aware of the fraud at Briar Holman?" she said. "Have you seen the evidence?"

"Yes."

"I found all the invoices."

"I see," Prosser said slowly. "And who exactly did you tell about them?"

"No one," Clarke said. "No one." She considered for a moment. "I told Tammy about the first one. Tammy Doncaster. But if she's been kidnapped or murdered, it can't be her who sent the note." Something dawned on her. "Do you suppose she told someone? Did they find out I discovered it? Should I be worried?" She *was* worried. She didn't need DS Prosser to tell her whether to worry or not.

"We're investigating the issue," Prosser said. "Let's give your note to forensics. They might get something from it." He frowned and his eyebrows mirrored his expression perfectly. "In the meantime, I would be careful."

Careful. What on earth did he mean by that? She needed to go to work. She lived on her own. Being careful wouldn't be enough. If someone wanted to harm her, they would have plenty of opportunity.

As soon as Clarke returned to her car, she wondered if she should have told DS Prosser about her visits to Tredington. But how would anyone have discovered she'd been there, unless they were following her? Well, she intended to go again on Saturday to check out the area where Jeffrey saw Tammy. She would be extremely careful. If anyone followed her this time, she would make certain she spotted them.

Clarke didn't get into the office until nearly half past ten. She intended to phone Andrew to tell him she'd be late, but with multiple problems buzzing around in her head, phoning the office completely slipped her mind.

Andrew looked up as she reached her desk. He made a point of looking really obviously at his watch.

"Sorry," Clarke said, turning on her computer. She didn't want to admit she'd been seeing the police. He'd want a full rundown of what she'd discussed. She didn't want to tell him about the fraud, especially not after that nasty note. And she certainly didn't want everyone treating her as a suspect. She grabbed her mug. She'd missed breakfast and felt a bit faint now. Anyway, it was so rare for her to be late. Andrew should cut her some slack.

"Clarke." Andrew's voice stopped her in her tracks as soon as she stepped away from her desk. "Tony needs to see you urgently. Can you phone him right away, please? He's phoned twice already this morning."

Clarke put down her mug. Tony was one of the managers she looked after. The costs on his biggest project were already spiralling out of control. If he'd phoned more than once, that meant he must be panicking about something. She would have to deal with it immediately. Reluctantly, she sat down and reached for the phone.

Her guess proved to be correct. Tony was panicking. He'd found masses of new costs coded to his project and didn't have a clue what they were for.

"I'm coming down," Clarke said, trying to calm him. He was on the floor below them. "I'll be there in a couple of minutes." She picked up her mug, hiding it behind a large notepad so that Andrew wouldn't spot it. Hopefully, she'd cadge some coffee in the second floor kitchen.

Tony's budget report glared out from his computer screen when Clarke arrived at his desk. She sipped her coffee while he explained the problem.

"There's over a hundred thousand pounds more of machinery costs that weren't there last week," he said. He rubbed his hands together distractedly and beads of sweat glistened on his forehead. "But I haven't ordered any more machinery."

"Ok, it's probably just a mis-code," Clarke reassured him, trying to drink some of the boiling hot coffee before she fainted from lack of breakfast. She reached for his computer mouse, clicked on a couple of things, and the screen flashed full of figures until a full transactions report for the overspent code appeared. She scrolled to the bottom to check the most recent additions.

One name stood out to her, as if in ten-foot-high neon letters. FIRESTOP. She looked at the report more closely. The three most recent payments, all dated last week, totalled over one hundred and forty thousand pounds.

Clarke pressed the print button to get a copy of the report. She would need to give it to Paul. "Don't worry," she told Tony. "I'll check it out thoroughly."

"Please," he said. "I'm going to get sacked at this rate."

She gulped down the remains of her coffee and took the printout. "Try not to worry. I'm sure there's a perfectly reasonable explanation." She felt guilty that she couldn't tell him what that explanation was to reassure him.

Walking back up the stairs, Clarke tried to work out the timing. If the fake invoices had been sent through the internal post and the payment runs took place twice a week, how long ago would it have taken for them to be paid? Was it before Tammy mentioned that first invoice to Bradley Acres? Or after? The degree of escalation suggested a final attempt to get as much money as possible before someone discovered the scam and put a stop to it? The culprit must be pretty sure of not being discovered. The invoices were much more spread out before. But now three invoices in one go, and nearly up to the maximum fifty thousand pounds each too, definitely indicated something. Clarke wondered if there were others, for the other three fake companies, paid on other codes. Another thing to discuss with Paul.

She found it difficult to concentrate on anything. The police came to the office twice during the morning. They kept asking about Bradley Acres, but he didn't seem to be in the office today. That was nothing unusual, as he frequently attended meetings at some of Briar Holman's other offices and factories. Clarke speculated whether they wanted to question Bradley about the invoices or about Tammy. She hoped Paul would show up, but they sent other officers both times. There were a few things she wanted to discuss with Paul, as well as some things she didn't.

Clarke still hadn't phoned Paul by the time she left the office for the day. She didn't want to have any discussions with him where it might get overheard. On her way across the car park, her phone pinged with a text message. She hoped it would be Paul, but the number flagged as unknown. She opened it as soon as she got into the car, expecting some dodgy spam message.

Hi Clarke, can we meet please to discuss the invoice you showed Tammy? I don't want to talk about it in the office as it may involve other employees. Please don't mention it to anyone else. Can you meet me at 7 pm tonight in the Ball and Chain pub in Havebury? Kindest Regards Bradley Acres.

Clarke read the message three times. Bradley had never shown up today. She would have remembered if he had because of the police looking for him. God knows how he had got her phone number. Would HR have given it to him, or maybe Andrew had? Andrew had her number for emergencies, so he seemed the most likely culprit. She would talk to him tomorrow about not giving her personal phone number to anyone without asking her first.

She dropped the phone back into her handbag and started the engine. At least now she knew for sure that Tammy must have shown that first invoice to Bradley Acres.

On the drive home, Clarke wondered what she should do. No, she knew exactly what she *should* do. She should phone Paul, tell him about the text message, tell him about the latest invoices. Havebury was in the opposite direction from her flat. She didn't have time to go home, then drive to Havebury, and find the pub by 7:00 p.m. She should have phoned Bradley back and asked him to make the meeting later, but she'd already reached the M25.

The junction off the motorway lay just ahead. Quickly, Clarke made a decision. She flicked the indicator and manoeuvred over to the inside lane. If she came off the motorway here and turned round, she should reach Havebury at around 6:45. That would give her time to phone Paul before she went into the pub.

The traffic on the M25 was much slower going in the opposite direction, so Clarke drove into the car park of the Ball and Chain dead on 7:00 p.m. Phoning Paul would have to wait, maybe until she got home. That was a much better idea, as then she'd be able to tell him everything Bradley said.

She walked into the pub, looking round for Bradley. A few people turned to stare at her as she wandered around, searching for him. Clarke didn't like the pub. The rather basic décor cried out for a facelift and the scratched tables added to the downmarket vibe. It wasn't crowded, but the few clientele present matched the state of the pub. Clarke still wore her smart work clothes, so would really stand out if she took her coat off. Best to leave her coat on until Bradley arrived. She wondered why he'd picked this place and assumed he must live nearby.

Clarke's tour of the pub ascertained that Bradley hadn't arrived yet. She ordered an orange juice at the bar.

"Haven't seen you in here before," the barmaid said.

Clarke handed her a ten-pound note. "I'm meeting someone."

She pocketed the change and settled down at a small table in the corner, which gave her a good view of the door. Then she pulled out her phone and dialled Bradley's number. Straight to voicemail. He must be on his way. Hopefully, she wouldn't be waiting long. To kill time, she reread his text message. Interesting that he only mentioned the one invoice. Was he not aware of the others? Or did he think she didn't know about them? The police had confiscated everything in the basement archives now. Surely he must realise that, unless he had been out of the office for a couple of days? A sudden chill hit her, despite the fact that she still wore her warm winter coat. Bradley had signed all the invoices. Perhaps he had summoned her here to warn her off.

Clarke stared at the door for the hundredth time. Still no sign of Bradley. It was nearly half past seven now. That seemed to be the story of her life this week, getting stood up in pubs. She scanned the room. Had Bradley got her here deliberately? No one looked friendly. No one looked as if they might come to her rescue if things got nasty. She began to think that Bradley might have taken Tammy. Had he killed her?

Pull yourself together, Clarke told herself. Of course not. Anyway, he would never do anything stupid in a public place. She had parked her car near the exit deliberately, to make a safe, speedy departure if necessary.

She took a sip of her orange juice. She would eke it out another ten minutes to see if Bradley showed, then she would go home. She wished she'd never come here. What a total waste of time.

Chapter 19

Friday, Week Two

Friday morning dawned cold and wet. DC Paul Waterford ducked under the tape cordon and veered off to the right behind the row of trees, which dripped residual rainwater onto the crime scene in the front garden. The early morning start and the nasty, wet weather did nothing to temper his excitement at being seconded to the Murder Investigation Team. Three officers in MIT had gone off sick, and the team already had another murder earlier this week to deal with, so Sergeant Prosser had put Paul's name forward for a temporary secondment and was also helping them out himself for a few days. Paul was buzzing.

The scene of crime officers had already arrived, carefully examining the sodden lawn where the body remained in situ. His legs were contorted at an awkward angle, crumpled when he had fallen. A dark blood stain congealed on the back of the victim's head, where it rested on the ground, the only remaining evidence of blood. Heavy overnight rain had soaked the body and its surroundings, washing away any useful blood splatter patterns. At least the leather jacket the victim wore had done a sterling job of keeping his torso dry.

"Yes, that's Bradley Acres," Paul confirmed to DS Prosser. He would need to be formally identified, but Paul was pretty certain, as he'd interviewed Acres only a few days ago. Acres wore a suit and tie then. Now he looked decidedly scruffy. Torn jeans, stubble on his chin, mud on his clothes.

"Any family?" Paul asked. He always dreaded informing the next of kin. No one liked doing it. Best get it over with.

"Not yet," Prosser said. "We've started searching the house."

"Quicker to get the details from his workplace," Paul said.

Prosser nodded. "Good idea."

"What's the time of death?" Paul asked. He stepped back as the SO-CO team began to bag up the body. He got a better view of the head wound now. It looked severe.

"Yesterday evening sometime," Prosser said.

One of the SOCO guys paused from his task and turned to Prosser. "Wait for the post-mortem," he said. "No point in guessing."

Paul checked his watch. Nearly 7:30 a.m. By the time he got over to Briar Holman, someone in their HR department would have shown up to find him an address for the next of kin. A missing person and a murder in the same company within a few days of each other couldn't be a coincidence. He would have to interview everyone in Acres' office. Better to do that sooner rather than later, but informing the next of kin took priority. Didn't want them finding out from somebody else. It might be useful anyway, talking to the family, discover any key events or issues in the victim's life, how much they knew, how much they didn't.

The traffic was a bitch. Forty-five minutes later, Paul finally turned into the Briar Holman car park. He wondered if he would bump into Clarke. HR shared her part of the office, so she may be around. Meeting her again after all this time had been a curious mixture of good and uncomfortable. He hadn't yet decided if he liked the feeling.

Paul nipped in and out of the office within minutes. Disappointingly, he didn't see Clarke. HR had provided an address. Bradley Acres' parents lived locally. He would visit them right away.

Clarke was freezing when she got into the office. She took the lift and headed straight off to make a coffee to warm herself up. One of the women from HR was perched on the arm of the sofa in the kitchen, tapping into her phone.

She looked up when Clarke came in. "Isn't it dreadful?"

"Sorry, what?" Clarke flicked the switch on the kettle.

"Bradley Acres," the woman said. "Haven't you heard?"

Clarke filled her mug with boiling water and picked up the milk carton. "Heard what?"

"He's dead," the woman said. "They found his body early this morning."

Clarke dropped the milk bottle and, for a moment, the spreading puddle of milk and boiling hot coffee distracted her. She jumped backwards to avoid it dripping on her but noticed her coffee-stained hands. How could she fail to feel boiling hot coffee sloshing on her hands, which now appeared red and scalded? She ran the cold tap and forced herself to hold her hands under the cool stream of water.

"Dead?" Clarke said slowly. "Are you sure?" He should have shown up to the pub last night. Why had he wanted to talk to her?

"Yes. The police were here earlier. It's awful. He wasn't even very old."

Police? That ruled out a heart attack or an accident. If the police were here, it must be... She immediately thought of Tammy.

"What happened?" Clarke's hand shook as she picked up the coffee jar. She replaced it on the kitchen worktop.

The woman shook her head. "Nobody's saying anything. I suppose we'll soon find out."

"Yes," Clarke said. The news would be all over the office before long. She hadn't known Bradley Acres particularly well. But she kept picturing his signature on dozens of fraudulent invoices and remained convinced that this was connected with Tammy's disappearance. She only hoped Tammy wouldn't turn up dead too.

Andrew was tearing his hair out when Clarke returned to her desk.

"Are you ok?" she asked.

"Bradley," he said. "Bradley bloody Acres."

"I just found out," Clarke said, sitting down. "It's terrible. Do you know what happened?" Her ankle ached. She needed to rest it.

Andrew wrung his hands together. "Murdered." His face looked ashen and sweat dripped from his brow, despite the chilly early morning temperature in the office.

"I'm sorry," Clarke said. "Were you very close?" She'd never noticed them being particularly friendly, but bad news affected everybody differently.

He shook his head. "It's not that," he said. "It's... the police want to interview everyone who spoke to him in the last few days. I spoke to him on Monday. Had a real barney in the middle of the office after you went home sick. Everyone saw us."

Clarke had been privy to Andrew's occasional temper flare-ups before. She easily imagined the spectacle he must have caused.

"People argue all the time. You didn't murder him, did you?" Clarke's voice wavered, and she wished she had managed to load the accusation with more conviction. Andrew didn't seem to notice. He was too wrapped up in worrying about himself.

"No," he said. "But I've seen it on TV hundreds of times. People have an innocent little argument then, before you can blink, the police arrest them for murder, even when they're innocent."

"I'm sure they're not going to arrest you," she reassured him, "but they will want to talk to you. You should go to the police. Be proactive, show them you have nothing to hide. It will be so much less embarrassing than having them come into the office looking for you." Maybe Andrew had done it. Perhaps they carried on outside the argument as they left for home? Clarke didn't know how or where Bradley had died, so she shouldn't be speculating about Andrew like this. Unfortunately, right now, she suspected absolutely everyone.

"Yes," Andrew said. "You're probably right."

Clarke wondered if she would take her own advice. Would she tell the police about going out to meet Bradley last night? She didn't really want to admit that to anyone. She was already too mixed up in this. It would look bad, and it wouldn't get the police any closer to finding out who murdered Bradley.

By 9:30 a.m., conversation about Bradley Acres buzzed around the packed office. Andrew took Clarke's advice and spoke to the police. They told him that Bradley was found yesterday evening at his home. Clarke wondered if he'd been dead already when she was waiting for him in the pub. That certainly explained why he didn't show up. If only she'd known what he wanted to talk to her about.

Clarke still wasn't sure what to do now. She hardly knew Bradley Acres, but the fact that he had asked to meet her last night and now he was dead meant she ought to inform the police. But she remembered the note and the brick thrown through her window. Someone was trying to warn her off. She shuddered and knew she couldn't tell the police.

"Andrew." Clarke walked the few steps over to his desk so she didn't have to shout. He looked up. "Did you give my mobile number to anyone yesterday?"

"No." Andrew looked puzzled. "Why do you ask?"

"Oh, it's nothing," Clarke said. She wondered who did give her number to Bradley. She'd probably never find out now.

The rumours about Bradley's murder flew round the office. Clarke couldn't tell what might be truth and what was fiction. She fought the urge to phone Paul. Best to stay out of it, although she desperately wanted to find out what happened.

She needed to complete some of Tammy's work, but concentration proved impossible with her colleagues all on tenterhooks and constantly talking. Her own brain whirled with Bradley, Tammy, and nasty notes on car windscreens. Tammy disappeared over a week ago. She hoped that Bradley's murder wouldn't hold up the police efforts to try to find Tammy. Did they even believe Tammy was still alive? Probably not. Definitely not now. But Clarke refused to give up on her friend. She needed to make sure the police continued to search for Tammy.

Clarke started thinking, if it were *her* in trouble, where would she go? Where would she hide?

She supposed her first thought would be to go to her parents for help. But with both of Tammy's parents dead, her second thought would be close friends. Who were Tammy's friends outside of work? Surely the police must have already asked Douglas that question? So would she go somewhere as far away as possible? Or go to a really familiar area? Everything seemed to lead back to Tredington. And if it didn't, then Tammy could be absolutely anywhere.

Clarke tried to imagine who might want to harm Tammy. Definitely her estranged husband was a contender. Everybody loved Tammy. She was fun and vibrant and chatty. No one ever said a bad word about her. It must be connected to the fraudulent invoices. So far, they added up to over one and a half million pounds worth, with probably more yet to find. If Tammy mentioned that first invoice to the wrong person, they would definitely want to shut her up. Had she mentioned it to Bradley Acres? But if Bradley was the person behind the fraud, who killed him?

Bradley Acres. Clarke hardly knew him. She rarely visited his end of the office, so even though they had worked every day in the same big room, she didn't have much to do with him.

She tried to picture Bradley in her head, with his thick mop of blond hair, much taller than her, and pretty fit. She wondered if he'd spent his spare time in the gym or playing sports. Everyone this morning speculated about how he'd been killed. Surely someone must have attacked him from behind, taken him by surprise. If he'd seen it coming, wouldn't he have run or at least fought off his attacker?

When was the last time she'd seen Bradley? It must have been when he had nearly caught her breaking into his cupboard, so early Wednesday morning. Clarke tried to recall if she'd seen him since. Her memory failed her on that score. When there are fifty or so people in the room every day, most of them blend in and she'd be hard-pushed to remember who she'd seen on any particular day, even today, apart from her own team and a couple of other people she spoke to.

Clarke vaguely remembered seeing Bradley with Tammy on the day Tammy had disappeared. Nothing unusual about that. Tammy had been working on a project with him for a few weeks. She met with him frequently. The events of that day were overshadowed by Brack Attack. Brack Attack really was the only thing that anyone remembered about that day. Had someone chosen that Wednesday deliberately to do something to Tammy?

Clarke considered her theory of Bradley and Tammy being together. If she was right, Tammy might be in danger. Or already dead. She reached for her phone and speed-dialled Paul's number.

Acres' parents didn't tell Paul anything useful. Despite living locally, they hardly saw him. Besides, they were too distraught and shocked to answer most of Paul's questions. He left as soon as the family liaison officer showed up. Hopefully, she would get some useful nugget of information from them that would crack the case instantly. But probably not. He returned to Bradley Acres' house. SOCO had left, but DS Prosser and DC Farrier continued to search inside the house.

Prosser was going through a cupboard in Acres' living room when Paul walked in. He stood up immediately. "You need to see this," he said.

Paul followed him to the corner of the room. "The parents didn't say much. Maybe they'll come up with something when they've processed things."

"It's always a shock to the families." Prosser pointed to a small table next to the sofa. The remote control sat within easy reach for lounging in front of the massive TV screen that filled most of the opposite wall. Next to the remote lay a small notepad.

Paul reached for it.

"Don't touch it," Prosser said.

Paul snapped his hands down to his sides before taking a proper look. Two words written on the pad jumped out at him. *Clarke Pettis.* He read the rest of the note. *7pm Ball and Chain, Thursday.* He took a moment to process the message. It sounded like Clarke met with Acres? He wasn't aware of any friendship, but he realised that Clarke must have moved on since he'd been with her. If anything was going on between her and Bradley Acres, he should tell her about his death before she heard it from somebody else. He read the note again. Not an affair, not with Clarke. Acres would never have used her surname on the note if they were in a relationship. Not even if they were simply friends, not with an unusual name like Clarke. He wouldn't need her surname to distinguish her from anyone else. It didn't make sense. Why meet up after work if they were neither lovers nor friends? No doubt Clarke would enlighten him.

"Can you check out the Ball and Chain," Prosser said, "before we talk to Pettis."

Paul had visited the Ball and Chain pub once before. Its general seediness and run-down appearance hardly made it Clarke's sort of place. The pub had been built years ago, next door to a prison, but the prison had been replaced by council housing back in the sixties. It took Paul less than five minutes to drive to the pub from Acres' house.

It was too early for the pub to be open, and the landlord took his time unlocking. Paul waited while he worked his way through multiple locks and bolts. They needed good security in a rough area like this. Hopefully, they would also possess decent CCTV.

The pub still smelt of last night's stale beer, and a couple of empty crisp packets littered one of the tables. Paul wondered what time the cleaner showed up. He tried to imagine Clarke sitting in here, sipping a glass of wine. In her firefighting days, she would probably have fit in ok here. Now? He wasn't so sure.

"Did this man come in last night?" He showed the landlord a photo of Acres.

The landlord stared at the photo blankly. "Never seen him."

"Are you sure?"

"Not one of our regulars. We don't get too many strangers in here. He'd stand out with that blond hair. Never seen him."

As soon as Paul arrived back at the station, he started looking at the CCTV. He would normally bend over backwards to get out of that job, but this time, he wanted to do it himself. He didn't know what he would do if he found any incriminating evidence.

He fast-forwarded last night's footage to just before 7:00 p.m. At 7:04, Clarke approached the bar. She ordered a drink and sat at a table near the door. He watched her sipping her drink, making it last over half an hour, repeatedly checking her watch. She got her phone out and dialled a number. After a few seconds, she hung up without appearing to speak, so she didn't leave a voicemail. Ten minutes later, she got up and left. Paul continued watching for a while. No sign of Acres. Was he already dead by that time? Hopefully, the time of death would be available by now.

Paul checked the CCTV footage of the car park, scanning through from 6:30 until 8:00 p.m. He saw Clarke parking her car at 7:00 p.m. and going into the pub, then leaving at 7:42. No sign of Acres.

He picked up the phone, dropping it straight back down. He would go to see the crime scene investigator in person.

The CSI in charge of the Acres murder was a bossy woman called Erica. She terrified most of the DCs, but Paul got on with her well. It took a certain type of person to be a CSI. Not everyone could stomach some of the stuff they dealt with, especially at grisly murder scenes. The horror of it would give most people nightmares. Once you understood all that, it was easy enough to relate to them and get some sort of working relationship going.

Erica seemed pleased to see him. "We haven't finished," she said before Paul even opened his mouth to speak, "but I can tell you he died from the wound to the back of his head. You're looking for a big blunt murder weapon. Something very heavy to cave his head in that much."

Paul nodded. He smelled freshly brewed coffee and regretted skipping breakfast. He didn't imagine Erica would offer him any. "Time of death?" he asked.

"Tricky." Erica glanced at her notes. "He's been outside in the rain all night. Best we can say is between 7:00 and 9:00 p.m."

Paul's heart sank. That would put Clarke in the vicinity at the right time. Had she gone to Acres' house after he failed to show at the pub? No way would she have killed him. No way. But she may have seen something. And he really needed to find out why she'd been trying to meet him.

"Thanks, Erica," he said, already halfway out the door. He needed to talk to Clarke before DS Prosser did.

Chapter 20

Friday, Week Two

Clarke came downstairs to meet Paul in reception.

"Is it true?" she asked before she even got close. "Is Bradley really dead?"

That confirmed to Paul what he already believed. Clarke couldn't have murdered Bradley Acres. Either that or her acting skills surpassed those of any Oscar winner. He shook that theory from his head. No, she was not a murderer. Not possible. Not his Clarke.

He followed her out to the car park. "Where did you go last night?" he asked.

He caught a split second of hesitation before she answered.

"Nowhere. I stayed home."

"All evening?"

"Yes," she said.

Paul saw her shivering and noticed she didn't have her coat on. Was she worried? Or upset? Or just cold?

"Alone?"

"Yes." Clarke shivered again. "Why are you asking? I didn't kill Bradley. You surely can't imagine I would do that?"

Paul didn't reply.

"You do think that, don't you?"

"No," he said. "Of course not. We have to rule you out." Paul shrank back against the wall of the building, trying to get some shelter from the wind. Why did he feel so defensive? It was Clarke who needed to justify herself, not him. She'd lied to him.

"How well do you know Bradley Acres?" he asked.

Clarke turned towards the door. "Can we go inside, please? It's freezing out here."

Paul grabbed at her arm. "Well?" He looked her in the eye and repeated the question. "How close are you to Bradley Acres?"

Clarke tried to pull her arm free, but Paul held her tight. "I barely know him," she said. "We work in the same office. That's all. I don't have much to do with him."

Paul pulled her back towards him. He wanted to see her reaction. "So why did you go to meet him last night?"

"Oh, shit."

Paul waited for her to say more, but she didn't. "I need to take you down to the station," he said. "You need to make a statement."

Chapter 21

The police interview room was stark and functional. It was nearly an hour already since Paul had dumped Clarke in here. She was getting a numb bum from the hard plastic chair. The disgusting machine cup of coffee Paul bought made her want to vomit. And the glare of fluorescent lighting on the white walls gave her a headache. She wanted to go home.

DS Prosser entered the room and sat down opposite her. "Just tell me, Clarke, why did you want to meet Bradley Acres?"

"I don't know." Clarke repeated the statement for the umpteenth time, struggling to keep the note of exasperation from her voice. She simply didn't have a clue why Bradley asked to meet her, so how could she answer his question? She could only guess the reason. And yes, she should have told Paul earlier about waiting in vain in the pub for Bradley last night. She wasn't sure why she'd lied. A spur-of-the-moment decision. The wrong one, as it turned out, although she doubted it would have made any difference. DS Prosser seemed to think she was guilty.

She repeated the whole thing again. "Bradley sent me a text saying he wanted to meet to talk about a suspicious invoice I'd found a few days ago. He's head of internal audit. It seemed perfectly reasonable."

"Outside the office? Outside of working hours?" Prosser didn't hide his disbelief. "Is that normal?"

"I don't know what's normal," Clarke said. "I've never discovered a fraud before. I supposed he suspected someone in the office." She didn't add that she had suspected Bradley, largely because of his signature on the invoice. In hindsight, it had been stupid of her to agree to meet him.

"The thing is," Prosser said, "we can't find his phone." He looked Clarke right in the eyes, his face coming close to hers. "What have you done with it?"

Clarke gave an exasperated sigh. She wasn't getting through to him. "I don't have his phone," she said. "I've never had his phone. He didn't show up, so how could I have taken it?" She glanced at Paul, who sat silently. Why didn't he do something? Why didn't he defend her? Surely, he didn't agree with his DS's opinion.

A knock on the door interrupted them and a young officer asked to have a word with Prosser.

"Interview suspended at eleven forty-five," Prosser said. He signalled to Paul, and they both left the room, leaving the younger officer with Clarke.

Clarke longed to stop wasting her time with these pointless questions and go home. DS Prosser said she was here voluntarily, insisting she could leave at any time, but actually putting that to the test scared her, in case it prompted DS Prosser to arrest her. Prosser seemed convinced she'd hurt Bradley, and nothing she said made him change his mind. Clarke wondered if she should ask for a solicitor or if that would make her appear guilty.

During the break in the interview, Clarke replayed everything in her head that Prosser and Paul had said. The CCTV footage proved she'd been in The Ball and Chain. They knew she'd got a text from Bradley asking to meet him there. They also knew what time she'd left the pub, but, unfortunately for her, she couldn't prove where she'd gone after that. The drive from the pub to Bradley's house took five minutes apparently, but Clarke didn't have Bradley's address. How could you prove that you *didn't* know something? Bradley must have been murdered outside his house when Clarke had been driving home. It might seem suspicious to them, but wouldn't they need more evidence than that to arrest her? She hadn't done anything wrong. Why didn't they believe her?

Tammy's disappearance, the fraudulent invoices, and Bradley's murder must be connected. Clarke hoped she might get a chance to talk to Paul on his own. Probably not. With a heavy heart, Clarke realised the only person she could rely on now was herself. She needed to find out what had happened to Tammy. If she solved that, maybe she would also discover who really killed Bradley Acres. But she couldn't do any of that while she was stuck in here. She needed to go home.

Chapter 22

Friday, Week Two

"She didn't do it, Gov." Clarke wasn't a killer. Paul regretted not admitting his previous relationship with Clarke to DS Prosser. If he confessed to it now, would it get him thrown off the case?

"Granted. There's no firm evidence yet," Prosser said, "but she went to meet him and won't tell us why. CCTV places her in the vicinity. She could have done it."

"You've seen the text on her phone. It doesn't say why Acres wanted to meet her," Paul said. "She's got no motive."

Prosser turned to face him. "Then find one. Interview their colleagues and friends. See if you can find any signs of a relationship. Maybe the love affair went wrong. People do act out of character sometimes if they're under enough stress."

"Yes, Gov." Paul would find some evidence somehow. Evidence that Clarke couldn't possibly have murdered Bradley Acres.

"Check CCTV in the area too," Prosser said. "It might show her driving towards Acres' house."

Or away from it, Paul hoped.

"Anyway, Douglas Doncaster's here and his solicitor's arrived. We'll leave Pettis to stew while we interview Doncaster." Prosser reached for the door handle of the interview room where they'd put Doncaster. "If Acres and Doncaster's wife were having an affair, that gives Doncaster a motive, but we haven't managed to place him in the area. As soon as the interview's finished, you need to find out which one of these women was carrying on with Acres. Could even have been both of them. Perhaps Pettis killed Tammy Doncaster in a fit of jealousy when she found out."

"Clarke's not our killer," Paul said. He would need to find some proof fast.

"Keep an open mind, Paul. Consider every possibility. We've got one, possibly two murders. Everyone's a suspect."

They let themselves into the first-floor interview room and sat down opposite Doncaster and his solicitor.

"Mr Doncaster is here voluntarily," his solicitor said.

"We're grateful for your cooperation," said Prosser. Paul was sure he didn't mean that at all.

"Mr Doncaster." Paul smiled at him. He wanted to put him at ease, so he would talk more freely. "Can you tell us your whereabouts for yesterday evening, please?"

Doncaster looked at his solicitor. She gave a tiny nod.

"I stayed in the office until late. Then I went home."

That repeated what Doncaster had told him earlier this morning. At least he was consistent. Paul would have to find his car on CCTV to prove his movements. "What time did you leave the office?"

"Around seven thirty p.m."

Paul did the calculation in his head. He could have got to Acres' house around 8:00 p.m. "And what time did you arrive home?"

"Eight-ish."

"Did anyone see you get home?" Paul would check with the neighbours. Someone may have witnessed it. They were a nosy lot in these posh areas, especially the areas with neighbourhood watch.

"How the hell should I know?"

Prosser butted in. "How friendly were you with Bradley Acres?"

Doncaster shifted in his chair. "He was a colleague."

"Did you ever go to his house?" Prosser asked.

"No." Doncaster seemed annoyed by the questions.

"Were you aware that Acres was having an affair with your wife?" Prosser asked.

Douglas Doncaster appeared genuinely surprised. "No."

Paul wondered why Prosser mentioned it. The affair was just a theory at this stage.

Doncaster's solicitor interrupted DS Prosser's next question before he even opened his mouth to speak. "My client is clearly unaware of any relationship between his wife and Acres, so this line of questioning is irrelevant. If you have no further questions, my client would like to leave. May I remind you he is here voluntarily?"

Prosser suppressed a scowl. "No more questions. But we may have to interview you again if there are further developments."

Paul showed Doncaster and his solicitor out. He badly wanted to punch something to dispel the frustration. Twice this week they had questioned Douglas Doncaster. They'd failed to find out any useful information, and now Doncaster flatly denied having anything to do with Bradley Acres outside of work. On top of all that, his solicitor made them look like idiots. If only Clarke could get a slick solicitor like that.

Some of the forensic results should be back by now, which might tie Doncaster to Acres. They had no concrete evidence to justify arresting him. Officially, he came into the station voluntarily, simply to help them with their enquiries. It looked like he wasn't going to help anymore.

"What a waste of time," Prosser said when Paul got back. "Get onto the CSIs. See if they've come up with anything. If they haven't, you can let Pettis go, but tell her we may need to speak to her again."

"On my way." Paul suppressed a smile until he slipped out of Prosser's sight and strode off purposefully towards the crime scene investigators' office. Anything to get away from Prosser, whose mood always plummeted downhill when he didn't get the outcome he wanted. Prosser liked to get results, and they weren't getting anywhere with this case. But at least he'd seen sense and decided to release Clarke, although, officially, like Doncaster, Clarke was simply helping the police with their enquiries.

"I've got some of the forensics back from the lab," Erica said. "The post-mortem's finished. It's most definitely the blow to the back of the head that killed him."

"Any signs of Doncaster visiting the house?" Paul asked. It might prove nothing about the murder, but it would help to rule him out if they found no prints.

"Her DNA is all over," Erica said.

"Her?" Paul was so fixated on Douglas Doncaster, he wondered if he'd heard wrong.

"Tammy Doncaster. Yes. It looks like she lived with Acres, at least part-time. There's some women's clothing still in the back of the wardrobe. We've matched prints to fingerprints we took from items on her work desk. Her prints are in every room in the house. If she didn't live with Acres, she certainly visited regularly."

Paul listened as he tried to process what Erica said. Was Bradley Acres Tammy's mystery man? It looked like Prosser's guess may be right.

Erica carried on. "There's no sign of her living there now," she said. "No toothbrush, cosmetics, underwear, shoes. There's a lot of stuff missing that she would need. I gather she's quite high-maintenance. So, hairdryer, straighteners, curlers, gels, shampoos, conditioners, make-up—I'd expect her to have enough stuff to open her own beauty salon. There's nothing. Either she's left for good or someone's cleared things out after her."

Paul realised he would need to rethink this case. Did Tammy kill Bradley and do a runner? Or did Bradley kill Tammy and clear her stuff out but miss a few things? Or maybe neither. It was usually the husband. He still didn't believe it was Clarke.

"What about Douglas Doncaster?" he asked. "Any of his prints?"

They would have trouble matching anything as Douglas Doncaster had refused to give his fingerprints. If they found enough evidence to arrest him, he would be forced to let them fingerprint him.

"Nothing yet," Erica said. "We identified Tammy Doncaster's prints and Bradley Acres himself. There are two other sets of prints. Neither of them is on the system. One is in every room. We're wondering if it's a cleaner. You need to trace her, if there is one, so you can rule her out, or not. The other prints are only in the living room and the bathroom. It might be Douglas Doncaster. Or maybe a friend or family member. Good luck with finding them."

Paul gave a half-hearted laugh. "Long shot," he said. Unless Doncaster volunteered to be fingerprinted. He wondered if he dared ask Clarke for her prints. It would help to rule her out, although, as Acres' body was found in the garden, it wouldn't completely put her out of the picture. He decided to leave it a while. If it became necessary to take Clarke's prints, he would ask DC Farrier to do it.

"Murder weapon?" Paul asked.

"Nothing obvious at the scene. I'm going back in the morning to recheck. Now I know what I'm looking for."

"Ok." Paul knew Erica would phone him first if she found anything.

Chapter 23

Friday, Week Two

Paul dropped Clarke back at the office. She didn't want to go back to work, not after the worst morning ever, not after they'd seen her go off with the police. Besides, she needed to prove that she didn't murder Bradley Acres and also find Tammy, not that she'd worked out yet how to achieve either of these things.

It was still lunchtime. She should make a start now before she lost the daylight. She sent a quick text to Andrew, saying she wouldn't be back today, and drove straight home. Half an hour later, she boarded a bus headed for Tredington.

As Clarke neared her destination, she noticed a thick shroud of fog starting to cover everything. So much for searching in daylight. Visibility would be dreadful. Clarke decided to crack on. The bus would reach Tredington in a few minutes. It was too late to alter her plans now.

This morning had been awful. She still reeled with shock that Paul even considered her a murderer, and even more shocked that he would inflict all that stress and humiliation on her. She understood now why Jeffrey was so upset with her. The whole experience annihilated her self-confidence. Had they treated him the same as they'd treated her? Did they make him feel so guilty that he almost doubted himself, almost would have said anything just to make them stop their incessant questioning? Did her colleagues think she'd done it? Mud sticks. Would they always suspect her every time something happened?

As soon as she got off the bus, she walked directly to Park Road, the place where Jeffrey said he'd seen Tammy. She'd already checked it out on Google Earth yesterday evening. Upmarket at one end, then at the other end stood a cheap looking block of flats. Clarke decided the posh end of the street was more Tammy. Either she rented a house in that road, or she'd been visiting a friend? Well, Clarke would knock on every single door if necessary. Somebody, somewhere must recognise her. She began working her way down the street.

After an hour, she'd knocked on every door on one side of the road and reached the block of flats at the end. When she got up close, the state of the flats shocked her. The fog completely hid the upper stories, but the whole block screamed of neglect and abandonment. The windows on the ground floor were meant to be totally boarded up, but some of the boards were missing, the bare windows exposed like gaping wounds in the building. The remaining boards were weather-beaten and covered in graffiti. The rude kind. These graffiti writers weren't 'artists,' not even able to spell some of the offensive words they had sprayed. A high chain-link fence surrounded the block, probably erected after the graffiti appeared, as it seemed much newer than everything else. The flats gave the impression that no one had lived there for many years. Clarke wondered how old the images on Google Earth would be.

At least she wouldn't have to waste hours visiting all the flats. Returning to the job at hand, if she pushed on, she would finish the second half of the street before dark. The good thing was that Tammy always got noticed. Tammy only needed to walk into a room and everyone turned around to stare at her. If she'd ever been here, somebody would have surely seen her.

By 3:30 p.m., Clarke had knocked on every door in the street without a single positive reaction to Tammy's photo. Jeffrey must have been wrong and mistaken somebody else in the distance for Tammy. If he really was obsessed with Tammy, he probably imagined her everywhere. Clarke tried to remember her sighting of Tammy outside the restaurant in Brackford. Had she dreamt up Tammy because of worrying constantly about her? It was an easy thing to do.

Clarke remembered she'd missed lunch, so she headed for a nearby café.

What a relief to sit down and take the weight off her bad ankle. She took a couple of paracetamol and a half empty bottle of water out of her handbag and swallowed the pills down.

She sat next to the window. The derelict flats on the corner loomed up like an eerie grey monster through the fog. Earlier this afternoon, she'd been able to see at least the bottom half of the block clearly. Now the fog wrapped itself round the whole block like a blanket. She would have to get back outside soon before she completely lost visibility with the worsening fog and imminent darkness.

"Penny for them?" The waitress put her toasted mushroom panini on the table in front of her.

"I'd want a lot more than that," Clarke said. She would eat up quickly and resume searching. The paracetamol was already kicking in, making her feel more human. She was ready to return to the houses where she'd got no answer earlier.

After the warmth of the café, the cold hit Clarke like a wall of ice when she stepped outside again. The damp fog added to the chill. She went straight back to Park Road. As she walked, she looked towards the empty block of flats. The five, or was it six, storey building was just a hulking grey mass from this distance. Clarke could make out only a vague outline of parts of the perimeter fence. Thick fog enveloped everything else.

Clarke needed to revisit ten houses. As soon as she'd done that, she would go home before the weather worsened. The roads would be lethal, but at least she might be safer on the bus than driving her little white VW Polo.

Suddenly, Clarke sensed movement behind her. Before she got the chance to turn, an arm grabbed her from the rear. With a sharp jerk, they pulled her close to their body, catching her off balance. She tried to scream, but a hand slammed into her face, forcing a piece of damp cloth over her mouth and nose. Clarke clawed at the hand, trying to pull it away, but the hand held tight. She struggled to breathe. Why didn't they just grab her handbag and leave her? Her head started to spin and, for a moment, she wondered if the cloth over her face had something on it. Again, she tried to pull the attacker's hand away from her face, but all her strength had dissipated, and the hand remained stuck fast. Then everything went black.

Chapter 24

DC Paul Waterford had worked late again last night. So today, exhaustion set in well before lunchtime. He yawned, just as DS Prosser walked towards him.

"Any developments on the case?" Prosser asked.

At least Prosser didn't bawl him out for yawning on the job. Most times he would have done. DS Prosser didn't miss a thing. Perhaps he'd actually noticed that Paul had been working his arse off on this case.

"Not on the murder," Paul said. This case was doing his head in. So many contradictions, so many loose ends. As soon as he seemed to be on to something, it turned out to be something else entirely. "SOCO's gone back to the crime scene looking for possible murder weapons. Blunt instrument, Erica said." He folded his arms defensively. It so often was a blunt instrument. And in his experience, that could be almost anything. The scene of crime officer would have her work cut out to find the right one. If it was still covered with blood, easy, but then they would have already found it. Or the murderer might have taken it with him. "I'm going to go back to the house myself. See if I've missed anything. There must be something."

Prosser looked displeased. Paul knew the DI was pressuring Prosser for results on this one before he left for his holiday.

"What about the fraud?" Prosser said.

Paul hadn't expected to hear from the fraud squad. Communication from them was way above his pay grade. But someone from the fraud squad had phoned him early this morning wanting sample signatures—Douglas Doncaster and Bradley Acres. Paul copied Doncaster's signature from his witness statement—not that he'd said anything much so 'statement' was a misnomer. He found Bradley Acres' signature on stuff that SOCO took from his house. The officer from the fraud squad had phoned him back an hour ago.

"Both signatures are forgeries," Paul said to DS Prosser. "Doncaster and Acres. They're good forgeries, but they're definitely forgeries. Handwriting expert confirmed it."

"So whoever committed the fraud might have killed Acres," Prosser said, "maybe trying to cover his tracks if he'd used Acres' signature. It's a motive."

"Yes, I agree," Paul said. "Do you think Doncaster's in danger, Sarge? Douglas Doncaster, I mean. His signature was used too. Should we give him some protection or at least warn him?"

DS Prosser leaned over Paul's desk. "That's possible," he said. "And Tammy Doncaster too, although I doubt she's still alive." He sighed. "But I don't suppose Douglas Doncaster would accept any help from us."

"Should I warn him?"

Prosser considered the question for a moment. "No," he said. "He's still potentially a suspect. He could have done Acres in if he realised Acres was shagging his wife. Could have topped his wife too. Let's monitor Doncaster."

Paul nodded. Maybe they could put a watch on his house this evening. See if he went anywhere.

Paul drove back to Acres' house for the third time that day. SOCO continued to search through Acres' things. He seemed to be a bit of a hoarder.

"Find anything?"

Erica scowled at him. "Didn't I say I'd call you if I did?"

"Sorry." Paul needed to keep Erica onside. Perhaps he should be more apologetic.

Erica smiled at him. "There's nothing concrete," she said. "At least, there is something concrete." She smiled again. "There's this." She held up a garden ornament. "It's possible that Acres was killed by a rabbit."

Paul spluttered, trying not to laugh. Erica looked serious.

"Concrete rabbit. The foot's broken off," she said. "The break looks recent, so it could have been busted when the rabbit got used to hit Acres over the head. No sign of the rabbit's foot. Maybe the murderer took it for luck."

Paul looked at the garden ornament. It stood about a foot high and would have been easy enough to grip around the middle and bash Acres with it. "Are you sure it's the murder weapon?"

"I can't confirm that yet. I need to take it back to the lab and try to match the marks on Acres' head. And we'll shine some light filters on Mr Bunny to test if it shows up any traces of blood."

"Where did you find it?" Paul said.

Erica transferred the concrete rabbit into a plastic bag and labelled it. "I found it in the front garden, under a bush," she said, "lying on its side, like it was dumped in a hurry."

"Suspicious," Paul said.

"Could have been there for years, except for that fresh break. See here." She pointed to where the foot was missing. "The rest of the rabbit is consistently weathered, like it's been in the garden for a long time. But this break is recent. It's too clean."

If the rabbit was in the garden, whoever murdered Acres probably picked it up in the heat of the moment. That meant it most likely wasn't a premeditated murder. Not self-defence as he was hit from behind, but possibly manslaughter rather than murder. A good lawyer would get the charges reduced. Doncaster's lawyer would run rings around them.

Paul started upstairs. He intended to turn the house inside out in case he'd missed anything, although SOCO would have already done the same thing. He would start in the main bedroom and work his way down. And when he finished that, he would check every bit of CCTV in the area, even if it took him all night.

Chapter 25

Clarke rolled over. Her head ached, and she felt really muzzy. For a second, she opened her eyes, then instantly shut them again. "Where am I?" She seemed to be in bed, but with no bedding, and a particularly offensive smell assaulted her nostrils. Clarke took a breath in. It smelt like the subway in Brackford on a Saturday night. Urine. She would recognise that vile stench anywhere. "Where am I?" she said again.

"Clarke," a soft voice called her, and she imagined she must be dreaming. She tried to open her eyes, but she still felt much too woozy.

"Clarke." The voice sounded comfortingly familiar. In a minute, she would be able to get up and see who the voice belonged to. She tried to raise her head. A stabbing pain shot through her temple. Gratefully, she let her head fall back onto the bed. She would lie here a little longer.

She decided to count up to fifty, then she would get up. *One, two, three... four, five, six... seven...* What came after seven? Her brain was all over the place. She didn't remember anything anymore. Someone was talking to her, but she barely registered what they said.

After a while, Clarke opened her eyes. She rolled over again and propped herself up on her elbow. Finally, she started to feel more normal.

The soothing voice stopped, and she saw someone walking around her, coming into view, at first just a rough shape, then Clarke managed to focus at last.

"Tammy?" Clarke sensed the presence of her friend and wondered if her imagination was playing tricks on her again. "Tammy?"

"Hi, Clarke."

Clarke smiled. "It is you," she said. She started to get up, wanting to hug her, but immediately fell back again, dizzy from the movement. It was definitely Tammy, but not a Tammy she recognised. Tammy's hair was greasy and tangled and she smelt like she needed a bath. "I thought... we all thought... you were dead."

Tammy shuddered. "Wish I were."

Tammy spoke so quietly that Clarke scarcely heard the words. She tried to sit up. Now that she could focus better, her gaze drifted from Tammy to their surroundings. She sat back with a shock. "What happened?" she said. "Where are we?" They were in an almost bare room, in such a state of disrepair that no one could possibly live here. She'd been lying on a mattress on the floor. Inspecting the mattress more closely, she realised it was filthy and covered in mould. Clarke didn't dare think how long it had been there or what it might be stained with.

From her position on the mattress, Clarke examined her surroundings. Tattered wallpaper peeled off the walls. Some of the floorboards were visible, with moth-eaten remnants of carpet covering the rest. A strip of light filtered up between a gap in the floorboards near her. A huge, damp patch streaked the wall opposite. The whole room smelt musty and mouldy and, Clarke realised now, the rank odour wasn't Tammy, it was this room, this house.

"I don't know," Tammy said eventually. She looked small and frightened. Where was the outgoing, larger-than-life, noisy Tammy, whose personality lit up a room? Where had that woman gone?

"I don't know," Tammy said again. "But it's really high up."

"How did you get here?" Clarke asked. "Have you been here all this time?" She wanted answers to so many questions. "Tell me everything, right from the beginning." Hopefully, by the time Tammy finished, Clarke figured, the fuzz in her head would have cleared and they could both go home.

Tammy sat down next to her. "I'm not sure what happened," she said. "I woke up in this room with no idea how I got here."

That was exactly how it had been for her, Clarke recalled. She didn't know how she'd got here. She didn't remember anything from immediately before waking up.

"Start at the beginning. At work. Do you remember the simulated terrorist exercise, Brack Attack? We were hiding in the cleaning cupboard. You left first. You were going to come back for me if the coast was clear."

"Yes, I remember that," Tammy said. "They must have caught me, the fake terrorists."

"They didn't." The police had checked. The mock terrorists had taken names of every one of their 'captives.' Tammy's name didn't appear on the list. Clarke had asked Paul to double-check. It meant Tammy must have got out when she left the cupboard. "You were going to a dentist appointment," Clarke said. "Do you remember that? Did you get there?"

Tammy shook her head. "I don't know. I don't think so."

The police had checked every dentist for miles around and come up with nothing. Clarke hoped going over it might jog Tammy's memory.

"What time did you wake up here?" She had last seen Tammy around 10:30 a.m. on that Wednesday. It may be useful to find out how long it took her to get here.

Tammy shook her head. "I don't remember anything."

Clarke's head felt less fuzzy now, and she managed to stand with no dizziness. Tentatively, she walked over to the door. Locked. She rattled at the door handle and leaned her weight against the door in case it was just stiff. It didn't budge.

"There's no way out," Tammy said.

Clarke ignored her. She needed to see for herself. It was possible she would find a way out that Tammy hadn't considered. Next, she investigated the window. It looked like it would open and was big enough to climb out. She looked out, then peered down, trying to count how

many floors were beneath them. It was impossible to tell from this angle, but Tammy's statement about it being high up looked right.

Clarke started to recall things now. Recent things. She'd been looking for Tammy. She'd knocked at doors to ask if anyone recognised
Tammy. There was a block of flats at the end of the street that seemed
ripe for demolition. Were they inside one of those dilapidated flats?
Judging by the dreadful state of the room, that would make sense. The
fog and the fading light outside made it difficult to confirm where they
were, but whoever had attacked her must have carried her or dragged
her here. They couldn't have carried her far without someone noticing.
She tried again to see what was below the window. There was a fire escape ladder attached to the wall. It looked precarious, but it might be
usable. Or it might not. As far as she remembered, the outside of the
building was as badly decayed as the inside appeared to be. The fire escape ladder might well come away from the wall if they put any weight
on it and it wouldn't be easy, anyway. She would find it difficult with
her ankle and no way was Tammy brave enough to even attempt it. She
discounted it. It was far too risky, maybe not even possible.

Clarke checked every inch of the room, tapping at the walls, testing
for any weak spots. She'd be damned if she would sit around and give
up, which was what seemed to be happening to Tammy.

The room was furnished sparsely, with a couple of blankets the
only concession to comfort. Clarke supposed if they were still here
overnight, she would have to share the mattress with Tammy. Yuk. She
didn't want to lie on that filthy mattress ever again. The blankets looked
newish. But whoever provided them obviously didn't expect an extra
person. They wouldn't be nearly warm enough at this time of year, not
shared between the two of them. Clarke shuddered. They needed to get
out of here.

The sofa had seen better days, with worn out upholstery, and dirtier
even than the mattress, a magnet for several years' worth of dust and

grime. How long had this place been empty? Everything in here seemed to be plastered in dirt and dust.

In another corner, a bucket with a thin piece of wood over the top emitted a vile smell. Clarke gingerly lifted the lid and saw that this was their toilet. It didn't have much in it. Did that mean that their captor emptied it regularly? Would that be a chance to take him by surprise? Clarke searched the room for something that might be usable as a weapon but found nothing.

The springs creaked as Clarke sank down on the sofa. The dirt disgusted her, but she needed to rest her ankle. She recapped the events of the day, remembering vividly some of the people who had answered their doors to her. Décor in the hallways and cars in the driveways sprang into her head. Then she'd eaten lunch, a late lunch. Before all that, in the morning, she'd been at the police station. It all flooded back to her now. The café where she'd bought lunch had been wonderfully warm. She remembered the pattern on the plate and the colour of the waitress's apron. But she failed to recall a single detail after that. How she had got here was a complete blank.

"Why do you think you're being kept in this horrible place?"

"I don't know." Tammy started to cry. "I just don't know. Somebody must hate me."

Clarke rushed over and put her arm around her. "It's going to be ok," she said. She wished she believed that herself. "Could this be connected to your husband? Is someone trying to get at Douglas?"

Tammy looked at her blankly. "Possibly," she said. "I hadn't considered that."

If Clarke had been stuck in this room for over a week, she would have thought of nothing else, except how to escape, of course. She chided herself. Tammy wasn't her. People react differently to things, she reminded herself.

"Could it be..." Clarke tailed off. She'd been going to ask if it might be connected to the fraud, but Tammy only knew about that first invoice. Best that she never became aware of the full extent of it. For that amount of money, their captor might kill them if he thought they knew too much. No point in scaring her and causing her to panic.

Clarke changed the subject. "How long have you been sleeping with Bradley?"

"Bradley?"

"Bradley Acres."

"What are you talking about? He's a colleague. We just work together sometimes."

Clarke laughed. "Your fingerprints are all over his house," she said. Paul had let that piece of information slip when he'd driven her back to the office this morning.

Tammy looked sheepish. "We weren't having an affair," she said finally. "Not at first anyway."

"Not at first?"

"He let me stay for a while when Doug kicked me out," Tammy said. "After I got back from my holiday, I was homeless. He offered to put me up for a while."

Clarke remembered Tammy's holiday, back in the summer. Two weeks staying with some friends who lived on the Dorset coast. She recalled being surprised as Tammy's usual holidays were of the exotic and expensive kind. This one seemed to be mostly sailing and walking, judging from the photos Tammy showed her afterwards. She'd gone without Douglas, which Clarke thought at the time was odd. Tammy must have gone straight to Dorset after leaving Douglas.

"That was good of Bradley," Clarke said, waiting for her to say more. Tammy must have moved out of Bradley's house at some point. Paul mentioned there was hardly any female stuff in the house.

Tammy turned to stare directly at Clarke. "Wait a minute," she said. "How do you know my fingerprints are in Brad's house?"

Clarke realised then that Tammy must be assuming that Bradley Acres was still alive and well. The murder only took place yesterday evening. How could she have forgotten? "I'm afraid I've got some bad news," Clarke said, dreading Tammy's reaction.

"What?" Tammy looked worried.

Clarke hesitated. How could she break this news gently? If an easy way existed, she wasn't aware of it. She got straight to the point. "Bradley's dead."

Tammy's lips quivered. "No," she said. "He can't be."

"I'm so sorry."

"What happened?" Tammy turned away from her and wiped at her eyes with the back of her hand.

"Murder," Clarke said. "Someone bashed him on the back of his head, outside his house."

"Murder?" Tammy's voice faded to a whisper. Clarke put her arm on Tammy's shoulder, but Tammy immediately shrugged it off.

"He can't be dead." Tammy stared blankly ahead of her, like she only existed in a parallel universe, not in this room. She didn't seem to be processing this news very well. Being in shock was understandable, but this was shock on a whole other level. "He can't be," she said again. Her whole body began to shake from side to side.

"Do you want to talk about him?" Clarke wondered if it might help Tammy to talk. It would help Clarke too, to puzzle her way out of this mess if she knew exactly what was going on. It was too much of a coincidence for everything not to be linked. "When did you get together?"

"Not that long ago," Tammy said quietly. "I don't remember. After I moved in."

Clarke thought that was strange. Most women can remember exactly when they got together with their partners. Most of them recalled the exact date, day, time, and place. Most of them expected to celebrate the anniversary. It must be the shock. Or perhaps Tammy only ever wanted a bit of fun to get back at Douglas. Maybe it had never been love.

"Where did you go after?" Clarke asked. "After you moved out of Bradley's place?"

Tammy got up and walked over to the window. "I got a shitty little flat," she said, "near here."

So Jeffrey *had* seen Tammy near here. That would have been quite a few weeks ago. Perhaps she'd been looking for somewhere back then. She might not have stayed with Bradley for long.

"Brad didn't want me to stay." Tammy began to cry quietly. "He didn't even want to tell anyone about us. He cooled off really quickly. I got the impression he was frightened of Doug, of what Doug might do to his career if he found out."

Clarke sympathised with her. It was a miracle Tammy had stayed so positive when she'd been in the office, with her whole life disintegrating. But now that she'd been trapped in this awful room for well over a week, Tammy was falling apart. Clarke wished she'd kept quiet about Brad's murder. She needed Tammy to stay strong. It might have been better for her not to have known yet.

"Douglas told the police he kicked you out because you were having an affair," Clarke said. Tammy's story didn't tie up with her husband's at all. Clarke wanted to know why.

Tammy laughed raucously. For a few moments, Clarke saw a glimpse of the old Tammy, the Tammy with attitude.

"That's a joke," she said bitterly. "I didn't even start seeing Brad until after I'd left Doug."

"Why would he lie?"

Tammy laughed again. "Do you really want to know?" she said. "Do you really want the real reason my husband kicked me out?"

Clarke looked at her but said nothing.

"My husband kicked me out because he cares more about his precious career than he does about me." Tammy got up and walked across the room to the window. "He kicked me out because I wasn't the perfect little corporate wife."

"But surely that doesn't matter. It's what Douglas does that counts and he's doing a great job, isn't he?"

"Oh, it matters," Tammy said. "It matters very much. The trouble is"—she turned around to face Clarke—"the trouble is, I'm too loud, too opinionated, and too black."

Tammy started to pace up and down. Clarke wasn't sure what to say.

"He wants the CEO job," Tammy said. "He's been promised it next year, when Alan retires. But some of the board members made it quite clear they didn't want a CEO with a black wife."

Clarke was horrified. "But surely that's illegal," she said. "The company's got an equalities policy. They can't do that."

"They can do what they like."

"But the company can't be racist," Clarke said. "They've got hundreds of black and Asian employees."

"Sure they have," Tammy said. "Hundreds of cleaners and factory workers. No top management and not much middle management either. That promotion I got. I should have got that three years ago. I'm sure I only got the job this time because no one else vaguely competent applied."

"That's shocking," Clarke said. "I never realised."

"And I never realised my husband lacked principles."

"But surely Douglas can't be racist?" He had married Tammy after all, Clarke reasoned.

"No," Tammy admitted. "But he thought he could beat the system. He thought he was so damned amazing that he'd get the top job anyway. Then he finally realised he wasn't, so he's sold out."

"I'm sorry." Both the men in Tammy's life cared more about their careers than they did about her. No wonder Tammy was upset.

Clarke's thoughts turned back to how to escape. She wondered who might notice she was missing. She realised with a shock that no one would know. She lived alone and had made no plans for this weekend, so she wouldn't be missed this evening. She wondered about her mum and Rob, but they wouldn't worry if she didn't answer her phone for one day. They might not even call her for a few days. Clarke was absolutely certain that no one would raise the alarm tonight. If she got out of here. No, *when* she got out of here, she needed to get a life.

Would Ken and Andrew worry if she didn't show up on Monday morning? She would have to rely on them to do something. Clarke remembered how unconcerned they were about Tammy disappearing and wondered if her reliance was misplaced.

"I wanted to call the police," she said to Tammy, "as soon as you didn't come in to work that first morning. Andrew persuaded me I was being stupid and I should wait a day." It wouldn't help Tammy to learn that Douglas had also told her not to bother. Tammy still exuded bitterness about her husband turning against her and putting his career first. She didn't need Clarke to dig the knife into the wound still further.

"I keep thinking it might have made a difference," Clarke said. "If I'd called the police a day earlier, perhaps they would have found you."

"I doubt it." Tammy lay back on the filthy mattress. "I've been here all this time and they haven't found this place, have they?"

"Yet," Clarke added. "Yet." It was important to try to keep Tammy positive. But she didn't feel completely confident herself. Tammy's words made sense. If the police hadn't found this place in over a week, would they ever discover it? Clarke walked over to the window again and stared out. If they weren't going to be found, she would have to find a way out herself. She just didn't know how yet.

Clarke had lost track of time hours ago. "My watch is broken," she said. "It must have got smashed when they brought me here."

Tammy rolled her sleeve back and looked at her watch. She wore the red sports watch that Clarke guessed she'd been wearing when their captor had taken her. Everything matching. That was Tammy. She'd bought the sports watch when she'd had a health scare and wanted to monitor her heart. Clarke wondered how much faster her heart beat now.

"Nearly four thirty," she said.

That figured, Clarke thought. Outside, darkness descended rapidly. It was still too foggy to see anything. In brilliant sunshine, this whole situation would be much less depressing. Clarke wished she had her phone, and she realised then that her handbag was missing too. She definitely hadn't found it anywhere in this room. Was it lying on the pavement outside? Would somebody find it? Or had her attacker got rid of it so no one would ever find them?

"How do you cope with this? With being stuck in here, I mean, not knowing what's going to happen?"

Tammy smiled. "I guess I've got used to it now. I just shut my eyes and go to my happy place."

"Where's that?"

Tammy shut her eyes. "Caribbean island," she said. "I can see blue sea, white sand, palm trees. The sun is shining, the waves are lapping in and out, and there's a calypso band playing."

"St Kitts," Clarke said.

"You remembered."

"It's where you're from, isn't it?"

Tammy opened her eyes again. "My dad is."

Clarke sighed. "I'm not sure where my happy place is. I used to think it was at the fire station, joking around with the lads. But that's not my life anymore."

"You need to find one," Tammy said. "It will help."

Clarke disagreed. Dreaming of tropical beaches wouldn't help them get out of this dump. They should spend their time trying to make a plan.

"Have you really got no idea why we're being held here or who is doing this?"

Tammy shook her head.

"When will he come back?" Clarke asked. "He must be coming, to bring food." *And to empty that disgusting toilet bucket.*

Tammy shrugged her shoulders. "He only comes in the middle of the night when I'm asleep. I wake up and there's food and water waiting for me."

"We should stay awake. Take it in turns to sleep." The mention of food made Clarke aware of her growing hunger pangs.

"What's the point?" Tammy said.

"We need to find out who it is." Clarke realised she was raising her voice. She took a deep breath and calmed down. "We need to know who we're dealing with so we can escape." *And so we can identify the bastard when we get out of here.*

"I don't think we will escape." Tammy's voice came out in a whisper.

Clarke looked at her friend. The Tammy she knew was a feisty, bolshy ball of fire. Had ten days in captivity broken Tammy? Would it break her too?

"There are two of us now," Clarke said. She lay back on the disgusting mattress next to Tammy. She needed to stay awake tonight, so she'd better get some rest now. Besides, she needed to think.

Chapter 26

Paul got a beer out of the fridge as soon as he got home. He was getting nowhere with this case. The fraud squad hadn't yet traced any of the money. Tammy Doncaster remained missing, probably dead. And they'd reached an impasse with suspects in Acres' murder case.

He now subscribed totally to Clarke's theory. The fraud, Tammy's disappearance, Acres' murder, must be linked in some way. If Tammy had been killed or abducted or had run and gone into hiding because she uncovered something about the fraud and been threatened, then Clarke might also be in tremendous danger. Paul should have told her about the forged signatures, but what good would it do? They didn't even have any suspects, not with evidence to convict them anyway. It wasn't as if Clarke would even listen if he warned her to be careful. He didn't know how to keep her safe.

He wondered if Clarke would ever speak to him again after his behaviour in the interview room. He never believed she was guilty. But he'd had to follow orders and act on the evidence. Perhaps he should phone her or go round with some flowers. He seemed to spend all his time now apologising to Clarke. She deserved better.

Why did Acres end up murdered? As head of audit at Briar Holman, he could have discovered the fraud and confronted the person responsible. But who was behind it? The two signatures on all the invoices, Acres and Douglas Doncaster, were forgeries, so that probably ruled them both out. That narrowed it down to just about every manager in Briar Holman and all the support service staff—accountants, HR, procurement, IT, even the chief executive. That totalled well over a hundred suspects. How would they ever get through that many?

Paul gulped down the rest of his beer. He grabbed another can from the fridge. He wouldn't be able to drive now, but that wasn't such a bad thing. Let's face it, he would be the last person Clarke would want to see this evening. He should stay away from her completely. Besides, with her being mixed up in the case and still being a suspect, it would totally kill off his career in CID if he got too involved with her now. He needed to remain professional.

Chapter 27

Clarke opened her eyes to bright sunlight streaming through the window. It took her a moment to remember her whereabouts. As soon as the awful mouldy smell of her surroundings wafted across her face, she remembered with a jolt. This place, Tammy, everything came flooding back in an instant. Clarke propped herself up on one elbow. She still felt a little woozy, as if she'd been whacked over the head yesterday. Automatically, she checked her watch. Useless. She'd forgotten it was broken.

Tammy still slumbered on the mattress next to her. She recalled now that they'd planned for one of them to always stay awake. They agreed that last night. Tammy would take the first shift. She had her watch, so she would wake Clarke at three in the morning. Which one of them fell asleep on the job? It must be Tammy. Clarke didn't remember being woken. Besides, she'd done loads of shift work when she'd been a firefighter. She'd never once nodded off in the middle of a shout during a night shift. Her body clock learned to reset itself to whatever was necessary. Then again, she might have lost the knack. Perhaps she had been the one to doze off. The bang on her head may have affected her more than she realised.

Clarke got up and moved to the window. With less to worry about, she might have admired the view. Now that the fog had cleared, the view stretched for miles. She recognised Canary Wharf and the Shard in the distance. Closer to the building, the window overlooked some deserted wasteland. They should try shouting if anyone ever came close enough to hear them. So far, Clarke had seen no one, not even a solitary dog-walker.

"We should keep a lookout from the window," she said. "If we spot anyone, we can shout for help." She rubbed her elbow across the window pane. A streak of grime planted itself on her coat sleeve, leaving a band of clear glass.

Clarke's parched throat grated like sandpaper. She didn't remember drinking much yesterday. Perhaps her extreme tiredness was down to dehydration. Maybe that's why she'd fallen asleep instead of keeping watch as they'd planned. She needed to drink... soon. Her skin itched with grime and sweat. She would love a hot bath too, but fat chance of that.

Behind her, Tammy gave a little grunt in her sleep, making Clarke jump. Best to leave her sleeping as long as possible to keep her strength up and give her less time to worry. Right now, she didn't have a care in the world. Perhaps she was dreaming of her happy place, on a beach in St Kitts.

Clarke scanned the room. Immediately a bag by the door caught her eye. The bag had appeared since last night. She picked it up and cautiously looked inside.

She'd briefly forgotten her hunger. The sight of a whole carrier bag full of food filled her with hope. Rifling through the bag, she found two packs of sandwiches, smoked salmon and cream cheese, and roast beef; some cooked spicy chicken wings, bananas, two enormous Belgian buns, a small loaf of sliced bread, a tub of houmous, and some cheddar cheese. A couple of large bottles of water completed the treasure trove.

Clarke opened a bottle and drank long and desperately until she had quenched her thirst. She stared at the half empty bottle, realising she should have conserved more of it for later. She remembered Tammy saying that someone always brought food during the night. This would have to last until tomorrow.

She sat on the sofa and wolfed down one of the Belgian buns. Even in her ravenous state, she promised herself she wouldn't touch anything else until Tammy woke up.

The bag of provisions seemed an odd choice of food, given their circumstances. Too nice, too expensive. The labels matched the small all-night supermarket she'd seen close by. If they got out of here, the shop's CCTV would be able to identify their captor. Six storeys up and locked in. Huh. Get out? Who was she kidding?

Tammy stirred on the mattress. Clarke waited until she sat up.

"We've got food," she said, holding up the grocery bag.

Tammy hauled herself up and put her shoes on. Clarke noticed then that Tammy wasn't wearing the same shoes she'd been wearing in the office during Brack Attack. Come to think of it, Tammy definitely hadn't been wearing those clothes either. She would never show up for work wearing tightly fitted jeans and trainers. Tammy wore a thick coat too, a dark blue one. She'd left her red coat in the office. She must have gone home first. That would explain why she ended up in Tredington, close to where she lived, instead of being near the office.

"You must have gone home on Wednesday," she said. "Do you remember?"

Tammy shook her head. "It's all a bit of a blur," she said. "Why do you think that?"

"Your clothes. You're not wearing work clothes." Clarke wrung her hands together. Her desperation to uncover something that would help them made her keep pushing Tammy for answers. "Try to remember, Tammy. It may be important."

Tammy shook her head. "I'm sorry. I can't remember anything," she said. She started to cry. "I don't know why I'm here and I'm sorry you've been dragged into it too."

The food parcel still bothered Clarke. "The food," she said. "It's nice food. If you're going to kidnap someone and keep them in a dump like this, why wouldn't you buy cheap rubbish? It doesn't make sense."

"I suppose," Tammy said.

Clarke carried on. "Smoked salmon sandwiches. That was one of your favourites."

"Lucky me," Tammy said sarcastically.

"I mean." Clarke sat on the floor, preferring it to the disgusting mattress. "I mean, do you think you've been kidnapped by someone you know?"

Tammy considered it for a moment. "I've been thinking about that," she said. "I wondered if it might be Doug."

Clarke shifted her weight on the hard floor. "Is it possible he would do that? Would he really do that if he thought you'd cheated on him?"

"Or if he wanted to save himself an expensive divorce," Tammy said.

"So he came up behind you and put his hand over your mouth," Clarke said, "the same way it happened with me. Could it have been Doug? Was he Doug's height? Doug's size? Did he smell like Doug?"

Tammy looked blank. "It all happened so fast."

Clarke nodded. That's how it went for her too. The attack was over in an instant. She didn't remember anything, except waking up in this hellhole.

"What's the time?" Clarke asked. "We should eat something."

"Nearly twelve thirty," Tammy said.

Lunchtime. Clarke grabbed the chicken and bread out of the carrier bag. "We should probably eat the chicken first." She forced a smile. Salmonella poisoning should probably be the least of her worries right now.

The houmous made a good substitute for butter to make chicken sandwiches. They were a bit rough and ready. A knife would have been useful—*in more ways than one.*

Clarke devoured her sandwich. Her fingers felt sticky with greasy chicken and hummus. Her hands were far too dirty to lick them clean.

She'd drunk most of her water. No way would she waste any of her precious remaining drink on washing her hands. She found a half-used tissue in her pocket and did the best job she could with that.

Now that she'd eaten, Clarke wanted to make a plan. She had no intention of sitting around, waiting for something bad to happen to them.

The wasteland below them remained depressingly empty. She would need to stay next to the window all day, in case anyone walked by. Eventually, she might see a dog-walker or some kids, who would hear them if they shouted for help. She tried the catch on the window. If she opened it, it would let in some fresh air instead of this stale stench. Clarke struggled with the handle for several minutes, but it remained well and truly jammed shut.

Tammy picked at her food slowly. Clarke longed to snatch it from her and devour it. Hopefully, she wouldn't waste it. "Can you help me open the window, please, when you've eaten?" Clarke asked.

Tammy finished chewing her tiny mouthful. "Don't bother. I've already tried. It won't budge."

"But if there are two of us..."

"What's the point?" Tammy said. "We're on the sixth floor. We're not going to jump."

Clarke searched round the room yet again, in case she'd missed something useful in all her other searches. There must be something she could use to bang against the handle and loosen it. She was angry enough right now to bang it pretty hard. Somehow, she needed to snap Tammy out of this attitude. Tammy may have given up, but Clarke certainly hadn't.

She scoured the room twice, exactly as she'd done yesterday. Again, she found nothing. She wondered about trying to break the glass with her shoe. But then tonight would be freezing cold and they might not survive that. Last night had been cold enough. Besides, if their captor came into the room while they slept, he would notice a broken window instantly and might move them somewhere worse. Clarke considered the possibilities in her head. The carrier bag of food was lodged against the wall inside the door when she woke up this morning. Had their kidnapper come in? He may have simply opened the door, dumped the food inside, then left. Now that there were two of them in here, it would be much riskier for him to come inside in case one or both of them woke up.

Perhaps either she or Tammy could stand by the door and bash him over the head with a shoe as soon as he reached in with the bag. He would have his hands full, so it would be the best time to tackle him. Clarke slumped back on the mattress. It would have to be her. She looked at Tammy, staring blankly ahead of her. Tammy wasn't in a fit state to do anything useful, let alone tackle a man without a proper weapon. Better not to tell Tammy of her plan, in case she worried. Clarke realised it would be all down to her. That meant she would have to stay awake all night. She lay down on the mattress. She'd been used to working night shifts a few years ago, so she'd learned to sleep anytime, anyplace. But back then, she'd been sleeping in a comfortable bed, with central heating and a room that didn't stink. It would be much more difficult to sleep here, unless she got really tired. She shut her eyes and tried to doze.

Chapter 28

Saturday, Week Two

Clarke opened her eyes. She realised where she was instantly when she saw the torn wallpaper and filthy carpet. Some weak winter sunshine tried to filter through the layer of grime covering the window. She sat up. Tammy sat slouched on the sofa across the room, staring into space.

"Are you ok?" Clarke asked.

Tammy got up and came over. "Just thinking."

"What about?"

"Just stuff."

Clarke wondered how long she had been asleep. "What's the time?"

Tammy looked at her watch. "Three p.m."

Clarke stood up, needing to stretch her legs. She'd slept for much longer than she'd planned, so now she ought to be able to stay awake all night. She was grateful for the nap, helping to while away a few hours of boredom. But now Clarke walked around the room like a caged tiger. How had Tammy coped with being locked in here for so long?

For a moment, Clarke imagined she heard the faint sound of her phone's ringtone. She strained to listen, but it disappeared. Her mind must have conjured it up because she longed for her phone to appear miraculously. If only she could phone for help. Being locked in was getting to her already. *Stop being so stupid*, she told herself.

"We should eat," Clarke said. It would start getting dark in not much more than an hour. Without lighting, the long hours of darkness would make even the most normal things difficult.

Tammy handed her a sandwich. Still hungry, Clarke ate it quickly. The roast beef tasted good, despite yesterday's bread starting to curl up at the edges. Clarke rummaged in the bag and pulled out a packet of

Jaffa Cakes. She swallowed them down, one after the other, until only half the packet remained. There was no point in saving them. Once it got dark, they wouldn't be able to see well enough to eat. Clarke's mouth felt fuzzy, and she longed to clean her teeth. She took a few gulps of water, swishing some round in her mouth before swallowing. There wasn't much water left. Would there be more in the morning when they woke up? She silently scolded herself. It didn't matter whether anyone brought them more food and water overnight. They wouldn't be here another night. Tonight, they would escape from here. She would make sure of it.

Tammy interrupted her thoughts. "Will anyone come looking for you?"

Later, Clarke wished she had weighed up the consequences before opening her big mouth, but the words tumbled out. "No," she said. "No one's going to come looking. Not yet." She'd thought about it since yesterday. No one would miss her until Monday. Maybe not even then.

"We're going to be in here forever." Tammy started to cry. "I really hoped someone might come to find you. Didn't you tell anyone where you were going?"

Clarke realised that, stupidly, she didn't. She tried to comfort Tammy, but Tammy shook her off. Instead, Clarke walked over to the window in case she'd missed anything outside that might help them.

The weather had improved dramatically since yesterday, but admiring the view wouldn't help their situation. She peered down. Concrete paving slabs covered the area around the flats. They must have looked smart at one time, but now they appeared dirty and discoloured. Some of the slabs were cracked, with weeds growing in the gaps between them. Many of the weeds were two or three feet tall and had gone to seed. No one seemed to have walked over this part of the garden for some time. Brambles encroached onto the paving from the communal garden. By next year, the whole area would be a wilderness of brambles and weeds.

Further along, the old panelled fencing had collapsed in several places and the whole block was now fenced in with high chain-link fencing, wrapping around the broken wood panels like a giant net. Clarke wondered if there were holes, big enough for a person to get through, anywhere in the chain-link fence. She and Tammy must have got in here somehow. So there would have to be a way out. At least, if they could reach the front of the building, someone might see them or hear them shouting. The difficult part would be getting down there, getting out of this room. Beyond the fence, a rough patch of wasteland looked as if it might attract dog-walkers, except that Clarke hadn't yet seen anyone and wasn't sure if she'd be able to shout loud enough to attract attention at that distance.

Clarke gazed at the ladder again, the one attached to the outside wall. The bottom of it disappeared from her sight. She would need to open the window and lean out to see it and the window remained stubbornly jammed shut. She wondered again about breaking the glass with her shoe. Perhaps if she saw someone outside, she would do that.

The best way out would be through the door. That meant overpowering their captor when he arrived with food in the night. The only way would be to take him by surprise. Clarke would have one chance, one chance only. She'd have to be sure to hit him hard enough and in the right place. What if she killed him? Would that make her a murderer? Surely the police would see this place and the state of it, the time they—or Tammy, at least—had been here, and realise how desperate they were. She tried to convince herself that everything would be ok. She couldn't afford to go at this half-heartedly. *It's him or us*, she told herself. Even so, she knew what she planned might be interpreted as premeditated murder if she killed him, which she wouldn't, she hoped. She needed to protect herself, and Tammy, protect their futures. Best not to tell Tammy her plans. It's not as if Tammy would be of any help, the state she was in.

"What time does food get delivered?" she asked Tammy.

Tammy sighed. "No idea. I'm always asleep."

"Surely, you've tried to stay awake to see who brings it?"

"I don't think he would come in unless he knew we were asleep," Tammy said. "Then what will we do, with no food or water?"

Clarke checked out the door to determine the best place to hide. If she stood a couple of paces back, flat against the wall, she wouldn't be seen through the keyhole, or even if he opened the door a crack. She stood against the door and crouched down. There would be a pretty good view of the mattress from the keyhole. She would stuff something under the blanket. In the dark, it would look like two people sleeping. Then he would open the door, not expecting any trouble.

She needed a weapon. The only thing that might do would be her shoe. Yesterday, she cursed herself for not wearing trainers, but now she applauded her choice of footwear. The low but solid heel on the shoes would serve her well. She would need to hit hard and on his head, where she might be able to knock him unconscious. Her height would be an advantage, helping her to get the right angle and whack the shoe down with enough force to stop him.

She sat on the sofa beside Tammy. The last faint traces of daylight were disappearing. "What's the time?" she asked.

"Nearly four thirty," Tammy said. "It's going to be a long night."

Clarke got up and walked over to the mattress. In the dim remains of the light, she tried to memorise the route from the mattress to the door, in case she needed to move quickly. Luckily, nothing blocked the path between mattress and door, aside from the sofa. Its light colour may just be visible if there was any moonlight. Clarke tried to remember what stage the moon had been in last night, but, once more, her memory failed her. A full moon would be perfect, but she doubted she would be that lucky. She lay down and pulled the blanket over her. She could do nothing now until their captor showed up. She needed to get some rest. It would be her second night in this awful place. Clarke decided that it would be her last. Somehow, she needed to get herself and Tammy out of here.

Chapter 29

Sunday, Week Two

Clarke had lost track of time. It still seemed like the middle of the night, but it was difficult to tell exactly when they were forced to spend so many hours in darkness. "Are you awake?" Clarke whispered.

"Yes." Tammy's voice came from across the room. Now that Clarke's eyes were becoming accustomed to the dark, she saw the faint outline of Tammy lying on the mattress.

"I've been thinking." Clarke rolled over. Her stomach rumbled, and she wished they hadn't run out of food.

"What?" Tammy sounded annoyed, like she'd been woken up and didn't really care what Clarke had to say.

Clarke ignored her. "Do you remember the invoice I showed you? The Firestop one, with the obsolete model of fire doors?" She wondered now if she should tell Tammy about the other fraudulent invoices.

"Yes, what about it?"

"You said you were already dealing with it. What did you mean? You mentioned a court case."

"Why are you worrying about work when we're probably going to die?"

"Who else knew about that invoice?" Clarke asked. Tammy definitely told her she intended to show it to someone. Had that someone been Bradley Acres? Was that why he had been killed and why they were imprisoned in this room?

"I don't remember," Tammy said. "The whole thing's a big blur. I probably didn't have time to show it to anyone before I ended up in here."

Clarke didn't want to push Tammy too much and risk upsetting her even more. Tammy had enough to deal with without adding to her stress. Clarke lay back and closed her eyes again. She got very annoyed if something like this bugged her. She wanted answers. She hated not knowing, not being able to fit all the pieces of a problem together. Whoever was holding them here, it must have to do with the fraud. Nothing else connected the two of them. If it was some personal grudge against Tammy, then why take both of them? Then there was the brick thrown through Clarke's window, the message on her windscreen, the car that had followed her. It couldn't just be a coincidence.

She'd already spent a long time considering who might be behind all the events of the last few days. She ruled out Bradley Acres. He'd been murdered before Clarke got locked in here and, whoever it was, had brought them food last night. Could it be Douglas Doncaster? Had he set up the fraud? But would it really be possible for him to leave no clue for Tammy to work out it was him? Maybe Tammy was too distressed to see it.

Had Jeffrey Todd done it? Clarke didn't think he would be capable. All he was guilty of was having a massive crush on Tammy. Jeffrey was a computer nerd. He did a lot of the robotics programming for Briar Holman. If he wanted to commit fraud, wouldn't he use his computer skills instead of messing around with manual invoices?

There must be someone else at Briar Holman with the knowledge and opportunity to pull off that fraud. But the list of possible suspects would be huge, starting with every single manager. Clarke didn't know any of the operational managers well. She'd never met any of the managers based in Briar Holman's three factories. But they would all be well practiced at completing a manual invoice form. Alternatively, any of the accountancy team possessed the required knowledge. Andrew or Ken? Ken was lazy. He'd certainly be attracted to making a huge amount of money for doing nothing. And what about Andrew? Clarke didn't recall the police interviewing either of them about the fraud. She wished she could talk this through with Paul. She would when she got out of here.

Getting out of here wouldn't be easy. She needed to be ready, so she could take their captor by surprise, enabling both her and Tammy to escape. For a moment, she wondered what she would do if Tammy was too slow to get out. Clarke would have to go without her and get help, or they may never get another chance, but it would be difficult to leave her. It wasn't in her nature. In the fire brigade, she'd been trained never to leave anyone behind.

Clarke questioned how someone holding down a day job was able to bring food here in the middle of the night every night for well over a week. It must be someone living close by. When she got out, she would ask Paul to get the addresses of everyone working at Briar Holman.

How much longer would she have to stay awake? "What time is it now?" Clarke pictured Tammy's sports watch with its bright red strap. Did it have luminous digits?

She barely saw Tammy moving her arm up and down in the dark. "It's no good," she said. "It's too dark to see my watch."

Suddenly, Clarke sat bolt upright. She was so stupid! Tammy always charged her watch in the office. Almost every day. No way would the battery have lasted eleven days without being charged. No way. And there was no electricity supply in here and no charger. It was so obvious. She scolded herself for not seeing it sooner.

Clarke's heart raced. She needed to stay calm and work out what to do. It simply wasn't possible for Tammy to have been locked in this room since last Wednesday. She couldn't have been staying here, not all this time. And she would be in a far worse state, both mentally and physically, if that were the case. So she must have a partner. Had her accomplice turned on her and locked her in here? Or had she been locked in willingly for a reason?

She should have considered the facts for longer, but instead, she just blurted it out. "Where have you been for the last eleven days?"

Tammy said nothing and Clarke struggled in the darkness to ascertain where she was. Had she moved?

"What do you mean?" Tammy said finally.

"You can't have been locked in here for eleven days," Clarke said. "Where were you before yesterday?"

"Here, of course. Why are you even asking that?"

Tammy had definitely moved now. Clarke spotted her shadow edging around the sofa. Suddenly, she realised how vulnerable she was and wished she'd kept her suspicions to herself. She stood up, ready to move quickly if necessary. Her height gave her an advantage over Tammy, but Tammy's weight would help her. Clarke wasn't sure who would win if she needed to defend herself. "I don't believe you," she said.

Tammy began to cry. "I don't know anymore," she said. "I was probably somewhere else first. They drugged me. I can't remember anything."

For a moment, Clarke wanted to comfort her but realised this was just another one of Tammy's lies. As for the tears, Tammy was an actress, a better one than she had let on. Clarke should let Tammy believe she didn't suspect anything more. She still needed to get out of here and, if Tammy was in league with whoever brought the food, Clarke didn't know how she was going to escape. Best to get Tammy onside.

Clarke's eyes began to acclimatise to the dark. It wasn't pitch-black in here. Any city gives off so much light pollution at night, from streetlamps, headlights, buildings. Even without buildings or roads on this side of the block of flats, a hint of light from outside still filtered through. Clarke wished she had cleaned the window, to take full advantage of it.

Clarke heard footsteps and noticed the shadowy outline of Tammy move closer. Instinctively, she stepped back. Her foot caught on the edge of something. Clarke let out a yelp as she fell backwards onto the mattress.

A moment later, Tammy launched herself on top of her. For a second, it winded Clarke, then she grabbed at Tammy's hair and yanked her head back. Tammy screamed and Clarke drove her fist into the side of Tammy's face. Finally, she bent her good leg up and pushed off of it until she managed to roll over and wriggle out from under Tammy's weight.

"Who are you working with?" she shouted at Tammy. "Who is it?"

Tammy grabbed at Clarke's sleeve and pulled her back down onto the mattress, then dragged one of her long nails down Clarke's cheek. Clarke jabbed her elbow hard into Tammy's ribs, forcing her to let go.

"Did you take the money?" Clarke asked. "I found dozens of fraudulent invoices."

Tammy hesitated, then said, "It's my retirement fund. I need it now that I don't have Doug anymore." She grabbed at Clarke's sleeve again, but Clarke was ready for her and twisted her arm free.

"This started long before you split from Doug." Would Tammy ever start telling the truth?

"You think you're so clever, don't you," Tammy hissed. She ducked as Clarke aimed a punch at her head. "I'll be in the Caribbean before they find you here. If they find you at all."

"You'll never get to St. Kitts. You're going to prison." Clarke stood up quickly and ran towards the sofa, staying behind it, out of Tammy's reach.

"You stupid bitch. I've got away with this for well over a year before you even noticed. Then you didn't have a clue who it was, did you?"

Clarke missed Tammy heading the other way round the sofa until she turned. Tammy shoved her hard with both hands. Clarke screamed as she fell backwards onto the floor.

"Why did you do it, Tammy? You didn't need the money, not at the beginning. Douglas earns a fortune." Clarke's head hurt like hell where she had bashed it against something hard. She put her hand up to her head. Her fingers came away damp.

"For Christ's sake, Doug's been threatening to kick me out for a long time. I need that money."

Clarke tried to get up. Tammy launched herself at her. Quick as a flash, Clarke folded her good leg in and kicked out with full force, delivering a well-placed kick to Tammy's stomach. Tammy reeled backwards, clutching her stomach. Clarke got up and moved to the other side of the sofa. The sound of heavy breathing filled the room.

"Did you kill Bradley?" Clarke asked. The police suspected Douglas had done it in a jealous rage. But that didn't add up. Never had. Douglas told Paul that he had kicked Tammy out for being unfaithful and, honestly, for not being the perfect corporate wife, for not being able to advance his perfect career. It might have been Tammy. Right now, Clarke believed Tammy was capable of anything.

She didn't answer.

"Did you kill him, Tammy?"

Tammy sat up slowly and groaned. "I loved him." The sobs grew louder.

"But did you kill him?" Clarke wanted an answer. *Know thine enemy. Know whether you're trapped in a room with a killer.*

"Yes," Tammy screamed. "It was an accident. I never meant to hurt him. I loved him. I begged him to come away with me, but he wouldn't." Big, retching sobs muffled some of her words. "Brad wanted to go to the police. He would have ruined everything."

"Tammy." Clarke tried to stay calm. Tammy was at her most vulnerable now. This may be Clarke's only chance to get her onside. "I understand," Clarke said. "I love you. I'm still your friend."

Clarke wondered what to do now. She needed to do something because she was pretty sure that Tammy saw right through her fake attempt at sincerity. Would Tammy kill her too? She edged slowly round the sofa. If she managed to knock Tammy onto the floor again, she might be able to tie her up. She fingered the belt on her trousers. She could tie her hands together with that. And then what? She was still stuck in this room.

Tammy sat on the floor, groaning. Clarke edged closer. She didn't think Tammy had noticed her moving in the dark. One step at a time. Her foot landed on something hard. Clarke had searched the room so many times and found nothing. She couldn't think what it might be, but anything would be useful to defend herself against Tammy. She bent down quietly, groping around on the floor for the object. Her fingers touched metal. As she picked it up, she recognised instantly the shape of a key. Clarke put it in her pocket. The key must have fallen out of Tammy's coat during the fight. Clarke shuddered at what that meant. It was the only possible explanation. The accomplice didn't exist. Tammy had brought her here and locked them both in. But why?

Clarke was overwhelmed with relief to have a way out. With Tammy blissfully unaware that she now possessed the key, Clarke would wait for Tammy to doze off, then let herself out, lock Tammy in and call the police. She hoped Tammy would fall asleep before she herself did.

"Tammy, are you ok?"

Tammy grunted.

"I'm sorry," Clarke said. "This isn't getting us anywhere. Why don't we both get some sleep and talk about it in the morning?"

Tammy didn't reply for a while. Then she said, "Ok."

In the silence, Clarke worried that Tammy gave in much too easily. Had the fight broken her spirit? Or was she planning something too? Like planning to leave and lock Clarke in. Well, she'd have a nasty surprise when she couldn't find her key.

Clarke didn't want to lie down next to Tammy. That would be a massive risk. She didn't trust Tammy one bit. "I'll take the sofa," she said.

Tammy sat down on the mattress and grabbed both blankets. Clarke curled her legs up on the sofa, huddling into her coat. She wished she knew the time. She'd never realised before how much reliance she placed on her watch. It was still dark outside. Hopefully, Tammy would fall asleep quickly, or the rest of the night promised to be extremely long.

When, at last, Tammy appeared to be sleeping. Clarke unfurled her legs from the sofa and stood up. She fingered the key in her pocket, reassured by the cold, hard metal. All she needed to do was creep quietly across to the door, let herself out, and lock the door behind her. She hoped the lock wouldn't be stiff. The flats looked like they'd been empty for several years. But at least Tammy must have used the key a few times, so it shouldn't be too bad. Clarke wasn't even certain that the key belonged to this door. She assumed it fell out of Tammy's pocket. What if some random key had been on the floor under the sofa the whole time? Well, she would soon find out and, right now, this key represented her only hope. She couldn't stay shut in here with Tammy for another night, not now that she knew Tammy was capable of murder.

Slowly, she tiptoed across the floor towards the door. Five metres felt like five miles. Halfway across, the floorboards creaked. Clarke froze. She looked round at Tammy's sleeping figure. In the darkness, she just made out her outline, immobile beneath the blanket. Clarke removed the key from her pocket, ready to use. If Tammy woke, she would have to move fast.

It seemed to take forever to reach the door. Clarke fumbled in the dark, trying to find the keyhole. In the darkest corner of the room, the tiny slither of light coming through the window didn't help her at all. She used her spare hand to feel for the keyhole. At last, she found it and tried to get the key in.

Suddenly, something whacked into the side of her head. Tammy.

"Give me that," Tammy demanded.

The punch caught Clarke off balance and she dropped the key. It landed on the bare floorboards with a thud. Tammy immediately bent down to find it and Clarke, grabbing the door handle for balance, kicked her in the chest. Tammy screamed.

Clarke spotted the key on the floor. She dived at it while Tammy groaned. A second later, Clarke's legs disappeared from under her as Tammy grabbed them, pulling them backwards. Clarke stretched for the key but knocked it with her hand, sending it skimming across the floor. Tammy lunged towards the key. Ignoring the pain in her bad ankle where Tammy had yanked it, Clarke got up and jumped towards Tammy, who fumbled for the key on her hands and knees. For a second, Clarke hesitated, then she stamped on Tammy's hand.

The scream Tammy let out tore at Clarke's heart. She felt terrible doing it, but this was about survival. Tammy clutched at her hand, wailing. "You bitch. You've broken it. You'll pay for that."

The key lay on the floorboards, glinting in a tiny chink of light. Both women attempted to grab it at once. Their hands clashed together and knocked the key spinning. Clarke watched dismayed as, in a split second, her one hope of freedom fell through a gap in the floorboards and disappeared.

For a few moments, both women were quiet and still as the enormity of their predicament hit them.

Clarke was first to break the silence. "If we can lever up one of the floorboards, we may be able to reach it," she said. They couldn't see the key, but it ought to be somewhere trapped in the floor space. She noticed now that, since they'd been fighting, it wasn't as dark outside. A faint glimmer of light filtered through the window. It would soon be daybreak.

It would be a while before there was enough light to see clearly. Clarke retreated to the sofa and rested her bad leg on the cushions, wishing for some painkillers. There were plenty in her handbag, but God only knew where Tammy had dumped that. Her head hurt too. She put her hand up to check the damage. In the dim light, she noticed blood on her fingers.

Clarke had no idea how they would pull up a floorboard. They lacked brute strength or any kind of lever. It would be easy if they found a spare crowbar lying around, but if there had been one, Tammy would have probably bashed Clarke's head in with it by now. Tammy sat silently on the mattress. Good. Clarke really needed to rest on the sofa until it was light enough to see properly. With any luck, she might have a brainwave by then.

They sat staring at each other in the dim light. Clarke didn't dare turn away even for a second. She didn't trust Tammy one bit.

"Why did you do it, Tammy?" Clarke asked after a while. "I want to understand." What would drive her to all this?

"Do what?" Tammy said sulkily.

"All of it. Ok, let's start with the fraud. Why did you do that?" Clarke wanted to believe that killing Bradley, and even abducting her from the street, was accidental, or spur-of-the-moment, that Tammy wasn't in her right mind and had panicked, causing everything to escalate out of control. But the fraud, that must have been carefully planned and executed over a long time period. That had been Tammy's choice.

It took some time for Tammy to answer. When she did, she just said, "Where did you grow up?"

Clarke didn't understand the relevance of that. She imagined the pretty little village in Hertfordshire where she and Rob lived as children, and where her parents still lived. She wasn't about to give Tammy their address. No way. "In the country," she said.

Tammy laughed. "You ever lived in a high-rise council flat in Hackney?"

Clarke shook her head, then realised Tammy wouldn't see her clearly in the dark. "No. I haven't."

"Well, I have," Tammy snapped the words out bitterly. "I've lived in a pokey little slum and survived on benefits. I bet you went on foreign holidays and got given nice toys and took ballet lessons."

Clarke stayed silent. She didn't want to admit that Tammy was right. Her upbringing, although pretty average, was considerably more privileged than Tammy's seemed to have been. Although Clarke had been a tomboy in her youth. She wouldn't have been seen dead in a tutu.

"But you've made up for it since. You're earning good money."

Tammy was doing much better than her. She bought loads of new clothes and travelled to exotic places that were well beyond Clarke's budget.

"Yes," Tammy said. "I have, haven't I? That's why I never want to go back. It makes you insecure, being poor. You never quite get over that."

"But surely Doug's earning a fortune." Clarke regretted the words as soon as they left her lips. She should have remembered Tammy's split from Doug.

"Doug," she shouted. "Doug's been threatening to throw me out for the last couple of years."

"I'm sorry."

"I can't go back to being poor. And I couldn't stand being at Briar Holman much longer. I hate seeing Doug every day."

"I totally get that." Clarke almost felt sorry for her. She remembered Bradley Acres and pulled herself together. She mustn't trust everything Tammy said. Tammy was a manipulator. She'd never seen it before, but it was painfully obvious now. As soon as Clarke let her guard down, Tammy would use it to her advantage. "Why now?" Clarke asked. "Why not carry on for longer and search for another job in the meantime?"

Tammy tossed her head, reminding Clarke of the old Tammy, the one with the haughty attitude. Had that Tammy ever gone away? Was this broken woman just an act?

"It was that stupid Brack Attack," Tammy said. "I went to Doug a few weeks ago and told him I'd been receiving death threats, and that was the best he could come up with to make me stop worrying—a bloody game!"

"But that still doesn't explain why you disappeared." Clarke wondered if the death threats were real and decided probably not. Another of Tammy's many lies.

Tammy slumped back onto the mattress. "Because I wanted to make him feel bad. I thought if I disappeared in the middle of his stupid game, he would feel guilty."

Clarke decided not to tell her that Doug hadn't seemed all that upset and definitely wasn't wracked with guilt. She didn't believe anything Tammy said now. "Are you sure you weren't just taking advantage of Brack Attack to give you the perfect alibi to disappear? People actually thought you might be dead. I thought you might be dead." The police had believed the death threats were real. Yet, Tammy was still here.

Tammy kept talking, seeming to want to unload everything to Clarke. "My retirement fund is big enough now. There's no point in staying any longer. Doug gave me the perfect gift in Brack Attack." She laughed. "The perfect excuse to disappear for good. Doug would hate it if he knew how easy he made it for me."

"So why are you still here? Do you want to make me feel bad too? What did I do to deserve that?"

"I'm sorry," Tammy said. "I never meant for that to happen. You got too close with all your meddling. How did you find me here?"

Clarke didn't want to drag Jeffrey into this. "Someone saw you on this road. I knocked on every single door looking for you. I was worried about you. What sort of idiot does that make me?"

"I'm sorry I hurt you."

"I wouldn't have found you, not here."

"You're clever. I couldn't risk it."

"You still haven't told me. Why are you still here?" Clarke couldn't fathom why Tammy hadn't got straight on a plane and gone as far away as possible.

Tammy got up and paced up and down. "The plan went wrong. I needed a fake passport. The guy who I found to do it let me down at the last minute. He gave me the passport a week late. By then it was too late to risk flying, so I've arranged something else. I sail off into the sunset tomorrow. So, you see, we both need to get out of here."

Clarke wondered how Tammy knew the sort of people who could get a fake passport. Did she still have contacts from her council estate upbringing? She wished Tammy would sit down again. She didn't dare take her eyes off her. "So where did you stay before I came along?"

"Here," Tammy said. "Well, in the room next door, actually. It's a bit more comfortable, but not much. It was only supposed to be for a couple of days."

"But?"

"I wanted to convince Bradley. But he threatened to turn me in. I offered him everything, but instead he wanted to turn me in to the police."

Bradley Acres was head of internal audit. Was Tammy really so mentally unstable now that she expected Bradley to throw away his entire career, his reputation, and all his principles with it, to run away with her, with no guarantees, and spend the rest of his life running from the police? Clarke wondered if Tammy retained any concept of reality because if she didn't, it meant that Tammy was capable of anything. Clarke found that frightening. On the other hand, some men would throw everything away for a beautiful woman and a few million pounds. Perhaps Tammy hadn't lost all her faculties yet. Perhaps she'd misjudged Bradley's strength of feeling for her. She wouldn't be the first woman to do that. Whatever was going on in Tammy's head, Clarke needed to keep her onside, make her believe for now that she empathised with her. She looked into Tammy's eyes, trying to gauge if any compassion remained behind them.

"But Bradley signed all the invoices. Surely that made him as guilty as you," Clarke said.

Tammy laughed. "Bradley didn't sign anything. I copied his signature off another invoice. Got quite good at it too."

"And Douglas's signature?"

"I've been signing Doug's name ever since we got married. I'm so good at that now, no one can tell the difference."

Clarke realised she'd been looking at everything the wrong way. Nothing was quite what it seemed, although she still found it hard to believe that Tammy had survived in this block of flats since last Wednesday.

"Couldn't you have stayed in a hotel? You've got all that money," Clarke said. Slumming it was so out of character for Tammy. Her whole lifestyle these days was *designer* and *luxury*. She didn't think Tammy even knew the meaning of *slumming it*.

"You must be joking. The police would have found me long before now if I'd stayed in a hotel. They haven't found me here, have they? I might not be totally honest, but I'm not stupid."

"What did you do about washing and charging your watch?" she asked. The watch had finally given her away. So many things still didn't add up. Judging by the state of this block of flats from the outside, there wouldn't be water or electricity in any of the flats, and no way did Tammy smell like she'd gone unwashed for eleven days.

Tammy laughed. "House next door," she said. "People are so stupid. I got a great view of them from one of the front rooms. I saw them go off in a minicab with enough luggage for at least a fortnight. Left the door key under a flowerpot. I guess I got lucky. Otherwise, I'd be in a real state by now."

That explained a lot. Tammy had lost none of her audacity. Clarke knew then that everything in this room since she had arrived had been an act, with Tammy very much in control.

Clarke pumped her for more, although she wasn't sure if she believed a word Tammy said. "Why come in here with me? Why not just lock me in and stay in your more comfortable room next door?"

Tammy thumped her hands down on the sofa, producing a cloud of dust. Clarke sneezed.

"It's not *that* comfortable next door, only marginally better than this, really."

"But you'd have your freedom to come and go. Why stay in here, with me?" Clarke wondered if she could use their friendship to get through to Tammy. She soon realised it was useless.

Tammy shook her head. "I'd hardly spoken to anyone for days. I was going mad, and I still had a couple more days to wait for my new passport. I stupidly imagined it might be like being in the office, where we could have a laugh together, but all you wanted to talk about was escaping, and Bradley, and how I got here." She gave a bitter laugh. "It turned out I didn't want to talk to you at all. I wanted to watch you suffer. Wish I'd locked you in here and left."

"Me? Why?"

"Why? Are you really that stupid? You found that invoice," Tammy said. "Once that happened, it forced me to go."

"But you said you'd already decided to go during Brack Attack." Clarke didn't understand. Tammy was so full of contradictions.

Tammy sat down. "Yes, but I wasn't ready. I considered carrying on longer and getting even more money. You forced me to go then. This is your fault. Bradley, everything, it's your fault."

Tammy surely didn't really believe that? Would she ever realise that all of this boiled down only to one person and that was Tammy herself? The sooner Clarke got out of here, the better. She didn't feel safe.

Dawn was breaking outside. Clarke wondered if the daylight was bright enough yet to see the key through the floorboards. Not that it would do her any good. They would never be able to prise the floorboards up. Tammy seemed to have dozed off on the mattress. Clarke went over to the corner of the room where they had lost the key, moving quietly so as not to wake her.

Sadly, neither of the gaps in the floorboards looked large enough for Clarke to get her hand in. She knelt down and peered between the dusty boards. A tiny shaft of light illuminated a small area of the ceiling beneath. She decided to move round to the other side to get a view from a different angle. That might help, with a bit of luck.

The floorboard groaned as she got up. Seconds later, as she knelt down on the other side of the cracks, Tammy came hurling towards her. She managed to jump to her feet in time to deflect Tammy.

"What the hell are you doing?" Tammy's voice croaked–they were both suffering from lack of water–which made her sound even more threatening than she probably intended. "You're not going to take the key and leave me here."

"Calm down," Clarke said, struggling to stay calm herself. She still ached from the previous fight with Tammy. She didn't need another one. "All I want is for both of us to get out of here."

Tammy backed off and began to cry. "Nobody's coming. We're going to die here."

The sunlight coming through the window behind her lent her a ghostly aura and, for a moment, Clarke wondered if they were both already dead. If so, then they were in Hell for sure. "We're not going to die," she said firmly. "Pull yourself together."

Tammy's sobs faded to a whimper. She sank to the floor, curling her legs up on the filthy carpet.

It would be unthinkable to die in this room. Somehow, they would get out. "Now listen," she said. "If we're going to escape from here, we need to stop fighting."

Tammy glared up at her. She opened her mouth, but Clarke cut her off before she spoke.

"We need to work as a team, then we stand a chance. If we're against each other, we stand no chance. Do you understand?"

Tammy nodded, almost imperceptibly. Clarke didn't trust her one bit, but they needed to call a truce or they were both doomed.

"I have an idea," Clarke said.

Tammy's face brightened ever so slightly.

Clarke walked over to the mattress. "Come and help me with this." It was a long shot, her idea, but the best she could come up with.

The fabric covering the mattress was old, cheap quality and beginning to rot. "Prod it until you find a weak spot," Clarke said.

"Here, the material's tearing." Tammy pointed to one corner.

Clarke smiled. "Teamwork."

"What are you going to do?"

Clarke didn't answer. She tore at the rotten fabric, managing to remove a big section, then pulled at a few of the springs until she found a loose one. "If I can break off a spring, we could use the wire to poke around under the floorboards and retrieve the key."

"That's brilliant." Tammy sounded more hopeful now. The dried-up tears left patches of dirt on her face where she had wiped it.

"I don't know if it will work," Clarke said, "but it's got to be worth a try." She bent the base of the spring back and forth, trying to weaken the metal so it would break. After a few minutes, it definitely showed signs of wear, but her hand ached like crazy. "Here, you take over." She showed Tammy what to do.

Tammy worked the spring in a different direction. They had been a great team once, Clarke remembered, but it would never be like that again. If they got out of here, Tammy had crossed far too many lines to ever be able to return to her previous life.

"There, I've done it." Tammy pulled the spring out, waving it above her head victoriously.

For a moment, Clarke regretted letting Tammy help. The end of the spring, where it broke off, looked sharp enough to do some serious damage. Clarke realised she had inadvertently found Tammy a weapon.

"Give it to me. I'll try to bend it into shape."

Tammy hesitated and Clarke wondered if she intended to keep it, and if she fully bought into the team concept. But then Tammy handed her the spring.

Neither of them was strong enough to bend the stiff wire with their fingers. Clarke gave up trying. She needed something to help her. Placing the spring on the floor, she trod firmly on the end piece of wire. Then she bent it across her shoe, unravelling the spring bit by bit until she transformed the spring into one long piece of wire. She put one last bend into it to form a hook on the end.

Clarke was tired after her exertion, but she forced herself to continue. The hooked end on the wire made it less of a deadly weapon if Tammy decided to stab her, but it still looked pretty useful if she wanted to try strangulation, or it might even do to tie her up. No way would she entrust it to Tammy. Besides, she wanted to get out of here as soon as possible.

"Let's see if it works." Clarke returned to the cracks in the floorboards. The light was better now, but still, the thick layer of dust obscured anything that might be down there. Carefully, she fed the end of the wire into the larger space.

"It has to work." Tammy leaned over, trying to peer through the gap in the floorboards.

"You're blocking the light," Clarke said. It might not do the job, but Tammy hadn't come up with any bright ideas, so this was their best hope. Clarke took a deep breath. *Stay calm*, she told herself. She would need a steady hand. And she needed to keep Tammy onside, not get angry with her. She began poking around carefully in the dust, but her efforts proved useless. Possibly they were in the wrong spot. Had they misremembered exactly where the key fell through the floorboards? Tammy leaned in closer, lying on the floor, too close to Clarke for comfort. She hoped Tammy wouldn't try anything now.

The wire had disturbed a lot of dust below the floorboards and, now that Clarke lay on the floor, the dust irritated her nose. Suddenly, she let out an enormous sneeze, then another two in quick succession.

"Let me try," Tammy said.

Clarke peered into the gap again. "I'm ok," she said. The sneezing had fortuitously blown some of the dust away and she caught a glimpse of a piece of brass-coloured metal. She really hoped it might be the key.

Reluctantly, Tammy edged back.

Clarke moved the end of the wire spring slowly, being careful to keep her hand steady. Since stirring up the thick layer of dust, a faint strip of light glimmered in the ceiling cavity. She lay on the floor to get a better view, trying to ignore the rancid filth beneath her. The dust still tickled her nostrils. She didn't want to sneeze again and risk losing the key.

"I think there's a hole in the ceiling below," she said. "The key's very close to it." If she tried to manoeuvre the hook on the end of the wire over the top of the key without touching it, she should be able to pull it back towards her, away from the hole.

"Let me see," Tammy said, bending down next to her.

"You'll have to lie on the floor."

Tammy made a face but did as Clarke asked. Clarke pointed into the gap. "You can just see that brass-coloured metal, on the left-hand side." She could see it better than Tammy, but she didn't intend to move over.

"Is that the key? There's so much dust down there, it's covering everything."

"I'm pretty sure that's it," Clarke said. The little shaft of light squinted up at her. She couldn't see the size of the hole and she daren't risk disturbing the dust too much. Getting that key back was vital. She needed Tammy to move back and give her some space, then it should be possible to retrieve it. Clarke glanced at Tammy, lying on the floor next to her. Once she got hold of the key, that wouldn't be the end of her problems. It would most likely be the beginning. She realised now how much more Tammy had to lose than she did if they didn't get out of this room. And the best outcome for Tammy would be to leave Clarke here and lock her in.

Clarke wriggled into a better position. She rested her right hand on top of her left wrist to steady it. Fighting the urge to sneeze again, she eased the wire hook above the key, intending to scoop it towards her, away from the hole in the ceiling below.

"You've nearly got it," Tammy said. "You just need to get the hook through the loop." She leaned across Clarke. "You're doing it all wrong. I'll do it."

Clarke's left hand was pinned to the floor, supporting her right hand. She couldn't release it quickly enough to stop Tammy. Before she even realised what was happening, Tammy grabbed at the wire.

"No," Clarke shouted. She couldn't see what was going on under the floorboards, but it needed a steady hand, and that wasn't Tammy right now.

"Oh hell," Tammy said. "I've lost it. It's your fault. You should have let me do it from the start."

Clarke stood up. "How is it my fault? I was doing fine before you barged in." She hoped the key was buried in the copious amounts of dust in the floor cavity. "It's probably in there somewhere. Let me see." If it had fallen through the hole into the flat underneath, they were doomed.

Tammy's knuckles showed white where she grasped the wire so tightly. Reluctantly, she relaxed her grip. Clarke took the wire from her.

As carefully as she could, Clarke poked around in the dust, methodically working her way around the space, checking every inch.

"It's no good," she admitted at last. "It's gone."

Tammy sank to the floor and screamed.

At that moment, Clarke felt totally alone.

Chapter 30

Sunday, Week Two

Paul was restless. Relaxing on his day off proved impossible, not with a murderer on the loose and Tammy Doncaster still missing. By lunchtime, he could no longer handle doing nothing and drove into the station.

Prosser sat at his desk, eating a burger.

"Any news?" The smell of Prosser's burger reminded Paul he'd not eaten since breakfast.

Prosser crammed the remaining piece of burger into his mouth and tapped at his computer keyboard. "Fraud squad can't trace the money," he said, spitting crumbs of burger bun as he spoke. "Looks like it's been routed all over the world. They lost the trail after the Bank of Dubai."

"What about the Acres' murder and Tammy Doncaster?"

DS Prosser took a gulp of his coffee. "Reckon she's probably dead," he said. "It's been eleven days. She hasn't used her credit cards or her phone. No sign of her." He slammed his coffee mug onto the desk. "I want to talk to Douglas Doncaster again, but the boss won't let me. Apparently, he's complained about police harassment. You'd think he'd want his wife found."

"He kicked her out," Paul prompted.

"Even so."

"Do you suppose he's got something to hide?" Paul didn't like Doncaster, but that didn't mean he believed Doncaster had murdered his wife and Acres. The evidence against him was remarkably slim. Yesterday, Prosser vetoed setting up surveillance on Doncaster's house. Staff shortages, he said. There was no chance of him agreeing to it now.

Paul's stomach rumbled, reminding him once again he hadn't eaten yet. "Do you want me to do anything?" He could grab a sandwich, then get stuck in.

Prosser shook his head. "Go home," he said. "Best come in fresh in the morning. By then, one of us may have had a brainwave so we can crack the case."

The constable at the front desk called out to Paul as he went to slip out of the side door into the car park. "I've just tried to phone you," he said. "Someone's waiting for you out front."

Paul grimaced. His rumbling stomach would have to wait. Served him right for coming in on his day off. "Give me five minutes." He hurried to the vending machine outside the locker room, shot in a pound coin, and grabbed his favourite chocolate bar.

Five minutes later, he found Rob Pettis sitting in the waiting area.

"Clarke's missing." Rob didn't even wait for Paul to speak.

"Calm down." Paul didn't feel at all calm himself on hearing that news, but his professional training took over. He showed Rob into one of the interview rooms. "Right, tell me everything, from the beginning."

"I can't find her." Beads of sweat stood out on Rob's forehead. "She didn't answer her phone, so I drove round to her house. Her car's parked near the flat, but there's no sign of her."

"Could she be visiting a neighbour or gone for a walk?" Paul started to sweat too. He hoped to discover a simple explanation.

"She isn't answering her phone," Rob insisted. "It's going to voicemail every time. I'm really worried about her. This thing she's got tangled up in. What if something's happened to her?" Rob's fingers tapped nervously on the table.

Paul knew he should calm Rob down, tell him that Clarke was a grown woman, and she'd only been missing for a few hours. "Have you got a spare key for her flat?" he asked. If Clarke was in trouble, he needed to act, not sit here trying to reassure her brother. Rob was right. Clarke could be in danger.

Rob nodded and pulled a set of his keys out of his pocket.

Paul grabbed them. "Don't worry," he said. "I'll find her." He got up.

Rob followed him. "I'll meet you there."

"Go home," Paul said, knowing he wouldn't.

Twenty minutes later, Paul pulled up in Clarke's street, looking for somewhere to park. He reversed his Audi into a tight space opposite her flat and switched off the engine.

No one answered when he rang the doorbell. He tried several times, to be sure. Still nothing. The keys to Clarke's flat felt heavy in his pocket. He would take a look inside, in case he could find any sign of where Clarke might be.

He was searching through Clarke's living room when Rob showed up.

"Have you found anything yet?"

"Not yet," Paul said. "Are you sure she's actually missing? She hasn't been gone long. She might be with a friend or a boyfriend?"

"She doesn't have a boyfriend and I've already tried her friends. They haven't seen her."

"I should call this in," Paul said.

Rob opened up her laptop and powered it up. "Will they take it seriously?"

Not necessarily, Paul thought, not when she'd only been missing a few hours. "I can go back to work. If I check the CCTV in the area, I'll probably spot her." If Prosser told him not to waste his time, Paul would remind him that Clarke was still a suspect, then Prosser would want her found pretty damn fast.

"I've found her search history," Rob said, tapping on her laptop keyboard. "She's been looking at Google Earth. The most recent search is Tredington. Do you think she's gone there?"

"Let me see that," Paul said. "She must be looking for Tammy. Does it pinpoint the area she wants to search?"

After a quick glance at the screen, Paul shut himself in the kitchen and phoned DS Prosser. He didn't want Rob overhearing everything.

"I haven't got the resources for a full search," Prosser said. "We don't even know if she's really missing. What if she's lost her phone? Anyway, we're part of MIT now. We should pass this back to CID."

"Sarge, she's gone to search for Tammy Doncaster. That can't just be a coincidence." Paul punched his knuckles down on the kitchen work-top in frustration, knocking over a jar of coffee. "You know CID won't do anything." His stomach rumbled, and he remembered he still hadn't eaten lunch.

"Ok. I'll ask if uniform can spare a couple of people for a door-to-door in the area. No promises."

Paul relayed the names of the roads in the area to Prosser. He would go straight there now. If uniform showed up, he would liaise with them then. He didn't want to waste any time waiting. Now that he knew where Clarke had gone, Paul was really worried about her.

DS Prosser found him two uniformed officers. Paul immediately allocated them a road each to go door-to-door.

"Which road shall I do?" Rob asked.

"Whoa. This is police business, Rob. You can't go knocking on strange people's doors." The uniformed officers had already made a start. Paul wanted to start helping them as soon as possible.

"Clarke's my sister. I have to do something." Rob started walking towards the nearest house.

Paul pulled him back. He would have to give him something to do. Otherwise, he might do something stupid and jeopardise the whole investigation and Paul's job too. "You can't knock on doors, Rob. People will ask for police ID. They won't even open the door to you."

"But—"

"Listen, Rob, why don't you scout around the area, look for any places Clarke might be." Paul hoped that would appease Rob. At least it would keep him busy. He hoped he wouldn't realise he'd been fobbed off.

"Ok. What am I looking for?"

Paul needed to stop wasting time and get started on the door-to-door. "You'll know when you find it," he said.

Rob didn't know where to start. He wished Paul would let him help with knocking door-to-door, but Paul obviously wanted to keep him away from any 'proper policing.'

There seemed no point in staying on this road. If Paul and the other police officers intended to check all the houses, then Rob would check everything else, garages, shops, parks, whatever he could find. He pulled out his phone and opened up Google Earth, looking up the same area he had seen on Clarke's laptop. With luck, he might notice exactly the same thing as her, then he could find her quickly. He certainly hoped so.

There were two large blocks of garages in the area. At least sixty garages in total. That ought to be worth a look. The shops were all clustered around the main road through Tredington. That was quite a distance from the area that Clarke had been checking, so it was less likely she would be there. The nearby park would be a better bet to start with. There might be some hiding places there. He would have to get a move on before it got dark.

The park was disappointingly small and mostly grass, so the only feasible hiding place was a large shed in the far corner. Rob guessed the park keepers used it to store tools, or maybe to brew tea when they were working. He headed towards it, his long legs eating up the distance rapidly.

When he reached the shed, Rob walked round the outside, looking for any signs of Clarke. He didn't really know what to look for, a Clarke-sized footprint, or a discarded credit card receipt. Who was he kidding? Clarke would laugh at him when she found out. He would never find anything that helpful. And if any real clues existed, he probably wouldn't even notice them. He marched straight up to the door and knocked loudly. "Clarke," he shouted, wondering how stupid he looked knocking on the door of a locked shed. He didn't care. If anyone asked him, perhaps he would say he'd lost his cat.

Rob put his ear to the door and listened. The shed was windowless. There wasn't even a keyhole to peer through as a metal clasp and a substantial looking padlock secured the door. Clarke wouldn't be in there, unless one of the park keepers had locked her in. Nobody would get past that padlock.

Rob decided to try the garage blocks. That seemed more likely. He started walking in that direction. It occurred to him that he should try Clarke's number again. It diverted to voicemail after three rings. Hopefully, Paul would have more success than him.

Chapter 31

Sunday, Week Two

"I'm scared," Tammy said.

Clarke ignored her. She was frightened too, but she didn't want to confess that to Tammy.

Funny how friends often used to ask her if she got scared when she'd been in the brigade. She refused to admit it then either. The truth was, sometimes she'd been terrified. But she'd been good at her job. She'd received first-rate training and gained lots of experience, and all the right equipment helped too. Yes, she'd been scared, but it was a good kind of scared. The kind of scared that made you safe. The kind of scared that made you avoid stupid risks. The kind of scared that made you not make mistakes. It had never felt like this. This was the kind of scared that made her feel like a beginner walking a tightrope across the Grand Canyon with no safety net.

"There really isn't anyone coming for us, is there?" Clarke said.

"No. We're going to die." Tammy still sounded panicky. She continued to wail.

Clarke wondered what she could throw at her to make her shut up before the noise did her head in. Besides, she needed some peace to come up with a plan. Giving in to her fears wouldn't get them out of here. They needed to get out. Failure didn't bear thinking about.

"Look, Tammy, this isn't getting us anywhere." Clarke tried hard to stay calm, but inside, she wanted to give Tammy a good shake and snap her out of this destructive mood. She walked over to the window. Perhaps if she cleaned off the layer of grime, she would see something outside that she'd missed before, something that would help her. She rubbed her elbow on the glass. A swoop of clearer glass appeared where she'd wiped it. The elbow on her coat was black. Encouraged, she kept rubbing at the glass.

"What are you doing?" Tammy sobbed.

Clarke wanted to ignore her, but perhaps if she could get Tammy engaged in what she was doing, she would stop her incessant wailing. She might even help. "I'm cleaning the window," she said. "If we can see out properly, perhaps we'll be able to spot something we missed before. Perhaps we'll be able to find a way of getting out."

"Huh. Only way we're getting out of here is if you rub it hard enough to conjure up a genie to help us."

Clarke wished she'd ignored Tammy, in case her negativity proved infectious. She stepped back to survey her handiwork. It wasn't perfect. There was nothing she could do about the film of dirt on the outside of the window. With no water to do a proper job, even the inside remained smeared in places. But it showed a massive improvement.

Now that Clarke could see out better, she tried to peer down at the old fire escape ladder attached to the wall. The top of it came really close to this window. If she stretched and found something to hold on to, she thought she might be able to reach it if she climbed out. The window ledge outside looked solid enough to support her weight. The ladder, she wasn't so sure about. It seemed to be firmly attached to the wall on the portion she could see. Further down, though, the black metal gradually faded into a red-brown hue. There was no way of telling if it was just surface rust or corroded metal. And the bottom of the ladder wasn't visible at all from this angle, although she would be able to check that out when she broke the window.

Tammy continued to sob on the other side of the room. Clarke knew for sure Tammy wasn't acting anymore.

"I'm going to get us out of here," Clarke said.

"You can't." The negativity remained. "There's no way out."

Clarke paid no attention to her. Granted, it would be tough, and she couldn't count on any help from Tammy, but she already knew she would have to do this on her own. She would never be able to trust Tammy again. She didn't need Tammy. In theory, it wasn't a difficult climb down the ladder, once she stretched across and got her feet on-to it. In theory. Clarke tried to ignore the memories that kept jumping into her head of the last time she'd been on a ladder. Painful memories. She'd slipped on the last bit, landed awkwardly. Her ankle twinged, as if to remind her of her injury. It had been life-changing for her.

She tossed the memory aside. At least Clarke still had a life, and she intended to keep it. Positivity would be key. If she entertained any doubts, she'd never do it. One quick glance round the room, Tammy crying, the filthy mattress, the smell, the dust, the empty food wrappers, confirmed her complete lack of choice. It was this or nothing.

"I'm going to climb down and get help," Clarke said. It would have to be now, before she lost the daylight. She wouldn't be in a fit state to do it tomorrow, not without food or water, not without sleep.

"No," Tammy screamed. "You're not leaving me."

"I'll get help. It's the only way." Clarke slipped off a shoe. She didn't possess anything else that would break the window.

Tammy ran towards her, her heavy footsteps an early warning for Clarke to turn around. "You'll get the police."

"No, Tammy." She needed to calm Tammy down. "I'll get someone who can break down that door."

"You'll hand me over to the police," she said. "I know you will. What's going to happen to me then?"

Clarke no longer cared. "We can't stay here any longer, not without food or drink." She wondered if she dared to climb out the window with Tammy standing so close. Would Tammy push her? It would be so easy and it would look like an accident. "Do you have a better idea?"

Tammy put her face to the window and peered down. "I'll climb out. I'll get help."

Clarke took a step back. No way was Tammy brave enough to go out that window. No way. They were wasting time they didn't have. It would get dark soon. Besides, she didn't trust Tammy to get anyone to help her. Clarke knew she would never escape this place if she let Tammy go. She picked up her shoe.

"Well, one of us has to do it, and it's got to be soon." Clarke counted on Tammy taking one look out of the open window and completely losing her nerve. She gripped the toe of the shoe and bashed the heel hard against the window. It broke easily, the shattered glass cascading towards the ground outside.

"What are you doing?" Tammy screamed. "We'll freeze." She went to grab the shoe, but Clarke saw the move coming and jerked her arm up to deflect Tammy's hand.

Clarke gave the glass another bash with the shoe.

"Stop." Tammy threw herself at Clarke, knocking her to the floor. The shoe fell from her grasp. "You can't leave me."

Clarke writhed around under Tammy's weight, trying to get her off. "Tammy, no." She struggled some more and managed to twist sideways before blasting her elbow into Tammy's nose.

Tammy screamed, putting her hands up to her face, and Clarke managed to push her off.

As Clarke got to her feet, she saw blood dripping from Tammy's nose. She dived for her shoe, but Tammy grabbed it.

"You're not leaving here," she said. A second later, she hurled Clarke's shoe through the broken window.

Clarke backed away from Tammy. Her chances of ever escaping from this nightmare were disappearing fast, along with the light outside. "Tammy, please, we need to work together on this or we're both going to die in here. Please." She didn't think reasoning would work. Something inside Tammy had flipped. Tammy was right about Clarke planning to get the police. And Tammy must realise, if that happened, the only life left for her would be in prison. Did Tammy want them both to die in here?

Suddenly, Tammy came at Clarke again. She held something in her hand and, a moment later, the light from the window caught it and Clarke realised it was a shard of glass. Clarke thought that all the broken glass fell outside. Tammy must have broken it off without her noticing, from the remaining glass in the window.

Clarke ducked sideways as Tammy brandished the piece of glass towards her. For a moment, Tammy lost her balance, enough for Clarke to grab at her arm and pull her over. Ignoring Tammy's screams, Clarke pulled Tammy's arms behind her back and sat on her. She needed to stop Tammy somehow. With Tammy struggling beneath her, Clarke managed to take off her belt. She wrapped it round Tammy's wrists and tied it as tightly as she could.

"You bitch, I'll get you for this. You'll end up like Bradley."

Clarke knew she must ignore Tammy, although it broke her heart to realise what her friend had become. She checked the belt again. The good quality leather should hold Tammy for long enough. For a moment, Clarke worried the belt might be tied too tight, potentially cutting off Tammy's circulation. She steeled herself to be strong. The light was already dimming. This would be her only chance.

Chapter 32

Sunday, Week Two

Clarke worked quickly. She picked up a blanket from the bed and took it over to the window. She threw the second blanket over Tammy. It would get cold in here with the broken window and Clarke didn't know how long this would take.

Most of the glass had been broken, but Clarke used her remaining shoe to remove any remnants. Then she folded the blanket, draping it along the bottom of the window frame so she could climb through without cutting herself.

She poked her head out the window. For the first time able to assess the challenge properly. It looked even harder than she'd imagined. The ladder on the wall didn't extend all the way to the ground. The final section appeared to be broken off. Clarke hoped that didn't mean that the whole ladder was rotten with rust. She couldn't tell from this perspective, but the bottom of the ladder looked close enough to the ground to jump the last few feet if she was forced to.

The sun was setting a beautiful orange in the distance. *Now or never*, she said to herself. Clarke grasped the window frame and pulled herself up, for once appreciating her muscular swimmer's arms and shoulders.

"Nooooooo." On the floor inside, Tammy became hysterical. Clarke glanced over. She had twisted her head round to watch Clarke, so she was contorted at an odd angle. Blood from her nose stained her chin, but the bleeding seemed to have stopped. For a second, they made eye contact. Clarke quickly looked away.

"Don't leave me," Tammy said, sobbing.

Clarke couldn't let Tammy get to her. She needed to do this for both of them. *Focus*, she told herself. It would be easier once she got outside and could no longer hear Tammy. Swiftly, she pulled herself up some more until the whole of her upper body poked through the window. She looked over at the ladder.

"Shit." The ladder was further away than Clarke realised. Could she actually reach it? She slid herself back inside again. Quickly, she scanned the room until she spotted the piece of wire they had taken from the mattress. It would be better if she could measure how far she needed to reach. That was how she worked. Clarke liked to plan things. If she proved to herself she could make the stretch, she would find the confidence to do it.

She pounced on the wire and ran back to the window, sliding it along the outside wall until it was touching the ladder. It was just long enough. As fast as she could, she pulled it back inside and measured the piece of wire against her outstretched arms. Yes, it was doable. Difficult, but doable.

The sunset was turning into a beautiful pink red that would have been breathtaking on any other day. There wasn't much daylight left to do this. Clarke hauled herself up again until she felt ready to step out onto the window ledge. *You've got this.*

Clarke pulled at the handle on the window. It didn't budge. Good, she needed something solid. Holding on to that, she stretched across towards the ladder. Her shoeless foot felt icy cold now, and she silently cursed Tammy. A few more inches, a bit more stretch. Now. Her fingers touched the ladder. She slid them across until she could wrap them securely round it, then started to edge her feet along the window ledge. She stepped one foot off the end of the ledge and felt across for a rung on the ladder. For a moment, the feeling of empty space below her was terrifying, then her foot made contact with the metal rung. Carefully, she tested her weight on it. She took a deep breath. In a minute, she would have to let go of the window and take her whole weight with one hand and one foot while she swung her other arm and foot across. She would count up to ten. One, two, three... this must be the hardest bit. Once she got onto the ladder, the rest would be easy... four, five, six... if she did this, she would be home in a couple of hours... seven, eight, nine... she could eat and drink as much as she liked... TEN. Clarke let go of the window and swung her arm across, grabbing frantically at the ladder. Phew. Her heart threatened to explode. She wrapped her arms around one of the rungs to secure herself until her breathing returned to normal. It would be ok. It was just a ladder. She was an expert at climbing down ladders, she reminded herself. Home and dry.

Here goes. The sooner she got her feet firmly back on the ground, the happier she would be. She took a step down. With only one shoe, it proved much harder than she'd expected. Damn Tammy. Her one shoe was on the foot with her bad ankle, meaning that leg had to support most of her weight. The worn ladder rungs dug into her socked foot, while her sock threatened to slip on the less weathered rungs. And each time she stepped down onto the next rung, she needed to test it, make sure it would hold her weight.

Everything took so long. She'd only managed to descend three steps so far. Her hands and her socked foot became increasingly numb with cold from the harsh November wind. A sharp pain pulsed through her bad ankle, bringing back memories of her last descent on a ladder, along with memories of the dark days following her accident. Clarke tried to blot them out and concentrate, steeling herself to do another three steps, wrapping her arms around the ladder to anchor her weight for a minute before she tackled the next section.

It felt like forever, but she'd made progress. She looked down. Only one more rung to go, but the ground seemed much further away than she'd expected. When she'd looked from the top floor, the bottom of the ladder seemed to only be a few feet from the ground. But now that she'd got down here, the distance was more like fifteen feet, too far to jump safely.

Clarke took the final step down, hoping it would seem much nearer the ground. It didn't. She wrapped her arms through the ladder rungs to hold herself firmly while she decided what to do. Now she really wished she still had her belt. If she could have used it to strap herself to the ladder, it would give her more time to make a plan. Again, she cursed Tammy. Then once more she worried that she might have tied the belt too tight and Tammy's wrists might be permanently damaged. For both their sakes, she needed to get down from here.

If she jumped from this height, onto concrete, it was game over. She would probably survive, as long as she didn't hit her head, but if she landed on her bad leg, it could be catastrophic for her. She knew her ankle couldn't endure another bad break. And even if she survived the jump, she wouldn't be getting up and walking away from a fall from this height. Someone would have to find her, and she didn't see anyone. The light was fading fast. Sunset had come and gone much quicker than expected. Soon it would be completely dark.

For a minute, she stayed still and listened. It was quiet round the back of the flats, but she could just about make out the faint hum of distant traffic. Would anyone hear her if she shouted? She didn't know, but right now, that seemed to be her only hope.

Clarke took a deep breath and used every inch of her lungs to scream for help.

Chapter 33

Sunday, Week Two

Rob's search of the garages proved fruitless, at least as far as he could tell. Most of them were locked, but he found no signs that Clarke might have ever been there. He'd rapped on all the doors until his knuckles became sore, in case someone had locked her inside one of them. Perhaps he could persuade Paul to get a warrant to search them properly.

It was nearly dark. Rob walked towards Park Road. It had been the last street on Paul's list for the house-to-house, so hopefully, Paul would still be in the area. Rob would phone him when he got there. Perhaps Paul would have better news to report than he did, although he didn't hold out much hope that Clarke had been found. He was quite certain Paul would have phoned him if he had good news.

The houses in Park Road looked very upmarket. Rob imagined the residents wouldn't be too happy about the police knocking on their doors. Too bad. The only thing that mattered was finding Clarke.

As he walked further, the houses towards the end looked a little less expensive. Then, in stark contrast, the eyesore at the end of the road really lowered the tone of the neighbourhood. As he got closer, it looked like the block of flats had been left to rot. He didn't suppose the neighbours were happy about it lowering their property prices.

The flats were obviously empty. Rob wondered if Paul had bothered to search them. Maybe Clarke searched for Tammy there and had an accident inside. He dialled Paul's number. No answer. Would Paul have stuck to the rules? The police would be trespassing if they searched the place without a warrant. Well, Rob had no intention of letting any stupid rules stop him. If there was the slightest chance that Clarke might be in there...

Rob scouted around the perimeter fence, wondering if he could climb over it. Halfway round, he found a hole in the fence. Carefully, he started to climb through. He was nearly through when his coat caught on the wire. He pulled at it, but he was completely stuck.

Suddenly, he heard screaming.

Chapter 34

Sunday, Week Two

Clarke was really cold and her ankle ached like hell with deep, stabbing pains that made her feel dizzy. She would have to jump soon or she would fall. Then Tammy would die in that awful room, and she might die too, freezing to death on her own on the icy concrete.

Someone shouted. It sounded like it came from below, but she must have imagined it. In any case, she didn't intend to look down anymore in case it made her dizzy.

The shout came again, louder now. "Kent."

Clarke smiled. It reminded her of the old days. No one had called her that in four years. The lads in the brigade all found it hilarious to call her Kent, after Clark Kent. Funny that someone should shout that. Would they hear her if she shouted back? She opened her mouth, but no sound came out.

The noise below her intensified, and a big red fire engine flashed into view briefly before disappearing behind her. She risked a quick glance down. Someone was erecting a ladder. They were coming to get her. Thank God.

"Kent, what are you doing hanging around here?" A pair of strong arms encircled Clarke, supporting her weight.

"Blue. Oh my God, Blue. Good to see you." She recognised his voice instantly. They'd nicknamed him Blue because of his penchant for blue clothes and general obsession with the colour blue.

"Good to see you too, Kent," he said. "If you'd wanted to meet up, I would have preferred the pub. You didn't have to go to such drastic lengths."

Clarke managed a weak laugh.

"Let's get out of here," he said.

"My leg. I'm not sure it can take enough weight to go down the ladder." It still pained her, worse than ever, agonising hot stabs of misery every time she moved it. She knew she would struggle to stand up when she reached the ground.

"Don't worry, I've got you."

Clarke smiled. Blue was big and strong and she'd seen him in action hundreds of times. She was in safe hands.

"Now, one step at a time," he said. "Put your weight on your good leg. Don't use your bad leg. I've got you."

They took it slowly. *It's only a ladder*, Clarke reminded herself. She'd already climbed down from the sixth floor. Just a few more steps now. She'd been up and down thousands of ladders in her fire brigade days. Not with a weak ankle that was absolutely killing her, though. Thank God for Blue.

"I considered jumping," she said, "before you showed up."

"Bloody hell, Kent. You really do think you're Superman, don't you?"

"Superwoman." Clarke corrected him.

"Nearly there," he said. "One more step."

Clarke stood on her good leg and leaned against the wall. What a huge relief to be back on the ground. Blue retrieved her shoe and put it on for her as Rob rushed up.

"Clarke? Are you ok?"

"I'm fine."

"You look terrible," Blue said. He scooped her up in his arms. "She needs a medic."

"No, Blue, stop." He was carrying her away from the building. Rob followed. "I need to talk to the police."

"Paul's here." Rob called out Paul's name.

Blue sat her in the ambulance, where a young paramedic started cleaning blood off her face.

"Clarke, what happened?" Paul stood at the door of the ambulance.

"It was Tammy," Clarke said before Paul got a chance to speak. "Tammy did it. She murdered Bradley, and she stole the money."

"I just worked that out," Paul said.

"She's upstairs."

Paul looked really worried. Clarke wasn't sure if he was worried about her or worried about losing Tammy. It didn't matter. Finding Tammy was the only thing that mattered right now.

"You need to find her," Clarke said. "She's locked in."

"Don't worry about that now. Leave everything to us and get yourself properly checked out." Paul called to one of the uniformed police officers and ran off towards the front of the flats.

Clarke relaxed. The gas and air the paramedic gave her helped. Her ordeal was over now.

When the painkillers kicked in and everything stopped hurting, Clarke insisted on a mirror to assess the damage. Her face was swollen around one eye and a big bruise was forming on her cheekbone. Her lip had split, and a scratch extended down her other cheek. The doctor spent a long time removing some small pieces of glass from her hands. They must have been embedded when she'd climbed out the window. Her hands had been so cold, it numbed the pain. Luckily, the doctor didn't believe there would be any lasting damage to her ankle. They'd put her on a drip to combat the dehydration. And they'd found traces of chloroform. That explained the woozy feeling when she'd woken up in that room, and Clarke figured Tammy must also have used it on her during that first night, so she could go out to buy food.

"The doctor says the bruising will soon go. You'll look great in a few days," Rob said.

Rob hadn't left her side for the last couple of hours, except when the doctor examined her. She was lucky to have such a great brother. Apparently, it was him who had called the fire brigade and ambulance.

Clarke tried to smile. "I look like a prizefighter."

"You look beautiful." Paul walked in, holding a big bunch of flowers. He put them down on the bed.

"What happened to you?" Clarke asked. "You're in a bit of a state yourself." A big bruise was beginning to form around Paul's left eye.

He laughed. "That was Tammy. She's a wildcat." He sat on the edge of the bed. "I untied her and before I could get the handcuffs on, she punched me."

Clarke laughed with him. "Yeah, she's a fighter." She had first-hand experience of that now. She wondered how many fights Tammy had got into on the council estate where she'd been brought up.

"We've found your handbag in one of the nearby rooms. We found a lot of Tammy's stuff in there too, including a fake passport and ferry tickets for this afternoon."

"I knew it," Clarke said. "She said something about sailing, not flying. Did she confess to murdering Bradley?"

Paul nodded. "And she tried to set you up. We found the phone that sent you the text message, pretending to be Acres."

"That's awful," Rob said.

A tight knot formed in Clarke's stomach. Tammy had been her friend. How could she have betrayed her like that?

"Anyway, I've come to take you both home," Paul said. "It's the least I can do."

Chapter 35

Clarke sat opposite Paul, sipping a vodka and orange. She wasn't sure why she'd agreed to meet up with him, but she'd been looking forward to seeing him again now that Tammy's trial was over.

It had been difficult being a witness against Tammy. A few times, Clarke felt like she was betraying her friend. She kept reminding herself of all the terrible things Tammy had done. The Tammy she'd thought of as her friend had never been the real Tammy. Did you ever really know anyone at all when you only worked with them? Were they always putting on a face, being guarded about what they told you and what they didn't?

"She's still not said where the money is," Paul said.

"I expect she's planning to spend it when she gets out." Clarke wondered how many pairs of shoes Tammy could buy with that amount of money.

"Twenty-three years." Paul screwed up the beer mat he'd been shredding. "She'll probably be out in twelve. They'll break her before then. She'll tell eventually."

Clarke wasn't so sure. Telling the truth wasn't one of Tammy's strengths, as it turned out. She'd stolen over three million pounds. The fraud squad searched through every single invoice in that basement archive, going back six years. She'd started over two years ago, small stuff at first, then got braver with larger, more frequent amounts. Clarke racked her brains as soon as they'd told her that, trying to remember any signs of Tammy's behaviour changing, or any worries she'd had around that time. Tammy was an expert liar, or perhaps Clarke didn't pay enough attention. She'd been wrapped up in other things, studying for her exams, working to get her new career going, struggling to rehabilitate her ankle, trying to survive. Anyway, three million pounds would make a fabulous pension. No, Tammy wouldn't tell.

"Another drink?" Paul asked.

He stared her right in the eye, looking expectantly at her. Clarke smiled at him, half worried about what might be coming next and half excited. She remembered the first time she met Paul, several years ago. She thought he was cute back then. She was surprised to find that she still thought that now.

"I should go." She got up.

"Please stay." Paul put his hand on her arm. Clarke didn't pull it away.

"Can I see you again?"

Clarke paused. She caught a glimpse of Paul's pleading puppy dog eyes and her last bit of resolve melted. Once, she'd thought Paul would be her forever partner, but he'd let her down badly. He was much more mature now. Perhaps she would give him a second chance. Life was too short to play safe all the time. Her experience with Tammy had taught her that.

Clarke gave Paul a massive smile. "Call me."

Acknowledgments

Thank you so much for reading this book. Readers are by far the most important people in an author's world. Of all the millions of books you could have chosen to read, a massive THANK YOU for giving my book a chance. I really hope you enjoyed it.

If you liked it, I would be grateful if you would consider leaving a review on Amazon and Goodreads. Reviews are so important to an author to raise visibility and help other readers find my work.

This book has undergone a thorough editing process, but sometimes mistakes happen. If you have spotted a mistake, please contact me so I can correct it promptly.

A huge thank you to my brilliant editors, Laurence Editing, and Ashley Smith-Roberts.

To my wonderful launch team. I couldn't do this without you.

To my cover artist, Get Covers.

To Rita's A Team: John, Makeda, Brian, Vanya, Tracey, Kerry, Tunde, IBK, and of course the fabulous Rita. You are the best team I've ever worked with, and not a bit like anyone who works at Briar Holman.

To all the authors who have ever inspired me.

To my parents for bringing me up to believe I could accomplish anything I wanted to in my life. And to my fabulous friends who have encouraged me on my author journey.

THE THEFT

Find out what Clarke did in her previous career as a firefighter. This action-packed book is a prequel to THE FRAUD. It's FREE to download when you sign up for my author newsletter.

This was twenty million pounds' worth of dangerous...

Firefighter Clarke Pettis' priority was saving lives, not possessions. But, when she discovers the painting that disappeared during the rescue of an injured man in a house fire was worth a fortune, Clarke couldn't leave things alone.

She puts herself in serious danger when she crosses paths with art thief, Antonio Balleri.

Can Clarke save herself from Balleri and find the stolen painting?

Be the first to find out about new releases, special offers, and other interesting stuff. Download the free book and sign up at https://dl.bookfunnel.com/hm3iserife

SECRETS NEVER DIE

Would you risk your life to save a baby?
Would you do anything you could to protect her from harm?
Even if that meant taking her and never giving her back?

Twenty-five years ago, Dan Peterson risked his life to rescue a baby from a dangerous cult, the Seventh Heavenites. That baby grew up to be the well-known model Pagan.

When Pagan gets the chance to be the face of a new perfume, she must spend a week working on the beautiful island of Jersey, the one place she will never be safe.

As Dan digs deeper into the past, he endangers both Pagan and her young daughter.

Can Dan protect Pagan from the Seventh Heavenites, and a secret that she knows nothing about?

Get SECRETS NEVER DIE on Amazon at **https://mybook.to/ 99nl4**

Coming Soon

THE COVER UP
Clarke Pettis series - Book 2

A small company of dysfunctional employees who all have their own issues, but which one of them will be driven to murder?

When forensic accountant Clarke Pettis is asked to investigate the finances of a pharmaceutical company, she didn't expect to get caught up in the middle of a murder case, intimidated by animal rights activists, and put in danger of being killed herself.

Can Clarke find out who is trying to bring down the company before anyone else dies?

About The Author

Christine Pattle writes thrillers with a bit of mystery and plenty of action. Her aim is always to write a good page-turning story that readers will love.

When she's not writing, she's busy riding horses, making fantastic cake sculptures, and walking round the countryside dreaming up exciting new plots.

Copyright

Printed in Great Britain
by Amazon